ABANDONED

USA TODAY BESTSELLING AUTHOR

A.M. WILSON

Editing: Jenny Sims Editing4Indies

Cover Design: T. E. Black Designs

(https://www.teblackdesigns.com)

Print ISBN: 9798363413117

CONTENTS

BOOKS BY A. M. WILSON

Standalone
Indisputable
Abandoned

PLAYLIST

Sky is the Limit - Mark Ambor
Nervous - John Legend
Little Bit More - Suriel Hess
Easy - James TW
Woke Up in Love - Kygo, Gryffin, & Calum Scott
Sleepy- Ashley Kutcher
Can't Help Falling in Love - Kacey Musgraves ELVIS
Missing Piece - Vance Joy
Feel Like This - Ingrid Andress
The Few Things - JP Saxe, Charlotte Lawrence
Give You Love - Forest Blakk
Last First Kiss - Abe Parker
My Home - AWIN

ABOUT THIS BOOK

A dog named Slipper almost ruined my life.

The uncatchable stray snuck on the patio where I was waitressing and knocked me straight into Lee Powell's lap.

My fist slammed into his junk.

Then I accidentally flipped his breakfast platter onto his pants.

I thought it couldn't get any worse, but when I bring my brother to baseball practice, I discover his new coach is none other than Lee, owner and founder of Powell Dog Sanctuary, and he's not happy to see me.

I try to keep my distance from the hottest grump I've ever seen and ignore what it felt like curled against his broad, muscled chest.

But a bad case of the flu changes everything.

He stumbles on to my biggest secret and reveals a few of his own. He can't seem to stay away from me. He says he's too old for me, but I couldn't care less when he makes me feel cherished.

But then his past raises its ugly head, and he breaks our connection in a moment of suspicion.

Lee's afraid of being hurt again, but I'm the one left abandoned.

To those adrift
May you find your way home
Or make one of your own

1

LEE

THERE'S NOT MUCH I despise more than wearing soggy, wet socks. A year on the streets as a kid, some twenty-five years ago, humbled me to the benefits of basic, properly fitted footwear. Something I could kick my own ass for neglecting as I stand in an inch of water at the foot of my stairs first thing on Monday morning. Not like a pair of house shoes would spare me from this shit. I need some rubber boots.

"Son of a bitch."

I drop the olive-green-and-beige tackle box in my left hand to the bottom step. I meant to go to the lake today and enjoy some quiet fishing, but the lake apparently found its way to the main level of my home. Slopping my way through the mess, I dig my phone out of my back pocket and text my brother, Corjan, to meet me at Mary's Diner in an hour for breakfast instead. The peaceful day I had planned will have to wait until after I clean up this mess.

The culprit to my sideways morning, a very obviously

burst pipe, resides in my laundry room just off the kitchen. Remnants of soggy drywall litter the floor, and the gaping hole in the ceiling is more than a neon sign. Sometimes I wonder why I stay in this old, collapsing rambler when I have more than enough money to afford a brand-new, custom build on a private plot of land. As I've argued with my six family members over the years, this place suits me just fine.

Suited.

After this rude morning mess? I'm damn near about to torch the place to the ground and start fresh on a plot of land far away from here.

I call the local plumber, only half listening while he informs me he can't make it until this afternoon. After shutting off the main water line, I lay out damn near every towel I own, turn on a couple of fans, and change into fresh socks before hitting the road. My place is only fifteen miles out of town, but with my mood, the drive feels like an hour with nothing but my bitter thoughts.

The tinkling bell above the door to the diner heralds my arrival. As does Corjan's booming laughter, where he sits at the counter flirting with a couple of mature ladies. The wide smile stretched across his scruffy face is genuine. Despite his wife ripping his heart straight from his chest with her departure only a year into their marriage. Ten years later and indefinitely single, he's managed to remain Mr. Sunshine around the opposite sex.

"Hey, about time! Any longer and Stella was about to take me home for lunch." Corjan winks.

"You scoundrel!" Stella swipes her brown suede bag at him with a laugh and a light blush on her wrinkled cheeks. "Lee, take your brother before he earns what I'm about to give him."

"He'd probably like it," I grumble and jerk my head at the door to the patio since Minnesota decided to finally grace us residents with her summer temperatures. "Got time for a bite, or am I too late?"

The mask never leaves his face, but the moment Corjan clocks my mood is obvious. We might not be blood related, but I spent enough time learning how his mind works to know the thoughts disguised behind the smile in his eyes.

"Ladies, thank you for the company. Lunch is on me." He swipes their check and tucks the paper into the breast pocket of his plain black cotton tee.

I fold my frame behind the red and white checkered table in the warm sunshine and turn back in time to see Dora appraise Corjan's backside before it disappears out the door. "You have admirers everywhere."

He palms the table and slides in with his attention on my face. "What's wrong?"

"What do you think?" I pin my younger brother with a hard stare. The guy wears rose-colored glasses most of the time, but even he can understand what might have me a little irked this fine morning.

"You're always so uptight." He flags down a server from behind the counter with a wave. "It'll work itself out."

"My main floor is flooded."

"So we can skip fishing, and I'll bring over a wet vac."

I grit my teeth. A steady throb begins in my temples.

"What can I get for you?" A woman with reddish hair

wearing a rolled apron tight around her curvy hips hinders my response.

My brother gives her a slow once-over. Not sure if I want to roll my eyes, laugh, or slap him for being such a dog, I resolve to simply observe the exchange.

"A black coffee, three eggs, medium, six slabs of bacon, and toast, please, darlin'."

An elongated pause follows his order.

"And for you?"

"Same." I grunt with hardly a glance. Corjan's undivided attention is probably more than enough testosterone for the poor girl. The quick peek upon her arrival spoke of her allure and also to the fact she's young. Way too young for an old man like me to be checking out while she's just trying to earn a paycheck.

But in the privacy of my own thoughts, I can admit she's downright gorgeous. Beautiful, and soft, and supple in all the places women complain about. Hips and thighs and *ass*. Full, pouty lips. Lightly freckled skin. And dark eyes the color of my morning cup of coffee.

"I'll be right back with your drinks," she says sweetly and departs.

Corjan snorts with derision and smacks his palm against the wooden table. "What's really crawled up your ass this morning? And don't say fishing. We both know you don't like it that much."

I give my brother my eyes. His playful exterior doesn't fool me. Only a few of us are privy to his hidden pain, which is reason enough for me to share. He's one of the few people in this world I trust. Even then, I keep him at a smart distance.

"Nancy."

"What's Mom got to do with this?"

The server returns to drop our coffees and scampers off.

"She's always harping on me to relax." I wrap my palm around the hot ceramic. "Ever since I received the call last year my biological brother died of a sudden heart attack at forty-five, she thinks I'm knocking on death's door and I work too hard. If she finds out I didn't make it to the lake today... I cannot handle another conversation about my impending doom."

Corjan runs his hand through his short, dark curls. "She's just worried about you."

"She shouldn't be."

"Good luck telling her that. She didn't take in six unrelated kids off the street to not give a fuck about them."

White tendrils of steam curl in the space between us. A welcome sip disguises my need to confirm he's right. "I'm nearing my forties. She's not raising a wild, angry teenager anymore. I can take care of myself. Hell, at her age, I should be taking care of her."

"You've worked hard your entire life." Corjan cuts me off, his face a mask of seriousness. "After Dad passed away, you helped her raise us. You stuck around long after you needed to so Aiden and I didn't grow up missing what it was like to have a dad. We all think you need to take a break."

When our adoptive dad passed away, Corjan and Aiden were barely preteens and new to our mismatched family. They didn't really get to know Terrance before we lost him. I put my college plans on hold in order to take half the load from Nancy, and finished my degree in business a few years later than I had originally planned, which

I ultimately used to help launch our family run dog rescue, Powell Sanctuary, not long after.

"This morning feels like a bad omen," I grumble, lowering my tone so the pretty server approaching our table doesn't hear how miserable I am.

"When's the plumber coming?" Corjan slides his mug to the side to make room for his breakfast platter.

I answer over the waitress's arm. "A couple of hours. He has a pretty cozy gig being the only plumber for miles surrounding Fairview Valley. I envy his workload, except when I'm the one in need."

"Can I get you two anything else?" our server asks.

Her sweet voice lures my attention away from the greasy plate waiting to be devoured. She reminds me of Nancy when she first took me in. Young and overworked but full of determination. The tired expression on her young face prompts a twitch to my lips. "We're all good here. Thank you."

"Great. Here's your check, and if you need anything else, holler."

"Slipper!" Corjan snaps and leaps to his feet. The stray white husky we've been tracking for weeks dashes onto the patio with a high-pitched bark, her elevated nose pursuing the smell of food. With hunger driving her senses, the dog races straight for our table and the fresh breakfast plates waiting to be consumed.

"Watch out!" I shout.

One moment our waitress is beside the table, arm extended forward with our receipt. The next, chaos ensues.

She doesn't have time to dodge before the dog's front paws land on her back. She gasps as her feet fly out from under her, and her fist slams into my junk in order to brace against her fall.

I wince and grunt, blinking back real tears as my balls crawl inside my abdomen for protection. The first time a woman literally falls in my lap, and I can't even appreciate her softness spread across my thighs.

"I am so sorry!" Her muffled cry sounds somewhere beneath the table near my aching dick.

"First day with your land legs, little mermaid?" I gasp. I attempt to lighten the mood despite the throbbing in my balls.

Her weight shifts, and the heat from her body starts to leave me. "I'm sorry," she mutters again.

Corjan's quick movement rattles our plates against the aged table. In one effortless tug, he helps slide her from the awkward position. Once she's on her feet, he makes a grab for the dog, who manages to slip right out of his grasp.

"Fucking hell, Slipper," Corjan groans and watches the animal sneak away with a piece of toast.

As if my morning misfortune just had to prove it wasn't through with me yet, the hand she sets on the table to steady herself lands perfectly on the edge of my plate. The dish executes a single flip. Creamy egg yolks and glistening, greasy bacon take no prisoners and land in the spot she just vacated.

My lap.

Fucking hell.

"Shit!" She claps a hand on her mouth as if she remembered she's on the job.

Not that I care about the blunder. A string of expletives dance on the tip of my tongue. I muster the remaining ounce of my willpower to lock it down and release a measured breath. She made a mistake.

"I'll get a towel." Corjan takes off, leaving the two of us stranded in an awkward hell.

"I'm—"

I pinch the bridge of my nose and cut her off. "If you say sorry one more time..." The unspoken threat trails into an awkward silence. I flip the plate over and start tossing breakfast items back onto the ceramic dish.

"I'll put in a fresh order right away."

"Don't worry about it," I grunt, angrier than my unfed stomach. Once I scrape my jeans off the best I can get them, I return the plate to the table and glance up, half expecting her to be gone.

A red hue covers her unblemished cheeks and the pinch between her eyebrows hasn't lessened. Concern wars with embarrassment as the dominant emotion.

Helping Nancy raise a couple of displaced kids more than prepared me to deal with the minor inconvenience of spilled breakfast. But the look on the pretty server's face reveals I must have forgotten how to use a gentle hand in the ten plus years since my youngest brothers grew up.

I sigh. "Hey. It's fine." I wave my palms at her. Fuck, I don't do tears. She better not cry. "No harm done. Go ahead and get back to work. Don't let this ruin your day."

"I can comp your meal." She shuffles from foot to foot while massaging her side.

My brow furrows, zeroing in on her hand. "Are you hurt?"

"I'm fine. I just bumped it a little on the table," she rasps. I bet she has an incredible laugh.

"Juniper." I read her name on the white tag pinned to her chest, testing out how it feels on my tongue.

Her breath hitches, and she wrings her hands at her apron-clad waist. "I've never spilled on a customer before. I don't know what else to do besides apologize. But I really need this job, so I'd appreciate it if you didn't tell my boss."

Corjan returns with his signature grin and a dripping white towel hanging from his left hand. "Darlin', don't let this idiot get you all tied up. Your apology is accepted." He throws the sopping cloth at the mess on my pants.

"Thanks," I mutter and begin scrubbing. The wet warmth of food and water against my junk makes me want to gag.

He sends Juniper a wink designed to weaken the knees of ladies everywhere and resumes his seat. "We're on a schedule this morning, so I'll share with him."

"You sure?" The heat of her gaze warms my face. She hesitates, waiting for my answer.

I muster up what probably resembles a grimace more than a sincere smile. It's the best I can do. "It's all good."

"Geeze, could you torture her anymore? This water thing must really be getting under your skin," Corjan admonishes once she walks off.

Stemming the quiver of guilt his words stir, I grunt and stab my fork into one of his eggs. "I think I was damn composed, all things considered."

"Well not to pile more on your very full plate"—Corjan smirks—"but are you still able to watch my dogs? I fly out this evening to Oregon to meet with a potential rescue partner and tour their facility."

Corjan keeps a couple older dogs who don't do well cohabiting with the rest of the pack at the sanctuary.

I scowl over his stupid joke. "I'll come over after Ollie's baseball practice tonight."

Our sister's son has played baseball since first grade, and it's become a sort of family tradition to watch as many of his practices and games as we can. The boy has a cheering section all to himself.

"Cortney's lucky she gave birth to the only grandchild. That boy is beyond spoiled." He pops a rasher of bacon in his mouth. "But I love it. I saw his first practice last night. He's only twelve, but I can tell he's going to go places."

A sip of coffee allows me to gather my thoughts. "It feels good."

"What's that?"

"Giving someone something we didn't have. I hope Cortney has twenty babies that we can all spoil rotten."

Corjan grins. "Good luck telling her that."

2

JUNIPER

"I NEED you to quietly get your cleats on so we can leave, buddy." I toss my burgundy hair into a mid-high ponytail and meet Lincoln's sad brown eyes in the bathroom mirror. One more growth spurt and my younger brother will tower over me. My heart twists at the similarities he shares with our mother. Same eye color and shape, and the little crooked left front tooth. If he were smiling, they'd share that joyful curve too. Smiles seldom occur since we lost her two years ago to a tragic accident.

"I heard Dad yelling at you last night." His twelve-year-old fists bunch at his sides. "Are you hurt?"

"I'm okay."

"He hit you again, didn't he?"

A silent spin sends me away from the mirror to face him while I blink away the memory of crashing against the basement banister the night before. Only luck saved me from a tumble down the stairs. I bite back a grin at his wild tufts of sandy hair and lay a tender hand on his shoulder, ignoring the smarting ache in my side.

"He didn't hit me." The partial lie leaves behind bitter grit in my mouth. "Now, I need to get you to practice so I can head to work."

"I thought you only worked at the diner today."

"I've picked up a few extra shifts at the club." The sooner I can get us out of this situation, the better, even if that means working double shifts most days. After working the morning shift at Mary's Diner, I serve at the strip club XO's in the evening.

Lincoln gnashes his teeth together, the clank dangerously close to a dental bill we can't afford. "I don't want to go."

"You have to." I touch his cheek and flick my attention down the darkened hall behind him where our father sleeps on his evening off. "You can't stay here alone. Oliver's mom will take you home until my shift is over."

"Why not?" The anger in his young face sends a bittersweet pang coiling my insides.

"Because you're half my age, and I'm not leaving you alone with him." Not as long as I have other options. Once I can afford to get out of here, I'm taking Linc with me. My father and his drinking problem can go to hell.

Lincoln's face twists into a sneer. "One of these days, I'll knock him on his ass."

"Shh!" I hiss to silence his dangerous threat. If Dad hears him talking like that, he might use the opportunity to teach Lincoln a painful lesson. My influential grasp on his shoulders forces him around. "Now go. I'll meet you outside."

"I hate baseball," he grumbles under his breath.

"You love it," I whisper to his retreating back.

With one last look in the mirror, I sigh and steel

myself for another long night. The embarrassment from this morning still hasn't faded, despite the hours since *the incident*, as I've been referring to it all day. There's a first for everything, though I didn't think dumping a platter of food and junk punching one of the hottest men to walk this town, quite possibly even the earth, was ever going to occupy a space on my list of accomplishments. I'd almost rather have fallen onto Corjan Powell, equally as devastatingly handsome with his dark curls and easy blue eyes, but where Lee Powell is steely rough edges, Corjan is soft and kind.

Lee Powell personifies broody. I don't think I've ever seen him crack a smile in the many years I've known of him. He's big and broad, taking up space with his sheer size. When he comes for a bite to eat, his intensity is palpable from across the diner. He's noticeable in a way I think he'd rather not be, but he's a whole hell of a lot of man to hide.

I'm not some creep keeping a ledger on the Powell family. Corjan happens to lives next door, and from time to time, Lee visits his brother. As do the other four siblings, their mother, and a massive pack of dogs from the rescue they own.

I brush my musings away as easily as I flip off the bathroom light. Lee's nearly old enough to be my dad, he might even have graduated in the same class and, from what I've seen, could be as mean as him too.

I snag Lincoln's forgotten water bottle from the kitchen table on my discreet trek out the door. My heart squeezes a little to find Linc already waiting for me in my used, cherry red Mazda, his scowl visible from the steps. This not-so-little guy makes me proud. Something I tell him as soon as I climb in beside him because he sure as hell doesn't hear it from Dad, and our mom isn't around to tell him anymore.

"You make me proud."

His shoulders lower a little from his ears. "Thanks, I guess. What'd I do?"

I back the car out onto the quiet street in front of our house. "I know this isn't easy, these last two years. You're doing good, kiddo, even when it doesn't feel like it."

Linc returns his attention out the window in silence.

I twist my fingers around the wheel, fighting with the worry I said the wrong thing. I'm not a parent. I didn't spend the first decade of his life practicing and learning what to say and when to say it. I'm winging this job of supporting my younger brother, and at this moment, I feel like I blew it.

Then again, I remember being twelve, the hormones and changes, and that was a trip I never want to experience again. I should give him some grace to be moody.

I switch on the pop radio station and notice the time. "Crap. We're going to be a little late." Musing about Lee Powell's good looks consumed enough time for a ten-minute delay.

Linc looks over before resuming his stare out the window. "It's fine. Our coach was late yesterday too, so I'm sure he doesn't care."

This is only the second practice of the season. I want to set a good example both for Lincoln and for the coach.

"I'll do better tomorrow." I speak my determination into existence and turn into the sparsely filled lot.

My brother shoulders his bat bag that I found at a resale shop for a steal of a price while I grab his drink. We cross the lot, him trudging and me ushering, my hand fluttering uselessly behind his back.

A small gathering of people ahead designates his team's location. I expected them to be on the field already.

"What's going on?" Lincoln asks.

"I'm not sure." My brows crease. Hopefully only a minor delay. I really have to get across town to the club before I screw up my second job today. I use my hand as a shield from the evening sun and scan the group. "Hey, Cortney."

Cortney Powell, yes, another Powell sibling, stands with one hand on her son Oliver's back and the other pointing at someone across the cluster of parents. "You're perfect for the job!" she exclaims proudly, a gleam in her dark brown eyes.

"What's going on?" I sidle up beside her while Linc moves to Ollie's side.

"The coach quit," Cortney whispers.

"Oh no. That's terrible."

"I mean, he was led away in handcuffs, so he didn't totally quit. More like he was forced to go."

"What did he do?" I turn more fully into her since I can't see through the tall bodies blocking my view.

Cortney and I aren't close by any stretch. It just so happens that her son and my brother are best friends, and since my dad is useless most days of the week, I'm the one she reaches out to for scheduling weekend events and sleepovers. Which she enthusiastically hosts one-hundred percent of the time.

Though I sometimes imagine we are friends even though she's twelve years older than me. I wouldn't have known if she didn't tell me. She looks as fresh as me at nearly twenty-five. I don't think I've even seen a single gray in her obsidian hair even though I pulled out one of my own just last week. She has an effortless beauty her makeup only accentuates and a naturally slim figure that doesn't require rigorous workouts and calorie counting to maintain.

I swear if I even look lovingly at a slice of pie, I gain five pounds, which doesn't stop me in the slightest from eating it. It just means I need to buy bigger jeans from time to time.

"That's what's so crazy about it all. He was preparing the field as players started to arrive, and then a cop car pulled up, and minutes later, he was walking off in Sutton Stone's handcuffs. It almost looked like he expected it to happen, but nobody knows what he did."

I jiggle my car keys. "Oooh, suspicious. I'm sure the rumor mill will churn out all kinds of speculation by morning."

"I know, right?" Cortney flashes a grin. Her true crime junkie side is fully invested in this small-town scandal. "Anyway, as you pulled up, we were trying to figure out who would coach these boys."

"Any takers?" I inch back. If I don't go soon, I'll be late for work.

"That'd be me." A deep voice rumbles to my left. A voice, if not for this morning, I wouldn't be as familiar with as I am right now. "And for the future, I expect my players to arrive on time. The first step in being a good teammate is reliability."

He did not just say that!

I look around the circle, hoping to catch the eye of a parent, *any* other parent, who's a little more equipped to coach a little league team than this jerk. Everyone seems to be avoiding looking at anyone else too closely.

"I'll keep that in mind." I inject a little zest into my reply. Cortney seemed fired up at the idea of her brother coaching her son, so I'm not about to interfere with her joy just because I find him to be a grumpy asshole.

Not that he even did anything to me. The blame is all mine. He just could have been a little nicer about it. Though he doesn't look like the type of man who has *nice* in his vocabulary.

I ignore the shivers accompanying that thought and address Cortney. "Hey, I've got to run. I should be by your place around ten thirty if that's still okay?"

"Of course." She waves me off. "If you're running late, Lincoln's welcome to stay the night."

"I should be on time, but thank you."

"Might want to set an alarm. I'm not sure you know the meaning of punctual." Lee lobs his comment before giving me his back. His words hit like a sinking stone in my stomach.

"I'll be on time," I reassure Cortney, who returns a sympathetic look.

With a subtle sigh, I turn to the man occupying my thoughts for most of the day. My lips twist as I examine the best way to get his attention. I hesitate with my hand raised before lowering it back down. Invading his personal space once today was enough. I settle for increasing my volume and attempt to be civil.

"Thank you for stepping in for these kids. I'm sure it'll mean a lot to have an influential person guiding them this summer while encouraging them to have fun."

Half the reason I signed Lincoln up this year was to

make sure he had male role models other than our father. Was Lee Powell the man I had in mind? No. Nuh-uh. Absolutely not. But if he can do the job, I'll be grateful for anything he can teach my brother.

Lee juts his chin over his shoulder. "Sure. For some of them, I'm all they get."

The insult is clear the way his light green eyes laser focus on my face. After my screw-up this morning, I probably deserve it. But his rejection hurts just the same. Tears burn the back of my eyes. My mouth opens, but nothing audible comes out. With a helpless glance at Cortney, I spin on a heel and head back to my car.

A muttered, "*Sorry,*" chases me on the breeze at my back, but I refuse to turn around.

3

LEE

"Great job today, guys. I'll see you tomorrow evening."

I lift my hat off my head and wipe the sweat from my brow with my arm. The grinning group of preteens jog off the dusty field to collect bats and bags and water bottles from the bench. I find a couple of stray balls and toss them into the bucket.

"Not bad for your first time." Cort appears at my side, extending a bottle of cold water.

"Thanks." I take a glug before handing it back. "They're a pretty good bunch for putting up with my rusty skills."

"Are you kidding? I don't think you pitched a single ball the entire practice."

I rotate my arm around. "I'm going to be feeling it tomorrow. Those muscles are out of use."

Cort jabs her finger into my shoulder, and I groan. "It's good for you, old man."

"You're three years younger than me. If you don't want me to call you old woman, I'd be careful."

"You wouldn't dare." She scowls.

Most the kids have walked off, but I notice one lingering by my nephew Ollie. That girl Juniper's kid. But that doesn't seem right. She can't be old enough to have a twelve-year-old.

I jerk my chin in their direction. "What's his story?"

The reason for my curiosity remains elusive, and I refuse to dig deep enough to decipher it. Some things are better left buried.

"That's Lincoln Kelly. He mostly keeps to himself. His mom died a couple of years ago, so his sister cares for him."

"No dad?"

Cortney shakes her head. "He's around, but I don't know the details."

"It's nice of you to help."

"Yeah well, none of us would be where we are today if we didn't get the help we needed. I'm just trying to do my part."

She's right about that. If it weren't for Nancy and Terrance, my adopted siblings and I might not all still be alive.

"So do you need to bring him home?" I vaguely recall the conversation earlier about him staying late.

"His sister will come when she's off work. Until then, the two will stay busy in Ollie's room."

I adjust my baseball hat, lowering the brim. "All right, I'm going to take off then. If you need help, I'm happy to give you a hand."

My sister waves me off. "It's not an issue, so don't make it into one. And maybe be a little nicer to her, yeah? She's got a lot going on."

"I apologized."

"Next time, make sure she can hear it."

I'm not interested in hearing what all pretty little Juniper has going on, so I let that one go. With a brief wave, I gather the coaching bag and bucket of baseballs, and head to my truck. I'd rather be going home, regardless of the hole in my ceiling, but I make the ten-minute drive to Corjan's place to watch his pups.

The property sits on the edge of town. The few houses lining the street grow more distant between the farther one drives, and for only being nine at night, most are quiet and dark. Corjan's still close enough to have some neighbors, though it won't do him any good if they're vacant more often than not.

I leave the coaching gear in my truck for the next practice and jog inside to let the dogs out. The geriatric yappers dance around my ankles in their excitement. If I'm not quick enough, Friskee will pee at my feet before I can get her outside. The one-eyed Pomeranian can't hold it when new people come to visit.

"Yeah, I hear you. Come on." I pick her up while Corjan's old Chihuahua named Pickles prances happily behind. The old man had a lot of dental work, and now his tongue seems to permanently hang out of his mouth. He looks like a potato with googly eyes.

The pair roams free in the backyard. A decorative fence between the properties keeps them from wandering too far. The scent of pine needles carries on a warm breeze from the woods behind Corjan's house. With the sun nearly set, the sky is a beautiful mix of purples and grays. Peace infiltrates the spaces still gripped by this morning's mishap, washing the remnants of frustration away and eliciting a quiet sigh.

Forget fishing on quiet lakes. I need to kick Corjan out of his house more often. For some reason, being somewhere other than home brings a serenity I've been missing.

With nothing better to do, I kick out the leg of a deck chair and drop my ass into the seat. I shut my eyes, enjoying the warm night.

A noise next door jolts me awake. The pool of headlights glances off Corjan's garage to my left. Two warm bodies snuggle together on my lap, warding off the slight chill overtaking the air. The moment my eyes open, alertness infuses my body, chasing away the sleep. I'm grateful for whatever woke me.

I could fall asleep outside on a bed of sticks with no problem, but the great outdoors isn't my location of choice. I spent enough time sleeping on park benches as an abandoned kid. I roll the ache in my neck for emphasis. Too fucking old for this.

A few car door slams later and the headlights extinguish, plunging me back into total darkness. My ears perk with the loss of vision. If I really strain, I can hear whispered voices before a door opens and closes.

I nudge the pups from my lap. "Inside, you two. Bedtime."

They both look at me with expressions clearly conveying their disapproval before trotting to the sliding patio door. I let them go ahead of me but then pause to peer over at the neighboring house.

A light clicks on in the window facing me before a woman appears yanking a hooded sweatshirt over her head. Red curls bounce around her bare shoulders when she tugs herself free.

After today, I'd recognize that burgundy hair anywhere.

The sight of Juniper flares something akin to indigestion. I rub my fist over the center of my chest. Corjan better have some antacids in his house, or I'm going to have to make a late-night gas station run.

With a harsh exhale, I stomp the rest of the way into the house and slam the door behind me.

> **ME**
> You didn't tell me Juniper was Corjan's neighbor

> **CORTNEY**
> What happened? You better leave her alone!

> **ME**
> Relax. I just saw her through a window

Her bedroom window. Undressing. Without a care in the world to who might be lurking outside.

This must be a midlife crisis. Nothing more. It's been decades since I've been in a relationship, and I haven't had sex in how long? Two years?

I lead the dogs to their beds with a treat and use my other hand to open my phone. I scroll the calendar in an attempt to jog my foggy memory. The history of the past few years of my life flashes by in a dismal blur. Business meetings, birthdays, holidays and events, rescues and vet appointments, road trips to help out-of-town shelters after hurricanes until finally I come across a date.

Three years ago?

That can't be fucking right.

No wonder my balls ache after this morning, and I'm not referring to the punch. I haven't been that close to a woman in a third of a decade. If I had any sense, I'd go out right now and find someone before the woman next door becomes more than a passing fantasy.

An email interrupts my musing with the subject COACHING DETAILS.

I scroll mindlessly through the temporary distraction. In the first line the director denotes that this change is permanent for the remainder of the season and follows with heavily worded apologies and gratitude for stepping in at the last minute. As if I had much of a choice. When my nephew threw my name into the ring and my sister cheered me on, I was done for before I even had a chance to beg my way out. The relief was evident on all the other parents' faces.

The bottom of the message includes a schedule as well as a guardian contact list. This newfound weakness has me opening the attachment and scrolling to her name.

An email address *and* a cell phone number.

I really should leave her alone, and I will. But I should apologize.

Before logic takes control, I type the digits into the keypad and connect.

The indigestion flares, and I'm out of my chair, digging through my brother's medicine cabinet as her voicemail picks up. I brush aside the flash of disappointment at the generic, robotic greeting and end the call.

I toss back two round tablets, crunching the chalky substance between my teeth, and muster up one last text for the evening before I put this entire fucking day to rest.

ME

I'm sorry.

4

JUNIPER

"Shit!"

I move my gaze from the rearview mirror over to my brother in the seat next to me. "Roll your window down, bud, and don't say anything."

Our father pulls into the driveway, idling his rusty blue truck beside my car. He steps out with a paper grocery bag in his hand and peers curiously through the open window. "Where you off to?" he asks Lincoln.

"Baseball practice," I answer.

"Since when?"

"Since he started three days ago."

His bushy blond eyebrows dip. "Got time for a bite first? I picked up the ingredients for fettucine alfredo." He volleys his question at Lincoln again, who simply shakes his head.

"We already ate. Sorry, but we have to go," I interject.

"I'll save you leftovers." He continues speaking only to his son.

"As if you'll remember," Lincoln grumbles under his

breath.

"What was that?"

"I said I can't wait," Linc replies a little louder.

I shove the shifter into reverse, but our father clamps his meaty hand around the open window frame and thrusts his head inside.

"You teaching him to be as ungrateful as you?"

"Not now," I bite out and level him with a look. My trembling fingers wrap around the black leather steering wheel, hiding the shake.

There's a hardening that occurs around someone who repeatedly hurts you. When the fear melts away to something like hatred and the shiver in your bones turns to flames.

For the man who raised me, I wish I could watch him burn for his choices. I'd even strike the match. If it means my brother gets out relatively unscathed.

I'd do just about anything.

He straightens. A sudden breeze tousles his sandy-blond hair. He's aged a lot in the last couple of years. New wrinkles line his face from the perpetual frown and heavy drinking, but unfortunately, his exterior isn't as ugly as the inside. He could easily date. Try to move on. Maybe finding someone new would soften this monster residing inside the man who used to give me hugs goodbye, but I can't find it within myself to wish for another person to share an existence with what he's become since Mom died.

With my father's eyes pinned on mine through the windshield, I back the car out of the short gravel driveway. I don't dare to speak until we're safely on the road.

But Lincoln beats me to it.

"Why does he do that?" The pain in his voice nearly slices me open. "How can he hurt you and offer to make me dinner like nothing fucking happened?"

"Hey. Language, bud."

"Fuck language!" His temper explodes along with his volume as the anger he holds inside rips free. "I hate him, Juniper. I *hate* him. Why did Mom have to die instead of him?"

"He wasn't like this before Mom died," I remind him softly.

The excessive drinking changed him. We all hurt when we lost Mom, but I can't pretend to know a spouse's level of suffering. His drinking is a sickness. How do I explain that to a child who only sees the sister he loves being hurt by someone who's supposed to protect and love them both? It isn't right, and it sure as hell isn't fair.

"I wish he wasn't around."

"I know it's easier when he keeps to himself," I reply and park in front of the baseball field.

For the most part, our schedules overlap just enough that we rarely interact. Lincoln is in school until three, and our father works the evening shift at a loading dock from twelve to eight. Most nights after, he drinks himself to sleep and doesn't wake until we're both gone for the day.

Enrolling Lincoln in baseball and having him over at Oliver's house helps to keep their interactions short when I'm not around to buffer. With waitressing two jobs, I try to keep that time minimal. Our father's never laid a hand on Lincoln... yet. I'd do anything to ensure he never does. The approaching summer will be a challenge to stay busy and away from home.

"Have a good practice!" The cheeriness in my voice falls just a smidge shy of cringe.

"Whatever." Even with the attitude, he manages a half-hearted wave before trekking to the field.

I reach over to dig my phone from my purse to call my best friend, Isla, on her break, but Lincoln's full water bottle resting under the edge of his seat delays the friendly call.

And here I thought I'd successfully avoided his hot, cranky coach today, and the following days, until their first game next week.

No such luck.

While grumbling nonsense under my breath about unreliable preteens, I pocket my phone, grab the beverage, and lock up in order to hustle across the lot. If I'm lucky, I might be able to just sneak the bottle to Lincoln without Lee seeing me.

Halfway to the field, my hopes are dashed.

The saliva in my mouth dries into a sticky substance at the sight of his biceps bulging beneath the sleeves of a black tee. His arms are crossed over his chest, feet planted wide, light wash denim stretched across sturdy legs while he chats with another parent. The edges of his soft brown hair curls beneath the sides of his backward baseball cap.

Ugh. Drool.

I shake my head, ridding the lust from my brain.

We do not cavort with grumps!

The mantra does the trick. I tamp down my natural people-pleasing disposition and adopt a blasé attitude instead. I will not be ruffled.

Without another glance, I skirt around the two and deposit the water bottle on the bench.

"Can I help you?" Lee's deep timbre sounds at my back.

I tack on a limp smile before facing him. "Lincoln forgot his water."

He removes his sunglasses. "Does he need a ride home tonight?" The question sounds sincere, but my defenses raise all the same.

"No. I'll be back for him."

From up close, his eyes appear almost a sea-foam green, and I wish I could un-see the sprinkling of gray at his temples that sends warmth to my stomach. It should be illegal for one person to be this attractive.

Lee looks at me as if he's waiting for something, and when he doesn't find what he's searching for, his lips flatten.

I glance behind my shoulder to the boys warming up on the field. Lincoln winds up and sends a practice pitch sailing into his partner's glove with an audible smack. "How was he? When he walked up?"

"I didn't see."

"Would you mind..." I pause to swallow passed the dryness in my throat and look back at Lee as he tosses an antacid in his mouth. "Would you mind just keeping an eye and let me know if anything seems up?"

A flicker of concern ghosts his features. "Something I should know?"

I shrug and force a laugh. "He's twelve, you know? He just had a rough afternoon."

"I will."

At least his no-nonsense, curt, grumpy persona is good for one thing. I appreciate that he doesn't pry.

"Well... Okay, then." With a flutter of my hand, I move

around him to return to my car. I have a best friend to call. It has nothing to do with this man I'm trying to avoid.

"Did you get my text?"

The words freeze me in my tracks. My mind riffles through the last day or so seeking confirmation. "Text?"

He clears his throat. "Last night. I called, and when you didn't answer, I sent a message."

The random number at ten o'clock last night and a vague *I'm sorry* was him?

Now I definitely need to leave and call my best friend. "Um, I'm sorry." I brush the hair from the sweat sticking it to my forehead. "It was late. I must have forgotten."

He settles the sunglasses back over his eyes, effectively shutting me out. Right before he turns back to the field in dismissal, I catch an angry expression crossing his face. "Have a good evening, Juniper."

"You too, Lee." I depart with an extra fire in my step.

***

"You're telling me that you sat astride Lee Powell and now you get to see him multiple times a week while he coaches your brother's baseball team?"

"Falling into his lap is not the same as sitting on it, Isla," I scold my best friend and dab my fried pickle into the spicy ranch.

"Close enough." She waves her hand between us. "Can you please explain to me how you ended up here when you could be sitting in the bleachers enjoying the view of his ass?"

After yet another awkward interaction with Lee, I

skipped calling my best friend and instead drove to the strip club where we both work while she's on break from her set.

We met here a year ago when I needed a second job. Although I'd do just about anything to earn money for Lincoln and I, I drew the line at stripping and applied to be a server instead. She was new to dancing at the club, and with her larger body, most of the other girls gossiped about her behind her back. Only shallow idiots care about the size of someone before deciding to strike up a friendship, as if the extra weight she carries has any correlation to who she is as a person. Without much effort on either of our parts, we became fast and easy friends.

"A stray dog named Slipper knocked me into his lap, I damaged his balls, spilled breakfast all over his pants, ignored his apology text, and somehow you want me to stand in his presence and not combust into a mortification-fueled bonfire?"

She shrugs and finishes her bite of pickle. "It'll blow over in, like, a day."

Complaints and rebuttals bounce around in my skull. "You know what? You're right. I'm not going to let this bother me. I'm just going to pretend nothing ever happened."

"That's my girl."

Her snark receives an automatic eye roll. "I'm lying, Isla! I can't just drop it."

"When do you see him again?"

The bartender, Benjamin, drops a water refill in front of Isla with a smirk. I wait until he retreats to the other side of the bar.

"There's another practice tomorrow, but I've already

asked Cortney to bring Lincoln so I can work. Then I'm off the hook until their first game next Tuesday."

She sips her drink and wipes the condensation on her hands onto a napkin. "See? That's plenty of time. I bet by next week, he'll have forgotten what it's like to have you snuggled up tight."

"Isla," I warn, but I can't stop the blush rushing to my cheeks. An image of the compromising position recalls easily. Too easily. Suddenly, I feel warm and a little electric, like a current zips through my blood.

The pretty blonde just grins at me and pops another pickle in her mouth.

"Let's talk about you. Any new boyfriends this week?"

She tips her head back and releases a throaty laugh. "Always. I can't keep them away." Her eyes stray to Benjamin's back.

Hmm.

Somewhere between her response and a sip of water, I rest my head on my arms against the bar with a sigh.

"You okay?"

"Fine. Tired." I stifle a yawn. "A few minutes and then I need to head back to the baseball field."

"How much longer?" she asks quietly. Without confirmation, her question is clear.

"I don't know. It seems like every time I get ahead, my dad forgets to pay some bill, and I pick up the slack. This month it was the electricity." The fee only set me back a hundred and fifty bucks, but still. That's an entire night plus tips of work that I could have used on gas or groceries.

"You should stop bailing him out."

"I can't. I'm not going to leave Lincoln to live in a

home without power or whatever Dad forgets to pay that month."

"Can I help?"

I lift my head and wipe my palms across my thighs. A soft smile graces my face. "I appreciate the offer, but no. I'm not far off. I'm going to start looking and hopefully put in some applications. I have the first and last month's rent. It's the utilities I'm nervous about. I just want a bigger cushion saved up."

Isla settles her palm firmly on my shoulder. "Let me know if I can help. I have savings too, and I wouldn't mind loaning you something to get started."

"I'll keep that in mind."

For Lincoln, I tell myself. It's the only way I can even consider and not be riddled by guilt.

"I should get going."

Isla waves off the twenty I move to put down on the bar. "It's on me tonight, babe. Tips are good."

"Will I see you tomorrow?" I shoulder my crossbody bag and tuck my phone into my pocket.

"I'll be here late afternoon. As usual."

I can't stop the frown settling into place, and my mouth opens.

Isla holds her hand up. "Don't say anything."

As her friend, I want nothing more than to engage in shit talk about how bullshit it is that, with the crowd she draws, she's stuck on an afternoon set, but I respect her request.

"Have a good rest of your shift." I squeeze her hand once. "I'll see you tomorrow."

5

LEE

BY THE TIME I pull into Corjan's driveway at nearly ten at night, I want to fall into my own bed and sleep off the last three days. I spend the ten minutes it takes to let his dogs out coming up with all the ways I can extract payment for helping him out. All my ideas fizzle to nothing because Corjan is the most selfless person I've ever known, so anything I come up with he'd tackle in a heartbeat with a damn smile on his face. Which makes the brainstorm session a lot less fun.

The dogs scratch at the door to signal they're ready for bed. After settling them down with a small snack, I steal a beer from the fridge and wander back out to the patio. Again, I'm struck with the desire to just sit and relax in the outdoors. Why don't I ever feel this way at home? It's probably because my deck consists of a cracked slab of concrete and a couple of plastic chairs for the occasional beer. Idle time doesn't exist in my usual day-to-day life.

Corjan, on the other hand, constructed an outdoor oasis. Cushioned seating litters the wooden deck that I helped him build. In the center rests a firepit he usually lights up after our family has enjoyed one of our regular Sunday meals together, and a table off to the left easily seats eight. Small, round bulbs strung across the pergola could light up the entire area with a flip of a switch, but I prefer the dark.

Just like Corjan on those quiet nights alone. He skips the home magazine version of peace and travels across his yard to the more secluded firepit he dug out near the row of trees where two lawn chairs wait.

I settle with my drink in one of the chairs on the patio, content to rest my eyes. But every few minutes, I find the traitors drifting to the house next door. Specifically, the window facing me.

That little fire flares in my chest. The beer probably doesn't help the indigestion.

My lips tug into a frown. Did she really not realize I was the one who called and text or was she playing games? Maybe my number was lost in a sea of unknowns. For all I know, she has an entire flock of age appropriate boyfriends attempting to chase her down. I wouldn't doubt it for a second.

Not because she invites attention. I couldn't even categorize her as flirty. My eyes drift over to her window again. The kind of beauty she possesses is quiet. Commanding. Her looks demand a man take notice without her even trying. I dig in my pocket for an antacid just as her bedroom light illuminates the darkness.

I tip my bottle to my lips and look away. My resolve only lasts for a few seconds before my gaze drifts back over just in time for her to step into view.

Her expression is difficult to read across the distance,

but her hunched shoulders tell a story. One I'm eager to discover, even though I shouldn't be. Red waves brush passed her collarbone as she moves closer. More of her fills the frame. My chest tightens, and I grip the armrest in an attempt to hang on. Or stay seated.

With a hinge at the waist, she dips out of sight, only to reappear a moment later. She glides her fingers through those reddish strands before gathering the mass atop her head with a practiced flick of her wrist. The style serves to highlight the curve of her soft neck, a gold chain glinting in the overhead light. A secretive place I could put my lips for a taste.

Fuck.

I jam my thumb and index finger into my eyes, rubbing harshly. I didn't mean to think that. The thought suddenly appeared, floating through. Invading me. Like all the others when she's near.

On the next glance, my jaw drops open, a harsh pant of warm air exhaling with force. Fuck. She's removed her shirt again, but unlike the last time, her proximity to the window means I can see more. I avert my eyes.

The imagery of her is void of detail, but the visual it provides brands itself all the same.

Whether or not her chest is freckled remains unknown, but the lacy white bra, the cups hugging ample breasts, is on full display.

Within seconds, my phone is in my hand, fingers gliding furiously over a text in an attempt to regain some control of this situation.

ME

Good afternoon, Juniper. This is Lincoln's coach, Lee

In my haste, I completely disregarded the fact it's night, and we should be in bed. Not together. We should be sleeping like proper mature adults getting a full eight hours of rest.

I resist the gnawing urge to see if she's in the window responding. Within a minute comes her reply.

JUNIPER

Funny. I have you as something else in my phone...

My heart thumps a little faster. Something else like what? Guy with a nice lap? Sexy coach? Or maybe she's decided to label me as an asshole. I couldn't really blame her, could I? I send two more texts rapidly.

ME

Are you still mad at me?

I said I was sorry

JUNIPER

What do you want?

ME

I wanted to ask you to please close your bedroom curtains before you give my brother a show

Her response is instant, a tell she's invested in what I have to say.

The belated realization hits me. In my rush to protect

my sensitive eyeballs from Juniper's hot body, I inadvertently told her I'm staying in the house next door and creeping on her like a perverted old man.

> JUNIPER
>
> Jealous?

I suck a hearty mouthful from my beer.

Of who? My brother? My thumb dashes across the keyboard before I regain sense and backtrack.

> ME
>
> Shut your damn curtains

Once the message zips off into the ether, I stomp back into the house, closing the sliding door with a slam.

She sends before I'm even across the kitchen.

> JUNIPER
>
> Your brother is a grown man. He can shut his eyes.
>
> Better yet, close his curtains for him

> ME
>
> Why are you so difficult?

I toss my bottle into the recycling bin beneath the sink where it clanks against the other glass. Friskee raises her head from her pillowed bed with a look that tells me to keep it down.

"Go judge someone else," I mutter to the dog without heat. Straightening from my bent position, I brace my hands against the kitchen sink.

JUNIPER

Why are you so mean?

A flush courses up my neck. I shouldn't care that she thinks I'm mean. It's better for both of us if she finds me unkind. For some reason, knowing she's displeased with me only increases the irritation I feel for myself.

I raise my head, jolting at the sight and swearing beneath my breath. The kitchen window before me is a direct view into her bedroom window, even better than from the back patio. I'm going to murder my fucking brother if I find out he's ever stood where I stand.

I palm the bulge in my jeans, willing my cock to stand down. Not only can I see the lacy white bra Juniper's wearing, but I can see the matching thong too.

With a shove, I'm off the sink and marching into the attached garage, straight to my brother's workbench to find what I need. My phone vibrates silently in my pocket as I storm around the privacy fence between the houses, a lot of good this useless fucking wood does, a six foot ladder tucked into the crook of my arm.

Her window provides an adequate yellowed light in the dark to aid me with my task. The phone signals again as I reach the top step. With gentle strokes, I pound the first nail in through the corner of a sheet and window trim, intentionally keeping my eyes away from the glass.

After the third notification, curiosity wins, and I pull out my phone.

JUNIPER

Based on your sudden silence, I'm guessing you don't have an answer to that. Have a good night

> Are you outside my window right now?

> Lee! What is that sound?

The slight panic I hear through her words tilts up the corner of my lips.

ME

> I'm hanging up some curtains since you chose to ignore me

I pocket the phone and tack the opposite corner into the other edge of the window. Then I carry the ladder back to the garage.

My phone burns a hole in my pocket as I get ready for bed, using the bathroom and splashing water on my face. I run a toothbrush through my mouth and swap my jeans for gray sweatpants. Once I settle in the guest bed, I resign myself to whatever may be waiting for me after my little stunt.

JUNIPER

> You can't hammer nails into my siding

An intensity blooms in my chest, and without thinking of the consequences, I fire off my final text.

ME

> Yeah? I just did. You might not care about showing off that beautiful body to the entire neighborhood, but I sure as fuck do…

I settle back into the lumpy pillow feeling like I might have just won this round.

6

JUNIPER

L EE P OWELL 'S seen me naked.

Well, almost. Mostly.

And he called me beautiful.

He's still a grumpy ass.

I inspect the white sheet draped over my window with a slight smile teasing my lips. His texts last night nearly took an offensive direction, but then he sent the last one, clarifying his thoughts. Instead of finding me repulsive, he said I have a beautiful body.

If only I had time to entertain such a notion.

A crash in the other room serves as my first warning of trouble and wipes the grin from my face. The sound of a fist on my bedroom door the second.

An urge to snarl sarcasm about remembering to knock curls my upper lip. The opening door brings a rush of cool air, whispering across my skin, and a reminder to adopt a passive expression.

My father stands half in, half out, one hand braced on the frame with the other clutching the knob so tightly he'd fall over without its support. His glassy eyes roam over my face before he sneers, opening a pit beneath my lungs. "What are you doing?"

"Getting ready for bed." I fidget with the hem of my silk camisole, the green sleep set I never intended to wear in his presence. Or anyone's for that matter. Long gone are the days when I'd skip out of my room in my pajamas and lounge on the couch watching early morning cartoons until it was time to get ready for the day. Now I'm the first to wake and the last to fall asleep, so what does it matter what I wear to bed if I'm the only one to see it?

"Where have you been?" he slurs.

I sigh, tired of our repetitive dance. "I was at work."

His fingers tighten on the knob, blanching the wrinkled knuckles. "When are you going to get a real job?"

"Waitressing is a real job." I can't help the hitch in my throat, knowing even through his drunken haze his words are meant to inflict damage. He's reminding me of the dreams I put on hold when our lives fell apart.

A short burst of mocking laughter falls from the same lips that used to tell me *I love you* every night.

"Dad," I warn.

His hand slides from the knob, and he nearly topples to the floor before righting himself. The glare pointed in my direction holds fury and blame. "You look just like her," he mutters with a tilt to his head.

"Don't." The single word scrapes up my throat, and my outstretched hands convulse. I'm torn between catching his next stumble or shoving him away.

"You could be her clone," he rants, moving a step closer.

I blink hard against the stinging flood of tears. His barbs hit with deliberate accuracy.

"It's not fair for you to look so much like her and live in this house when she's dead because of you."

"Go to bed. *Please*," I tack on. My eyes flash behind him in the hall to the closed door at his back. I pray Lincoln isn't listening to his horrid, hateful words, absorbing them and the blame they carry.

The sway of his unsteady feet sends him lurching backward, and I use the opening to leave. His fingers curl cruelly into my bicep, whether to inflict pain or maintain his stability I can't be sure. I gasp at the bruising contact and press my lips together to contain a cry.

"Let go," I whisper, glancing again at my brother's bedroom door.

"It should have been you." He roughly shoves me away, releasing my arm, as if touching me repulses him, and I stumble.

The meaning scores into my soul. This time, I can't contain the whimper. The sounds of my bare feet tapping against the hardwood and my harsh breathing follows me out the sliding door. When I reach the grass in our backyard, I pause with my hands braced on my knees, swallowing against the acid in my throat.

Tears hit hard, coursing in rivers down my heated cheeks. Gravity sucks them beneath the edge of my jaw, and some continue down my neck. I move farther into the darkness to my mother's raised garden boxes. Picking up the hose, I flick the nozzle and swipe the spray over the flowers I managed to keep blooming and alive over the last two years.

"Fuck," I mutter out loud, unable to stem the shake of

my shoulders. His words tore a new hole inside me, killing the last shreds of hope that our family could ever be unbroken again.

It should have been you.

A strangled sob rips free before I can choke it down. The wet hose slips sideways in my hand, the skyward nozzle sends droplets flying.

"I wasn't aware it was raining."

My racing heart stops before kicking back to life in my throat at the sound of Lee's voice from the other side of the fence.

"I'm sorry," I rasp, fighting for control of my tears.

"It's fine."

The nozzle sprays upward again before I can turn it off, nearly soaking my face.

"Now that seemed intentional." A hint of amusement colors his tone. The shadow of his head appears over the top of the fence. Through the light of the moon and the lamp at my back door, I can just make out the small nod he gives me. "Come over."

I glance back at my house. Between the two, going with Lee seems like the safer option.

Even if I'm not sure he likes me much either.

"Um, sure." The unmasked uncertainty floats between us. I drop the hose and wipe my tear-streaked face discreetly with my bare shoulder. The darkness might provide just enough cover to hide my swollen eyes.

Lee meets me on the paved driveway, and we walk silently to where he must have been sitting before I rudely interrupted him with my late-night sprinkle. A pit of glowing red embers and empty lawn chairs awaits his return.

"Where are your shoes?" He looks pointedly at my bare toes, drawing my gaze there too.

"I forgot them."

He cocks a brow but doesn't question me further.

"Sorry about the water," I say as I sit. A stretching silence between us brings a flush to my already hot cheeks.

He plucks the front of his tee away from his chest before letting it drop. "I was getting warm anyway."

"What are you doing here?" I ask the question I've been ruminating on since last night. The reminder of his texts brings another hot rush to my skin.

"My brother's out of town, so I'm watching his dogs." He adds another log to the fire and a flickering flame licks up the sides, consuming the fresh wood. "Technically, they belong to the rescue we run, but Corjan's a foster failure. I think he belongs to the dogs more than they belong to him."

I smile in the darkness. "That's nice of you."

"I'd do anything for the idiot."

"Yeah." The sentiment strikes close to my own sacrifices and reminds me of Lincoln.

"Do you want a beer?" Lee retrieves an open bottle from beside his chair.

"No, thank you. I don't drink much."

Lee clears his throat. "Everything okay? I don't mean to pry, but it sounded like—"

I cut him off before he can acknowledge my tears out loud. As if every other interaction with Lee hasn't been embarrassing enough, what's one more? "Yeah. A fight with my dad, you know?" The admission makes me feel incredibly young and small. Embarrassment streaks through me.

"I used to fight with my dad. I was a little shit when he and Nancy first took me in. Then again, we all were. I miss him." Lee brings the bottle back to his full lips, his gaze fixed on the golden flames.

"I'm sorry for your loss." My voice is soft.

His eyes meet mine across the way. "I'm sorry for yours."

"How did you know?"

"Cortney mentioned something about your mom. She didn't share anything else. We're close, all of us siblings are, but she'd never betray your trust."

I nod. A warm breeze flits across my face. Tipping my head back, I close my eyes. "We're close too, Lincoln and me, though I'm more of his guardian than his sister." The strangled quality of my voice betrays my emotions.

Lee laughs softly, the rare sound urging me to open my eyes. God, he's beautiful when he laughs. With the glow of the fire and darkness behind him, the angles and shadows somehow make him impossibly more handsome. My belly tightens and floods with desire.

"I should warn you it doesn't go away. After my dad died, I dropped everything to help care for the youngest siblings. They were actually around Lincoln's age. Even all these years later, I can't seem to stop stepping in to help like a mother hen."

"Great," I mutter without any heat. The corners of my lips tip into a grin as I imagine Lee chasing around his little chicks. "Do you regret it? Dropping everything to help?"

He pauses with his bottle halfway to his mouth, then

lowers it. "No. At the time I was frustrated, but I've been able to do everything I wanted and then some things I never even dreamed about."

My head bobs in a tight nod. "I'd meant to be out on my own by now, but when we lost my mom, I couldn't leave Lincoln like that in his grief. He struggles a lot still. I work two waitressing jobs just to make sure he has everything he could want."

"Doesn't your dad work?"

His curt question catches me off guard. His eyes appear dark behind the glow of the fire. Some might find it rude, but I'm learning it's Lee's nature to be direct. The trait feels honest, like he has nothing to hide. Though we all have our secrets.

"He does. It's just not enough." I leave out the part about my father drinking his paycheck away. Nobody needs to know that fact. At least not until I can get Lincoln out of the house. Then he can do whatever he wants.

Lee's tight expression implies he finds my answer lacking. As the silence stretches, his roaming gaze wanders to the rest of me, the attention bringing heat to my skin that has nothing to do with the fire. His eyes linger on the hem of my shorts and the bare skin of my thighs.

My nipples tighten beneath the thin camisole.

"Tell me about your siblings," I ask to diffuse the rising tension.

His wandering eyes snap back to my face, and his tense body relaxes back into the chair. "There are five of them. You know Cortney. She's three years younger than me. And I'm sure you've met Corjan. He's the second to youngest. Then there are the twins in the middle, Jack and Jude, and Aiden is the baby at twenty-nine. Except for the twins, none of us are blood-related."

"That's incredible. And you said they took you all in?"

He nods. "Yep. They couldn't have biological children."

A small smile graces his face, and my breath catches at the subtle beauty. I want to trace his full, tilted lips with my index finger.

"What's incredible is how selflessly they took us in. They found me first. I'd been out on my own for a year. Winter was around the corner and I visited one of the local churches to see if they had anything I could eat. Nancy found me walking along the sidewalk with a can of green beans and no coat. She managed to talk me into coming over for a hot meal and I never left." He chuckles and drains the rest of his drink. "You'll meet her at the baseball games, I'm sure. She talks to everybody. Are you coming next week?"

"Of course." For the first time, the thought of Lincoln's baseball game doesn't fill me with dread. Getting to see this version of Lee has been nice. And unexpected.

"Good," he answers, a little less coolly than usual.

I cover a yawn with my palm, thoroughly worn from the evening, and stand. "It's late. I should go," I announce before he feels the need to ask me to leave.

Lee rises too. "I'll walk you back."

A laugh sneaks free. "It's not far."

"This is an argument you'll lose." He holds out his hand in a gesture for me to lead.

A giddy energy infuses me at his tone. I should be careful. It's been a long time since I've had someone who cares for me. His chivalry would be easily mistakeable for something else.

Silence accompanies our walk along the fence. The swish of grass beneath my feet reminds me it's time to mow. Far too quickly, our late-night stroll comes to a halt at the end of my driveway.

"I'll see you around." A war of indecision twists my fingers where they rest against my belly. I put an end to the night, but I'm not ready to let him go.

"See you."

Before I can second-guess myself, I curl the digits into the sides of his cotton tee, yanking him close enough to settle my lips against his. Fuck it. He made his move with the comment about my body, I'm claiming mine. Taking something for myself to tuck away when I return to my reality in a few minutes.

Lee holds deadly still, his hands fisted at his sides. As I close my eyes and indulge us, a muted grunt vibrates his soft lips. Just for a breathless moment, I pretend to be someone else. Someone who gets what they want.

His breath fans across my lips in heated pants, and much too quickly, I pull away and scamper to my house without looking back.

The weight of his eyes track me the entire way to my door. I'd bet he didn't return to his brother's house until he knew I was safely inside.

The silent and dark house brings a breath of relief. Once I shut my bedroom door, I throw myself onto my full-sized bed without even turning on the light, feeling oddly comforted and safe. The image of Lee's face, shadowed by the glow from the fire, plays in my head, while the feel of his mouth against mine still tingles my lips.

7

LEE

I STEP through my kitchen into my bare laundry room carrying a large piece of sheetrock. "I'm back with another one. Give me a hand."

Corjan pushes himself from his position against my wall and helps me set the piece into place, where we secure it.

"Last one?"

"Yep," I mutter, pulling off my hat to run a hand over my dusty hair.

"Thank fuck. If I would have known this would be your payment for watching the dogs, I would have asked someone else." He grins.

"Feel free." Ignoring the sinking in my stomach, I shrug, trying not to think about Juniper's hurried good-bye. I would have missed out on a nice night with her if he had asked someone else.

"What's that look?"

The look of a fool who wants to kiss someone again.

Someone much too young and unblemished. "What look?"

Corjan slams his beer down on top of the washer currently residing in my kitchen. "Something's going on with you."

"You mean besides patching the hole in my ceiling?" I bend over into my fridge and retrieve my own drink.

"Yeah. That's exactly what I mean." He gives me a critical once-over.

"You must be imagining things."

He takes a pull of his drink. "I don't think so."

"I hung out with the neighbor last night. That's all," I admit with no small amount of guilt.

"Yeah? How is Tom?"

"Tom? No. I meant Juniper."

"His daughter? The server? What is she, eighteen?"

Fuck. I hope not. I rack my brain for any mention of her age, but come up empty. She's not that young, though. Right?

"Nah, she's...older."

I don't drink much. Her words from last night come back to haunt me. Thank fuck I didn't put my hands on her. I nearly had to strap them down to my sides to stop from reaching out and sliding a finger under the strap of her silk top. Did she even realize what she was wearing last night? My eyes had a mind of their own, wanting to trace every inch of her hemline where the bare skin met small scraps of fabric.

Corjan sets down his bottle and begins mudding and taping the seams. "So what did you do during this hangout?"

Let her kiss me and should have kissed her back.

I run my tongue over my bottom lip as if I can still taste her and elbow his shoulder.

"Nothing like that. She seemed upset. I could hear her crying on the other side of the fence, so I invited her over to sit by the fire."

"She's pretty hot." He dances his eyebrows at me with another grin.

"How would you know?" I scowl.

"I have eyes."

"You're an ass." My stomach clenches at the thought of him checking her out or peering through her bedroom window. But I don't ask. We're all better off if I don't fucking know.

"So if I ask you to watch my dogs again week after next, I'm guessing it'll be a yes."

I flick a dab of mud at him with my spatula. "I said I hung out with her, not that she's my girlfriend."

A wave of indigestion crests with the thought. Now why did I say that? I haven't had an official girlfriend since college, when I realized it wasn't fair to string women along when I had no intention of marrying one. After enough dead-end relationships, I was done. Something I've happily accepted and plan to maintain until the day I die.

"Is that still a yes?"

"What day?"

"It's a Sunday."

"Yes. But it's because your dogs are sweet and zero work. I could even take them back to my place and sleep in my own bed."

"But then you'd miss *hanging out*."

I lunge, but he jumps out of the way with a laugh.

"It's not a bad thing, you know. You taking an interest in a woman."

The only suitable response is a grunt while I move on to the next seam in the sheetrock. "Where is it you're going this time?"

"Vegas. I'll be touring a ranch a lot like Jude's property."

Corjan's been traveling to make connections and also to view other facilities. Our brother Jude houses the family rescue as an extension of his home. He lives alone on the ranch and our dogs there are his pack. He keeps the most difficult cases, and the ones easily rehabilitated, we foster until they can be adopted. Corjan's main job is to make sure we're up-to-date with our methods and to find any ways we could possibly improve.

"Keep me posted. How long will you be gone this time?"

"Two days."

I try not to think about why that makes my chest feel hollow. "Sounds good. Will you be back in time for Ollie's game on that Tuesday?"

"Aw, shit, I don't think I will. I hate to miss one." He wipes his hands on an old rag.

"Can you catch an earlier flight?"

Corjan shakes his head. "Can't, unfortunately."

I clap my brother on the shoulder on my way back to the kitchen. "It's all right. The Powell cheering section is loud enough to keep him from missing you too badly."

THE NEXT DAY, I drag myself out of bed bright and early to head over to Jude's ranch. My secluded brother lives even farther out of town than I do on several acres of land surrounded by dense trees and greenery. The man is practically a recluse. If it weren't for Nancy dragging him out to Sunday dinners and his weekly grocery run, I'd imagine he'd never leave his place.

The turnoff from the main county road leads down a winding dirt driveway. Half a mile in sits a silver gate blocking my path and the beginning of the fenced property. A pack of dogs waits on the other side, panting and prancing in greeting of their new visitor.

I hop from my truck, rubbing my quad as it aches in protest. Tension coils my body tight. Not for this visit. I'm tense and frustrated because I can't get sweet Juniper's face out of my head. It doesn't help that I won't see her again until next week since Corjan is back home, and the baseball team doesn't meet again until the season opener on Tuesday, which leaves a lot of time for my brain to torment me with images.

She's fucking pretty. Just using that word makes me feel like a teenage boy with his first crush, but it's the god's honest truth. I want to thread my fingers through her soft red waves and brush my palms across her lightly freckled skin. Just the thought of her lips touching mine the other night in that skimpy little shorts set turns my cock to stone.

Which makes me angry all over again.

I march to the keypad and punch in the code before climbing back into my truck, a new scowl firmly in place. The dogs shift away from the moving gate, and I creep the vehicle in just enough to hop out and shut it behind me.

The group trails behind as I slowly travel the rest of the way down the mile-long drive to Jude's house.

The final curve exposes the more stoic of my middle brothers. He sits on an Adirondack chair with his black French bulldog, Ramona, in his lap, trimming her nails as she hollers out to anyone in the vicinity that he's attempting to kill her.

I park and join him with a trail of canines close behind.

"Jack or Aiden coming today?"

He shakes his head. "Just Cortney."

Our sister runs her own veterinary practice in town, and today is vet check day for all the dogs. Which means a marathon of blood work, stool samples, and charting.

"Is she on her way?" I sit in the chair next to his and stretch out my legs. His fourteen-year-old German shepherd, Winnie, drops her head into my lap. I scratch behind her ears, and she softly woofs in pleasure.

Jude quirks an eyebrow in my direction. "In a hurry?"

I let the steady *snip, snip, snip* of the clipper and Ramona's screams stretch between us. "I don't have all day to sit around."

Lies. I have exactly all day to sit around. I promised Nancy I'd come by and mow her lawn, but that isn't until tomorrow. I run a hand through my hair and bend my knees to plant my feet flat on the deck boards.

"Something's up with you."

"Nope."

My left knee bounces so hard it dislodges Winnie's head. She settles down by my chair instead.

"Is that why you're so fucking restless?"

"Since when are you a body language expert?" I snap.

Jude just snorts and shakes his head.

"Can I do something to help?"

"Lucy's nails are next if you need something to do with your hands."

"I'm on it."

I'm just thankful to be done with the investigative questions. First Corjan, now Jude. Maybe I'll postpone Nancy's lawn until I know she's not home because if I'm wearing my thoughts as openly as it seems, she won't stop asking questions until she's satisfied with the answers. I refuse to delve into the why of my current emotional state and leave it at that.

We work separately on the easier dogs before tag-teaming the wiggly ones. A while later, the crunch of gravel heralds Cortney's arrival. She hops out with a smile, and her tech, Bridgette, retrieves a bag from the trunk before meeting us on the porch.

Cort claps her hands together. "I love vet day!"

"You would with how much we pay you," I tease, a little surly.

She sticks her tongue out at me. "Whatever. I'd hang out with these pooches for free any day." She floats effortlessly up the steps, tapping heads and scratching chins as she goes. The dogs compete around her knees for the best positions for attention.

"I'll set up inside," Bridgette says.

"How's Juniper?" Cort asks suddenly.

"Who's Juniper?" Jude sets down Winnie's paw and retrieves another.

I glare at my sister. "Huh?"

She twists her black hair into a clip behind her head.

"I'm just wondering if you've talked to her and apologized."

"Oh." I scratch my left pec. "Yeah. We're fine. I mean, she's fine. I apologized."

"Makes sense." Jude grunts.

"What?" I snap. The cryptic statements toward me deteriorate my already thin patience.

"Ohh." Cortney shares a knowing look with Jude. "He's grouchy."

"Yep," our brother replies with a rare grin. "Probably has to do with Juniper."

Cortney's mouth makes a little O, and her eyes widen. "Did you sleep with her?" she hisses, slamming her hands on her hips.

I want to smack myself across the face. "No, I didn't sleep with her."

"But he wants to," Jude adds.

Cortney jams a finger into my pec. "Don't you dare. You're too old for her."

"I'm not that old," I grumble, rubbing the spot.

"She's like twenty-five!"

Thank fuck for that. Better than eighteen. The guilt I feel for letting her kiss me lifts, and regret that I didn't kiss her back materializes in its place. Twenty-five is still pretty fucking young, but she's well out of high school and old enough to make bad decisions.

"I'm serious," she goes on. "Don't muck her up with your baggage."

"What baggage?" I brace, tensing my thighs, and cross my arms.

"She means you're closed off."

I lift a brow at my brother. He's the last one who

should accuse someone of being closed off since he lives on a ranch like a fucking hermit.

Cortney picks up Ramona and moves toward the door. "No, what I mean is she's too nice for you. You'll hurt her." Her brows dip in concern.

For some reason, her truth makes my chest muscles ache. Old abandonment issues rise rapidly to the surface. *She'd walk away like everyone else.* "Am I really that bad?"

Her eyes lock on mine, a lifetime of conversations passing between them, and her face softens. "No. You're not bad. You're a good man, Lee."

I nod once. Quick. Ready to move beyond this shit. "It's a moot conversation because I'm not sleeping with her."

I repeat the phrase twice more in my head for good measure.

"Good. Let's get started so we aren't here all night, then. Jude sucks at cooking dinner."

Cortney dashes inside with a girlish laugh.

"Assholes. All of you." But even Jude can't hide his grin as he ducks in after her.

8

JUNIPER

IMPULSIVELY KISSING Lee good night has followed me around like a ghost this past week. Any moment not consumed with serving customers or asleep has been occupied by the memory of his soft lips beneath mine.

Kissing him was stupid and selfish. An attempt to convey my thanks for his invitation that evening and a memory to carry with me back home. Words didn't suffice and would come with the requirement to spill all that transpired before he found me crying in the garden. Something I'm not willing to do no matter how fast he urges my heart to tick in his presence.

Faced with seeing him tonight at the first baseball game of the season, I battle with the anticipation.

I should be embarrassed for presuming he'd want me to touch him like that, but he didn't push me away. He just stood there, vibrating with energy, like he fought an internal war with himself and almost lost. And the way I just went for it and took what I needed? Whatever. It's cool. I'm fine. This is fine.

"Do you have your bag?" The metal of my car keys bites into my fingers as I grab them more forcefully than necessary and look to where Lincoln rounds the corner into our kitchen.

"Dammit."

"Language!" I chase two steps after him.

He returns moments later with a lopsided grin and a twinkle in his eyes. "You don't really care that I swear."

"Stop testing me, and get out there." I throw the screen door open for him to exit before following close. Cortney and Oliver wait outside to pick him up so I can work a four-hour shift to make a little extra money before the game. I plan to meet them there later after it starts.

"I'll see you at the game!" I call to Lincoln's back. Cortney sticks her arm out of her window with a friendly wave. On the way to my car, I return the gesture and watch them back out through my rearview mirror.

A surge of exhaustion engulfs me, and I sink down in my seat. This schedule runs me ragged. I picked up doubles Friday through Sunday to get the best tips, and my body pays the price in aches and pains. A dull headache throbs across the back of my head. Only four hours of work and then I can relax for the rest of the evening at the game before coming home and snuggling in bed.

With this most recent paycheck, I'm ready to put in a rental application. There's a cute little two-bedroom house on Main Street that I've had my eye on. Rental properties are scarce in this small town since the population remains stagnant. If I don't act soon, I might miss my chance. Once secured, I can back off a little on the extra shifts and work to maintain my small savings.

This isn't the time to let up yet, so with a deep breath, I straighten in my seat, blink the exhaustion from my eyes, and drive to XO's for my shift.

The loud music and stage lights aggravate my increasing headache. I tie my black apron around my waist with a wince.

"You okay?" Isla asks, appearing from back stage having just finished her afternoon set. She's already removed her heavy makeup, tied her blond curls into a high ponytail, and changed into simple black pants and a white fitted top.

"I'm tired and have a headache. Maybe I'm coming down with something." I press the heel of my hand against my forehead.

"Oh, I'm sorry. I might have something to help." She digs in her clutch purse and pulls out a packet of blue pills. "If you feel the sniffles. It's just cold medicine."

"Thank you. I might need this later."

She brushes her hand down my arm. "Hang in there, beautiful. On your next night off, we need a girls' night."

"That's tomorrow, so if this develops into something worse, I might already need a rain check."

Isla beams and gathers her clutch. "This weekend, then."

"It's a date." I pocket my order pad and move wearily into my section.

By the end of my shift, my muscles ache, and my joints feel stiff. Punching out and walking to my car nearly depletes me of energy. I sit for a moment, forehead touching the cool steering wheel, and close my eyes. My last table put me over forty-five minutes, making me extra late. I should call Cortney and ask her to just bring Lincoln home after the game, but the thought of him not seeing a familiar face in the stands fills me with sadness. He doesn't have anyone else to be there for him. I can't let him down.

On sheer willpower, I manage to drive to the sports complex. As I walk the paved path to the four baseball fields at the back, a light drizzle begins. The gentle droplets cool my flushed skin, and I tip my face to the patchy gray sky.

Maybe this isn't a bad thing. If the first game gets rained out, then I don't have to feel guilty for missing the first couple of innings, and we can go home early.

The Powell family takes up most of our team's bleachers, all huddled together with hoods on and black umbrellas overhead. I catch Cortney's eye and wave.

She gestures beside her, but I shake my head. It's probably not a good idea to sit in the close-knit crowd when I feel like shit. She returns a shrug and resumes watching the game. I'll text her later and explain my rejection.

I meander farther down to the other side of the dugout. Fewer people sit in lawn chairs along the fence. There's a large tree another hundred feet or so that I mentally mark as my destination, feeling my determination leak away with each step. I don't have a chair or a blanket or an umbrella, so the leafy branches will provide the perfect amount of cover.

Sitting at the base sucks the remainder of my energy. A sudden cough catches me by surprise, and by the time I regain normal breath, tears sting my eyes. Heat envelops my hand when I bring the back to my forehead. Like I have a fever. Shit.

I close my eyes and rest heavily, the tree bark rough against my cheek. The rain picks up, a temporary remedy for my condition. The chilly drops cool my fevered skin. Can I make it through his game like this?

I have meds! Oh, thank god for Isla. I dig through my crossbody, past old receipts and wrappers, and emerge with the packet clenched between two fingers. Without any water, I force the pills down dry. If they work quickly, I should be much better by the time the game's done.

In the sea of orange jerseys on the field, I search for Lincoln. He stands near first base with a look of determination that makes him appear much older than his age. I don't bother seeking out the coach, but I can't help the small part of me that wonders if he's scanned the bleachers in search of me.

Time passes with the crack of bats hitting baseballs and cheers from the fans. The rain soaked through my clothes long ago, leaving me shivering and wet. I curl my knees into my chest and huddle against the tree. Dizziness and fatigue muddle my head.

Either this is one hell of a flu or Isla accidentally gave me the wrong medicine. I should care. I should get up and ask someone for assistance, but I can't. Despite the cold, I'm comfortable, and the game won't last forever. Lincoln will find me when it's done.

By then, I'll be much more rested. If I'm not, we'll find someone to help us get home.

9

LEE

"See you, Coach!"

"Great job tonight, Roberts. See you Thursday." I wave at one of the grinning boys and turn back to my family. Most of them wear proud smiles despite the shift in the weather.

"That was a great hit to left field in the third inning." Jack wraps a tattooed arm around Ollie's shoulders and gives him a shake.

"Thanks." The young kid tries to remain passive but a satisfied grin breaks free anyway.

"And that pop fly you snagged? I've never seen you move so fast." Aiden holds up his fist to bump knuckles. After a moment of hesitation, Ollie taps his uncle's fist.

"Too bad the weather turned to shit. I'm ready to get out of this wet mess." Corjan wraps Ollie in a brief hug. "Nice game, kid. Can't wait to see how far you come this season."

"Thank you." Ollie steps back only to be engulfed by Jude.

"All right, say your goodbyes before you inflate his ego anymore." Cortney folds her blanket over her arm.

Nancy pulls Ollie in to kiss his cheek. "Proud of you, baby."

"I'm not a baby, Grandma." He scrubs his face with his forearm.

The rest of the family lets out a series of *oooh's*.

"You should probably run." Aiden cracks his signature smile. "I'll race you to the car."

With a wave around the group, he takes off.

"Hey, cheater!" Ollie chases after his youngest uncle. Jude slinks away behind them.

I wipe a palm down my face. "I could have done without the rain, but not bad for the first game."

"Talented group of boys. So talented, they don't even need you." Corjan slaps my shoulder before sauntering off.

Nancy watches her children ribbing one another with a satisfied smile before Jack threads her hand through his elbow. "Come on, Mom. Let's get you out of the cold. I know your knee acts up with the weather."

"I suppose." She sighs. "Love you all. See you Sunday."

"Love you too." I wave goodbye to Nancy, Cort, and Jack.

I turn to grab my coaching bag from the dugout, rubbing the back of my neck, and realize I'm not alone.

Lincoln stands on the edge of the field in the rain, his gaze scanning the empty complex, squeezing his glove with both hands. The image of him alone, looking for someone who isn't here for him, strikes close to my chest.

I know what it's like to feel abandoned at his age.

"You need a ride?"

The kid startles. His wide eyes glance my way for only a second. "No. She's coming."

"You sure?" It's not as if her track record of being on time is squeaky clean, though she has done better getting him to practice before it begins.

"I said she'll be here!" he suddenly shouts. One hand clutches the cap at the top of his head.

I move calmly beside him and cross my arms. "I'll wait with you." The rain continues falling, but it doesn't matter much when we're already soaked.

"She said she'd be here," he mutters after a few quiet minutes, broken only by the raindrops pelting the dirt beneath our feet. The tension from the kid is palpable through the thickness of the humid summer storm.

"She doesn't seem like the type to go back on her word."

He shakes his head. "Do you think something happened to her?" A quiver of worry permeates his voice.

"I'm sure she's okay. Let me make a call." A gnawing ache warns me to remain in check. Feel out the facts. Emotions only cloud good judgment. I yank my phone from my pocket and angle to the side.

"Hey, did we forget something?" Cortney greets.

"Did you by chance see Juniper at the game?"

"I did. She waved, but when I tried to make room for her to sit, she went somewhere else."

"That's all I needed. Thanks." I keep my eyes on Lincoln as he starts to pace farther away.

"Wait. Is something wrong? I can come back."

I shift my weight to my other foot. "Lincoln's still here, but I have it under control. I'll call if I need you to." I end the call before she can say anything else.

The options are pretty slim, but standing out in the rain isn't doing us any good. If we walk to the parking lot, we can check for her car, and if it's not there, I can run him home before coming back. At least get the kid somewhere out of this shit weather.

But first, I tap her name in my contacts and walk slowly after Lincoln. Maybe she ran off on a quick errand and didn't know the game ended.

Before the phone can even ring once, the kid takes off in a sprint down the third baseline.

"Juniper!" The sound of his scream sends every hair in my body on end.

I pocket the phone without even ending the call and run after him. Down the fence line, I follow his trajectory to a pair of black sneakers sticking out from the other side of a tree.

"Fuck."

He reaches his sister first in a skid of mud and grass and drops to his knees. His fingertips clutch her jaw and shake her face. "Wake up!"

My hammering heart has nothing to do with the burst of cardio and everything to do with the frisson of rage zapping beneath my skin. If someone hurt her while I was a hundred feet away, I don't know what I'll do. A relieved exhale puffs from my lungs when her eyelids flutter, but she doesn't fully wake. Wet grass soaks through my jeans where I drop to my knees beside her brother.

"Does she have a medical condition? Seizures, diabetes, anything she takes medicine for?" I gently prod her wrist to feel her pulse. A racing tempo jumps beneath my fingertips. Faster than it should for someone at rest.

"No." He shakes his head.

"Let me see," I order calmly.

He's wide-eyed with fear, but hastily shifts out of my way, defaulting to the adult to assess the situation. I replace his hand with my much larger one, immediately noticing the heat of her skin.

"She has a fever." I brush the dampened hair from her forehead, placing my palm more firmly against her. Definitely. She's burning up. I look at Lincoln. "She's going to be okay, buddy."

"Hey, Juniper, can you hear me?" I shake her a little forcefully. Her lashes flutter, but her eyes remain closed.

"Can you grab our bags from the dugout? I'll carry her to my truck."

He takes off while I hoist Juniper into my arms. Her little moan sends another shot of comfort to my heightened nerves. She might have a fever, but the rest of her is damp and clammy. The sooner I can get her someplace dry and warm, the better.

Her head lolls against my shoulder, tucking into the hollow of my throat. The hot even breaths chase away some of the chill from the rain. She's so close I can almost imagine the press of her lips against my Adam's apple, and the tropical scent of her skin rises to greet me.

I grip her tighter against my chest. My sense of purpose is renewed with each determined step to get her safe and out of the rain.

Once she's settled in the passenger seat of my truck with the heater on low, I wipe her hair back from her face again, not liking the blue tinge to her lips. Who fucking knows how long she's been sleeping out here? I turn to load the gear from Lincoln, but stop short.

"It's okay, buddy."

A tremor bursts through him that has nothing to do with the weather, and his expression is wide with fear.

"She's going to be okay," I repeat, dropping down on one knee.

The kid's shoulders rise and fall rapidly as if he's breathing fast, but he doesn't look like he's taking in any air.

I yank the bag straps from his shoulders, and they fall to the pavement with a crash. Then I put one hand on each bicep and tap one at a time as if I'm counting the seconds. Alternate tapping is a decent trick to regulate the nervous system. "I think you're having a panic attack. It's okay, Lincoln. I'm right here."

The expression on his face doesn't clear, but he locks eyes with mine as if he's begging me to do something.

"I'm right here. We have your sister, and I'm not going to let anything bad happen to her, okay? I'm going to get you in the truck, and I'll take you both home."

"No!" he shouts abruptly, breaking through his panicked fog. "You can't take her home."

My brows cinch together. "Why not?"

"Because..." He finally looks away, and his fear abates some. "Because there's nobody there to take care of her. I can't do it by myself."

"Where's your dad?"

"He's at work." He clenches his hands into fists.

"Tell me what you think I should do."

He chews his lip for a moment before his face settles with resolve. "Bring me home, but Juniper needs an adult. Can you bring her to the hospital or something?"

I glance back at the truck. "I don't think she needs a hospital."

"Can't you take her home with you?"

I nearly balk at the suggestion before remembering this is an innocent twelve-year-old kid asking someone he trusts for a favor. We don't have time to hash out other options.

"I can do that. As long as you promise you'll be okay until your dad gets home."

He nods once.

"Good. Climb in then."

After loading up our bags, I drive to Lincoln's house to drop him off before bringing Juniper to mine at the request of her little brother. Someplace I never imagined she'd be.

Juniper still hasn't stirred or blinked or even hardly twitched on the drive. I leave the coaching gear in the truck and approach the passenger side. She fits into my arms easily, her back nestled in the crook of one elbow while her knees rest in the other. The dead weight isn't a challenge. I fight back the urge to bury my chin in the damp hair surrounding her neck and breathe in her scent. Because that would be fucking weird. Except I'm surrounded by her, the dampness from the rain making her skin and perfume and shampoo stronger. Something sweet and tropical.

I slip into the side door by the kitchen, grateful Corjan and I finished patching and painting the laundry room so the kitchen isn't still a fucking mess. Her head lolls back over my arm and I'm careful not to bang it around as I carry her up the stairs to my room.

I lay her on my king-sized bed, her red hair fanning across my charcoal pillows. I have to step back and rub the burn in my chest. The sight is so beautiful I want to take a picture so I can pull it out and stare at the serene image whenever I want.

I force myself to enter the attached bathroom instead of gawking. After popping in an antacid, I grab a fluffy bath towel, a clean tee shirt, and send a text off to my sister that all is well and Juniper is fine—as fine as she can be unconscious in my bed. I'm not sure she'll think this is fine whenever she wakes up, but I'm doing the best I can here. Where do I get the handbook called *How to Be a Knight in Shining Armor*? Because I can't be more than a step or two away from fucking this all up.

I wonder how she likes her coffee and if I can have one waiting for her when she's conscious again. She might need the caffeine to keep her awake enough to tell me what happened, and I might be able to bribe her with it not to be too pissed over my next task.

Because I can't leave her in these wet clothes any longer.

A roll of my shoulders and neck isn't enough to prepare me for what I need to do. As gentlemanly as I can, I untie each of her shoes and pry them from her feet. Next off comes her socks. What is wrong with me that I find even the sight of her delicate toes with orange-pink-painted nails cute?

I work succinctly. Popping the button on her jeans and easing the zipper down, I'm extra careful not to touch anything I shouldn't with the backs of my knuckles. It takes more effort than I expect to ease the sticky material down her legs. I toss them behind me before moving to work on her torso.

I bite the hem of the clean tee, holding it ready, and ease her into an upright position. A small moan floats past her lips, but the poor girl still doesn't wake. Stabilizing her around the back with one arm, I use the other to shimmy the wet cotton up and over her head. It joins her pants on the floor behind me. I shove the fresh shirt over her head quickly to protect her modesty, but she starts to tip, so I ease her onto her back.

Circling one of her wrists with my grip, I slide it into a sleeve, receiving only a gentle flutter of her lashes in response. Then I move to the other one, trying to ignore the way it feels to have her dainty arm wrapped in my hand. But she shifts before I can finish the task, and my traitorous eyes accidentally flick down at her exposed torso.

The warm fantasies vanish the instant I spot the purplish marks on her ribs. My eyes flash to her face before returning to soak in the bruises marring her skin, noticing more on her hip and the arm still held in my fist.

"What. The. Fuck," I rumble, low, dangerously low.

A drumbeat starts in my head near the base of my skull, tugging my muscles rigid. The urge to rip all her clothes from her body to inspect her flesh for more blemishes nearly wins, but I beat back the need. My scrutiny would constitute a violation, regardless of the intention.

What I've seen already crosses that line.

Someone hurt her. Bruised her. Gripped her hard enough to leave marks or, *fuck*, hit her. The idea of a man raising his hand to a woman fills me with such a deep desire to inflict damage that a shudder rolls through me.

When I loop her other hand through the hole in the tee shirt and tug the material to her hips, I use ten times the amount of care as before the discovery.

I rearrange her limbs on the bed as if moving a priceless doll and carefully guide the duvet up and over her body. I find myself unable to do anything other than stare as a range of scenarios runs rampant through my head.

"Uhng," she groans and stirs. Her long dark lashes flutter against her pinkened cheeks.

"You're safe, Juniper. I've got you." I curl the blanket down just a bit so she doesn't overheat.

She settles back without waking, her little congested snore sounding cuter than it should. The anger inside tamps down a little.

"I've got you," I repeat, planting a few fingers in the mattress near her hip as I toe off my shoes.

"I'm right here," I vow, leaving only long enough to drag a chair over and position it at the end of the bed.

"I'm not going anywhere."

10

JUNIPER

When I open my eyes, warmth suffuses me. The last thing I remember is shivering beneath a tree in the rain after taking Isla's cold medicine. I could kill her for not telling me it was the drowsy kind. She accidentally drugged me and rather than eliminating my cold symptoms, she sent me off to dreamland.

My heavy eyelids flutter and blink a few extra times against the harsh sunlight streaming through the unfamiliar window. My head feels stuffed full of cotton, and I can't breathe through my nose. I'm in a bedroom. Whose remains a mystery, but it isn't mine. The charcoal sheets and duvet pillow me in a cocoon so warm I don't want to crawl out until I'm one-hundred-percent better, which could be days. This doesn't feel like your run-of-the-mill cold.

On the table to my left lies a box of tissues next to a paper coffee cup. I take a second to blow my nose before wrapping my fingers around the cardboard, testing the weight and feeling the heat seep into my palm. The fresh and hot brew calls to me. As the fog clears and my mental faculties fire to life, panic swiftly kicks in. Where the hell am I?

"Good morning."

A gasp leaves my lungs in a wheeze, and I start coughing, nearly spilling the hot coffee on my lap. I set it aside before it becomes an unfortunate casualty and seek out the source of the low greeting.

"The coffee is for you," Lee continues when I just stare at him with my mouth gaped. Not from the shock, but because I can't properly breathe through my nose.

As I recover from the information of exactly whose bed I'm lying in, I bring the plastic lid to my lips for a sip. I'm startled to find it tastes like my favorite hazelnut creamer. I move in for another taste, savoring the bitter sweetness on my tongue. "You?"

Oh jeez, Juniper. Apparently we aren't firing on all cylinders this morning. You? You what? You brought me home while I was unconscious? You brought me coffee? You're waiting for me to wake up to make sure I'm okay?

A flutter activates in my stomach at the stream of questions. I drink more coffee to silence them.

Lee sits at the end of the bed in a stone gray accent chair. A casual light gray tee stretches across his broad chest. His elbows rest on the armrests, legs spread wide, hands steepled in the middle of his face as he watches me with wary eyes. At my soft accusation, he simply smiles. Even though I don't know him that well, I can tell it isn't happiness lifting his lips.

"Who else? Unless you have a boyfriend I didn't know about."

Something about the way he says the question is accusing.

"If this is about the kiss—"

"This isn't about the kiss." He spits the word as if allowing it to pass through his lips is bitter. "Dammit, Juniper, I hope like fuck you don't have a boyfriend who'd leave you out in the rain like that."

"I-I don't," I stammer, struggling to keep up with the conversation. Heat infuses my cheeks that has nothing to do with the fever. "What happened?"

A stretch of silence follows my question before Lee leans forward and drops his linked hands between his knees.

"That's the million-dollar question, isn't it? What happened?" His voice takes on a new quality—soft and filled with concern—while his brows pinch together on his forehead.

"I think I caught the flu." As if to punctuate my statement, I rub the tissue beneath my nose again to catch a drip.

If I weren't so sick, I might care about how hideous I look, but the fact Lee hasn't run screaming from the room yet keeps me optimistic.

"There's medicine on the nightstand."

I eye it warily.

"The non-drowsy kind," he supplies. "Unless you want another nap, then I can get you something stronger."

"Thank you." I grab the orange pills and wash them down with a mouthful of coffee.

"Who did this to you?" The soft question catches me off guard.

I slowly lower the cup from my lips. "Did...what?"

"Who hurt you?" His low voice drops ominously with the question.

"I'm not following."

"If you have some boyfriend who thinks it's okay to rough up his girlfriend, give me his name, and I'll take care of him."

"I don't know what you're talking about." I twist to set the drink aside. The movement allows me to neutralize my expression.

Lee's fist clenches on his thigh as if he's physically restraining himself. "I saw the bruises on your side. On your bicep. On your hip."

I can't help the startled intake of breath and stall with a question. "You undressed me?"

Belatedly, I notice the large unfamiliar shirt draped over my body. I open the collar and peer inside, nearly sagging into the pillows in relief. Oh, thank god. My underwear is on.

"I had to get you out of the wet clothes. Your lips were fucking blue." He says it as if there's not a regret in the world that he stripped me nearly bare.

My heart rate kicks up. It's the fever making the organ race, not the fact Lee's discovered my very personal secret. "If you don't mind, I think I'd like a shower."

I move to stand, but a wave of dizziness forces me back onto the bed.

Lee leans forward. "You can have a shower, and you can drink your coffee in bed, and I can get you something to eat. Later when you feel up to it, I can drive you back home to your brother, who's worried about you. But before all that, I need you to tell me how you got those bruises." He swallows thickly and glances down at his knuckles before returning his gaze. "I need you to tell me because if someone is hurting you, I will make them stop."

His green eyes flash with sincerity as he stares me down. The way he's perched on the chair feels like a coil wound tight, about to spring out of place at the slightest provocation.

"I bruise easily, okay? I got them the day on the patio with the dog. I hit my side on the table when I fell, and your brother might have pulled a little too rough on my arm when he helped me up."

His expression doesn't change, and I can tell he doesn't fully believe me.

"That's your story?"

"That's what happened." My version isn't totally a lie. I did bump my side when the dog pushed me, though I can't remember if his brother actually grabbed my arm. It would be best for everyone if Lee doesn't ask him.

A provocative silence stretches between us.

"Okay," he says and rises. His full height towers over my perch on the bed. "Let me help you to the bathroom then."

"I got it. I can walk." I wave his hand away. "Don't get too close, or you'll get sick."

"I'm not afraid of a little virus, but I am afraid of you falling and cracking open your head."

I ignore the thrill his words provoke.

He doesn't intervene again, but he leads me across the room into the attached bathroom, keeping me in proximity. The room isn't luxurious, but it is clean for a bachelor. The glass-walled shower with a large showerhead looks heavenly. I need to wash off the sweat from the fever.

Lee steps through the glass door and twists on the

knob, and the room immediately fills with the sounds of the shower and steam. "There are fresh towels in the cabinet. I'll leave you to it."

He grabs the doorknob and pulls it closed on his way out.

"Lee! Wait."

"Yeah?"

"Thank you. You didn't have to do this." My brows draw together. "Actually, why are you doing this?"

He sighs and props one forearm against the wood trim, looking hotter than a single person should in a plain gray tee and blue jeans.

"I found Lincoln alone last night looking for you. When we found you, he asked if I could take care of you because you didn't have anyone to do it. He's a nice kid, and I couldn't let him down. He kind of reminds me of myself at that age."

At the mention of Lincoln, something snaps into place and parts the fog from the fever.

"Where is he?"

"I dropped him off at home last night."

"I need to get back there." I stumble forward, pitching with a wave of vertigo.

Lee stops me by bracing his hands against my shoulders. His thumbs draw gentle circles against the fabric of the borrowed tee shirt. "He's fine. I spoke to him this morning when he called your phone."

To keep all the words I want to say inside, I bite my lip. Lee doesn't know the right questions to ask, and Lincoln wouldn't tell him anyway. This is our shared secret. Not wanting to draw more attention to the situation, I resolve myself to a simple plan of showering and getting dressed.

"Okay."

"If you're that worried, I'll take you home as soon as you're finished."

"Thank you. You've done more than enough. I think I'm just ready to be in my own bed."

His eyes lazily trail across my face and dip quickly down to his oversized tee that reaches my knees.

I swear something sparks in his green gaze, but it's gone before I can be sure.

"I washed your clothes. I'll leave them on the bed for you."

With that, he departs, leaving me in the room quickly filling with steam.

THIRTY MINUTES LATER, I'm surrounded by the scent of a man's body wash. The label said Big D Energy, as if that's supposed to invoke a smell other than dick cheese, but really smells like citrus and sandalwood. I feel a thousand percent better. It's amazing what a hot shower can do. The sickness remains, but between the meds and getting clean, I feel like I can at least make it back to my house before collapsing into the nearest bed.

Though I can't deny the appeal of waking up in the place where Lee sleeps, investigating that feeling will have to wait for another day.

With the lukewarm coffee in one hand and my cross-body in the other, I descend the steps to the main floor in search of my grumpy caretaker. The staircase opens into a simple living room with white walls and dark hardwood floors. A stone fireplace is centered between two floor-to-ceiling windows. Does he spend cold nights with a fire roaring, sipping a beer or spirits as the snow falls outside? For some reason, I can picture it. Lee alone, bare-chested in a pair of sweats, living a quiet, peaceful existence when he isn't out there saving dogs, stepping in to coach Little League or rescuing sick women from the rain.

He's easy to spot out the glass patio door, standing on the edge of the concrete slab and gazing out into the greenery surrounding his property.

I make more noise than necessary as I step into the kitchen with dark cabinetry and stainless steel appliances, and slide open the door outside, stopping beside him.

"Your body wash is something else."

A sound escapes his lips, like a cross between a grunt and a laugh. "Christmas white elephant gift."

"Christmas was six months ago." I face him and rest my hip against the railing.

"It was an industrial pack. The name is shit, but it smells all right."

"You have a nice place." I sip my drink, moving us away from Big D Energy.

He glances at me from the corner of his eye. "You ready to go?"

"Yes. This was really nice of you. You even happened to have my favorite creamer on hand." I smile.

Lee doesn't say anything, but his large hand engulfs mine and tugs me along. "This way. We can enter the garage from the back."

My heart beats in a tizzy. The last time someone held my hand escapes recent memory, and I don't want him to let go. It feels that good. But all too soon, he stops at the passenger door to his truck and loosens his hold. And if I want to be a little bit delusional, I can almost pretend that he seems reluctant to do so when his fingers give a final, lingering squeeze.

The drive to my house is too silent, yet before I can come up with a topic of conversation, he's pulling his truck into the gravel drive.

"Thank you again. You've been a really good friend."

He turns in my direction with a neutral expression. His wrist rests on the steering wheel and with the other hand, he removes his sunglasses. "Is that what you think we are?" His tone matches his face—hard to read but not unkind.

I shrug. "Why not? I don't have many friends. You've seen me cry, and you've seen me nearly naked. I think that makes us closer than acquaintances." Why did I say that? I shouldn't want to draw attention to the fact he's seen more of my body than anyone else in the past few years.

That produces a rare, small smile. "Point made. Rest up, *friend.*"

Before I can get myself into any more trouble, I leap from his truck with as much energy as I can muster, and walk to the house without turning around.

I pause just inside the storm door. With a breath of courage, I steady myself with my hand on the knob before twisting and pushing my way inside, not entirely sure what I'll find.

My father and Lincoln at the kitchen table, a Monopoly board open between them, is not even in the realm of what my mind could have conjured, even under the influence of a fever and meds.

"You're back! Are you better?" Lincoln stares and gives

my appearance a once-over as if he can spot any lingering damage.

"I'm a bit better. How are you doing?" I try to keep my gaze from wandering to our father, who's attempting to ignore me.

"Dad made pancakes this morning, and now we're playing Monopoly." He fans out his stack of properties. "I'm kicking his butt."

"Looks like fun." I smile at my brother. "I'm going to lie down. I think I may have the flu, and I don't want you to get sick."

"'Kay." He turns back to the game and tosses the dice.

Moments like these are rare around here, but I can't help but wonder if maybe I've become the problem. I've spent the past two years trying to be there for my brother. First, to help him through his grief and get him into therapy when our father couldn't be bothered to look after anyone but himself. Then as a buffer between him and our father's drinking. It seems clearer by the day that I'm the one Dad despises.

It should have been you.

His words echo through my head.

Maybe this is all for nothing. Maybe if I removed myself from the equation, Dad and Lincoln could go back to living life as normal, and I could go back to chasing the dreams of a twenty-five-year-old.

But what if leaving home only opens the door for our father to push Lincoln around? I'd never forgive myself for being wrong.

11

JUNIPER

WORKING SO many extra shifts set me firmly in my boss's good graces. I've always had a strong work ethic, but being available to cover for my coworkers means they didn't hesitate to help cover for me. My boss, Kathy, at Mary's Diner wanted to give me an entire week to rest, but after I promised her I was on the mend, she said I could come in on Friday at the earliest. Manny, my boss at XO's, was a little less concerned about my condition and said as long as I felt good enough to work, I could return whenever. Not wanting to have another mishap and miss Lincoln's other baseball game this week, I told him it would be Friday for that shift too.

After my schedule was squared away, I texted Isla to assist picking up my car the next morning and spent most of Wednesday in bed, alternating between hot and cold before my fever finally broke around eight o'clock that night. After receiving one text from Lee checking in, I promptly fell asleep and woke up this morning with minor sniffles lingering but the other symptoms resolved.

Thursday afternoon, I sit at the kitchen table with my planner open, outlining my upcoming shifts and the baseball schedule. Lincoln only has one more week of school before the summer break. I'll need to get in touch with Cortney tonight about setting up some playdates to get him out of the house while I wait to hear back from the rental company. I managed to drop the application off this morning while running some errands. They said they'd look it over and call me as soon as possible if I've been approved. My hopes are high, and despite the lingering flu symptom, my mood reflects the optimism.

I always dreamed of moving out of state once I finished college, but after we lost Mom, my dreams died along with her. I was needed here. Even if moving out on my own is one tiny step, finally accomplishing something for myself feels good.

The alarm on my phone sounds, warning me we have thirty minutes until we need to be at the field.

"Linc! Get ready to go!" I tuck my planner into my crossbody and dump the dregs of my coffee down the sink. After plopping my sunglasses on my head, I slip on my shoes and purse, and grab my keys just as my brother rounds the corner with a scowl. I choose to ignore drawing attention to the twelve-year-old beast that has overtaken my brother.

"Meet you out there." I skip out the door without waiting for his response.

He wanders out a few minutes later and climbs into the passenger seat. Without a word, I set a wrapped box in his lap and back out of our driveway.

"What's this?"

"A gift."

The weight of his glare is heavy. "No shit."

I fix a scowl on my face. "Lincoln," I warn, exasperated.

"Sorry." He grins, and the sound of paper ripping fills the car. "Is this for real?"

"Yeah."

"You got me a phone?"

"I feel guilty for what happened the other night. You need a way to get ahold of someone if I'm not there." Not much would have changed the situation, but he could have tried calling Oliver or Cortney, or even our father as a last resort. "I've already programmed a few numbers in there."

"But Dad said I couldn't have a phone until I'm a teenager."

"Don't worry about him. I put it on my plan. Maybe try not to shove it in his face, though."

We don't even have a landline at the house. What happened the other night, plus school letting out, is more than enough reason to get him a phone in case of emergencies. Our father will just have to deal.

"Thank you."

"You're welcome."

"Now I'm sorry I said shit earlier. I take it back."

"You just said it again!"

I look over at him in time to see him grin. The easy smile reminds me that whatever life throws at us, we'll get through it together.

THIS TIME when I approach the Powell cheering section, I don't turn down Cortney's invitation to sit. Nerves fire at the thought of being surrounded by Lee's entire family even though we're just friends. They have no way of knowing he's seen me nearly naked.

"Hey, I'm sorry about the other night."

Cortney surprises me with a cardboard cup, tendrils of steam rising from the opening. "Lee called and asked if you'd been at the game. Everything all right?"

I wish I could read her mind and know how much Lee told her. The warm coffee with hazelnut creamer gives me a much-needed boost of courage to open up to a new friend. After a stalling mouthful, I settle for a simplified version.

"Thanks. I was coming down with the flu, and it hit me out of nowhere. I fell asleep under a tree over there." Downplaying the situation, I wave my hand in the general direction.

"Oh, you poor thing! My brother sounded worried when he called."

I grimace. "Yeah. I scared Lincoln, I think."

"You scared me too! I was about ready to turn my car around, but knowing Lee was looking for you, I felt it was okay to wait." She nudges my side. "I think he likes you."

"Saving me from my own stupidity doesn't mean he likes me." I turn my attention to the field, pretending to be engrossed by our pitcher throwing a strike.

"I'm serious." She elbows my ribs. "He's grouchy and old, but his face changes when your name gets brought up."

"Changes how?" My curiosity wins out.

"He looks unsettled. Like hearing your name and not seeing you nearby makes him want to jump in his truck until he finds you."

"Why is my name getting brought up?" I raise an eyebrow at her, finally looking away from the game.

She throws her head back and laughs. "I maybe prodded him a little bit about you. I'm sorry. I'm nosy, okay? Just be careful. He can be difficult to get close to."

"Careful is my middle name."

Cortney and the rest of the Powells jump from their seats in a roaring cheer as our boys make a double play. Catching the pop fly and tagging the runner at second, they end the inning. I clap loudly from my seated position.

While eyeing the boisterous, loving family, I feel a pang of longing. I miss my mom. Our family has always been small. Both my parents were only children, and after we lost her our unit shrunk even more. What it must be like to have so many people loving you unconditionally, flaws and all.

Once the ruckus settles down, I ask Cortney about her summer plans with school ending.

"You know I will do just about anything to get Ollie out of his room and off the video games. Lincoln is welcome at our house any time."

"I hope I can repay the favor soon. I put in an application for a rental, and once I get settled, we can plan a sleepover for the boys."

"I'm excited for you!" She grasps both of my folded hands in my lap. "My first time moving out was less than glamorous. I thought I was about to start a family, but Ollie's dad turned out to be a cheating dirtbag."

I give her a sympathetic look. "Ouch."

"Mm-hmm. Did I ever tell you he got another girl pregnant at the same time?"

"You're kidding!" I turn to face her while the other team throws a few warm-up pitches before starting the inning. I'd heard stories about how much of a loser Ollie's dad was, but this one is new to me.

"Nope. I always said the best thing that ever happened to us was him choosing her and moving out of state. Last I heard, they're off in Iowa somewhere."

"Good riddance. Thankfully, I have nothing major going on in my life. It's just time to start out on my own."

"You should be proud of yourself. You've worked so hard since your mom passed and it really shows."

I only half listen because Lee chooses that moment to step onto the field, and I suddenly can't decide if I like the view of his front or back better. The man can wear a pair of worn denim jeans so well, he could be in a Wrangler's ad. If the dog rescue doesn't work out, he'd have a career in bull riding for sure with an ass like that. Slap on some boots and a hat, and he'd make a damn fine cowboy.

"Thanks," I belatedly respond.

"Oh look. Lincoln's up to bat."

My attention shifts to where my little brother approaches the plate, a black number four on the back of his orange jersey. A second later, the pitch whizzes by, followed by the umpire calling, "Strike!"

Tension curls Lincoln's shoulders. I can tell the error discourages him.

"You got it, Lincoln. Next one's yours, buddy!" I call out. My own body fills with tension.

"Strike two!"

His swing at the second pitch isn't quite quick enough. The third pitch sails in, hitting the catcher's glove, and the umpire calls, "Strike three!"

Lincoln turns around, takes a few steps from the plate, and slams the top of his bat into the dirt in an incredibly unsportsmanlike display.

"Oh no," I mutter, starting to rise from the bleachers.

Cortney places her hand in my elbow and tugs me back down. "Let Lee handle it. I know you want to help, but you'll only embarrass him by going over there."

My fingers twist together in my lap. "He's embarrassing himself. I don't know what's gotten into him lately."

"I think it's the age. These boys don't have periods starting, but they go through hormonal changes too. Ollie's had a few outbursts lately that even resulted in tears, and he's a pretty levelheaded kid."

A strand of hair tickles my cheek, and I swat it away. "I'd take tears over whipping around baseball bats." Concern fills me as I watch, barely containing the question fighting to burst free so someone else can tell me I'm being silly. Could Lincoln's sudden aggression be something that runs in the family?

"Take it easy, number four," Lee says.

But Lincoln doesn't give him the time of day. He brushes past, knocking into Lee's elbow, and throws his helmet into the dugout, where it clangs loudly against the chain link. My heart skips into my throat.

Lee follows him inside. "You're going to strike out sometimes. But how you deal with it—"

"It was a bullshit call!" His outburst startles me, and some of the team turns around to look at him.

"We don't argue with the ump unless you want to get thrown out of the game."

Lincoln sits back on the bench and crosses his arms over his chest. "I don't care then. Throw me out."

Without hesitating, Lee looks at the lineup and calls out, "Dawson, you're taking over for Lincoln when we're back in the field this inning."

"Okay," Dawson says, looking back and forth between Lee and Lincoln, but my brother simply continues sulking.

"He shouldn't have done that," I argue to Cortney. "He could have talked to him before pulling him."

"I think he's pretty old-school. If Lincoln wants to sit out, maybe it's what he needs."

She's probably right. She's the one with twelve years of parenting under her belt. But what happened to dusting yourself off and getting back out there? This feels a little like giving him what he wants.

I try to enjoy the rest of the game, but I can't let it go. So much that when the team pulls off a win and the Powell clan descends on Oliver, I tell Lincoln to wait at the car, and I find Lee in the dugout. "Got a second?"

"Hey. You look like you're feeling better." He looks up from zipping a black bag.

"I am. Look, I just wanted to say what happened with Lincoln, well, I'm not sure exactly what happened with him, but I think maybe the next time he could benefit from a little more discussion before yanking him out for the rest of the game."

Lee stands and shoulders his bag. "When I'm in the middle of coaching a game, I don't have time for a long discussion, but if you'd like, I can take some time now to talk to him."

"It just seems like you were rewarding his bad behavior."

"I don't know what you want from me." Lee's tone becomes irritable. "He got a little hot-headed and chose to sit out the game. If at any time he wanted to join in, we could have made that happen."

I check over my shoulder to where his family still gathers before looking back to find Lee glaring down at me. "I think he just needs someone to show they understand and validate his feelings."

"You're coddling him," Lee says suddenly.

The muscles in my back tense, pulling my spine straight. "No, coddling would have been coming into the dugout while you allowed him to sit on the bench and talked to you then. I'm calling you out after the fact for being too hard on him."

"I don't see much of a difference."

"I'm just asking you to be a little nicer, considering he's going through a lot."

Lee shifts his gaze from over my shoulder back to my eyes and huffs in annoyance. "I won't give him special treatment."

"Not even for a friend?"

"We aren't really friends," he says with enough condescension that it burrows deeper than it should beneath my skin.

I move an automatic step back in self-preservation. I don't know what happened in the last two days for this one-eighty change toward me, but I'm smarter than to stick around to be his practice target. "Okay then."

The sound of his family's laughter draws me from the

dugout. I might hear my name called behind me, but I keep walking straight to my car. I have enough experience to know when I'm not wanted somewhere and just enough dignity to remove myself from the situation.

Before I get irrevocably hurt.

12

LEE

I'VE BEEN STOMPING around like a bear forced out of hibernation in the middle of winter for the past two days, and it doesn't take a rocket scientist to determine why. Hell, I bet even Ollie could take an educated guess and come out pretty damn close to the mark. My sour stomach is a product of my own selfish attempts at preservation.

The extra pent-up energy hasn't completely gone to waste, and my house is clean from top to bottom. While I vacuumed behind my fridge, I thought about how to apologize to Juniper for my attempt to keep her at arm's length. During the time spent scrubbing my oven, I mentally drafted an apology letter I thought I could stick under her windshield wiper before nixing the idea. Too impersonal for an apology and too intimate for a friend. The hours washing the exterior windows were just a distraction from the memory of her sleeping peacefully in my bed.

(Which didn't fucking work.)

After days of avoiding everyone and anything with a heartbeat, I have my boat hooked up to the back of my truck, and I'm almost to Corjan's to pick up my fishing pole he accidentally took home after our last trip. I conveniently forgot the extras in my garage and set out on my mission to retrieve this particular rod. It has nothing to do with the person who lives next door to him.

And I refuse to examine too closely why I have a fresh cup of coffee with hazelnut creamer sitting in the holder next to my americano as I pull past Corjan's house in order to back the boat into his driveway.

Keeping my eyes away from the neighbor's house isn't an easy task. The damn things act magnetized to seek her out whenever I feel she's near. Not that I have the slightest clue if she's home or not, but I want to pretend she is so I don't have to feel like a schmuck for all this extra effort.

The fishing pole is right where Corjan said it would be, leaning in the corner of his garage. I snag the rod, but indecision stalls me. Without much forethought, I dig out my phone and start to text.

ME

Juniper

I need to talk to you

I mean, would you please talk to me?

Shit, I'm fucking this up

I called after you the other night but you kept walking

I run a hand through my hair and pull my palm down over my face. It's too damn early for this. I stalk out the door, but my phone buzzes in my hand, halting my steps.

JUNIPER

Why would I stop? You were pretty clear

Just the fact she responded fills me with relief.

ME

Can you come over next door?

While waiting for her to text back, I secure the rod in the boat. Looking up from my task, my mouth hangs open at the vision of Juniper walking toward me along Corjan's side of the fence. A pair of tiny cutoffs hug her little belly in the front while sitting snug on her upper thighs, and a white tank clings to her curves, leaving very little to the imagination.

"Thanks for coming," I stammer through a dry throat.

She stops across from me, the boat a buffer between us. "I'd like to hear what you have to say, even if it is seven in the morning."

Her gaze issues a challenge and her cool confidence forces me to straighten. A worthy opponent. Not that I doubted her strength before, but her backbone is fucking sexy.

I lean into the truck before coming back out and hold the coffee out to her across the bow. "Here."

The silence speaks volumes, but she easily accepts my first gift.

Words I want to say tumble around my skull in a jumbled mess. "How much do you love surprises?" I blurt.

She tries to hide her reaction with a sip, but her eyes widen, and her expression clears. A one-shouldered shrug serves as a partial answer. "Seven out of ten if it's from someone I actually like."

I fight my own reaction to her jab. "Come on the boat with me."

"What? When?"

"Now."

"I can't just get on a boat with you for the day."

"A few hours max," I coax. "I can have you back by lunch."

"I really don't think I should."

"And I'd really like it if you'd say yes."

We're forced into a staring match. I brace my hands against the edge of my boat while Juniper worries her plump pink lip between her teeth, drawing my attention someplace it has no business being. Her mouth.

"What's holding you back?" I ask after a stretch of silence.

"That things will go south again, and I'll be stuck with a grump on a boat and can't escape."

Her words draw a sudden laugh from my gut, so acute I press a hand against my abs as if to ascertain it really happened. Recovering from the shock of my reaction, I can't wipe the smile from my face. "I promise if he shows up, I'll drop you off at the nearest shoreline."

"Funny," she deadpans. "Then I'll be left stranded."

"It's a good thing it's a made-up scenario and won't happen. I promise to be on my best behavior. I just want to show you a good time."

"You promise you won't keep me out all day?"

"I'll bring you home whenever you like. Just say when."

"Fine." She saunters to the front and swings open the door.

All the reasons I should stop her from taking this little adventure with me storm my mind, but I can't muster the strength to employ one of them. After checking that everything is secure, I hop into the truck and smoothly pull us onto the road. The air is warming already, but I keep the windows up to trap in her flowery scent.

"I'm sorry for the other day. I didn't mean to say what I said."

"What, that we aren't friends?" The emphasis she places on the verb establishes her hurt.

I resist the urge to hang my head. "I'm not used to letting people get close to me."

"Not to call your sincerity bullshit, but you seem to have a lot of people close to you." She sips the caffeinated beverage, eyeing me over the lid.

"That's my family, and they've earned their places, but even they'd tell you I keep them at a certain distance."

The way she teases her bottom lip with her brows pulled together urges me to keep talking.

"I've called my parents by their first names, Nancy and Terrance, ever since they took me in twenty-some years ago. I never could call them Mom and Dad. Nancy and my siblings, they're all I have," I confess quietly. "And now you've come around..."

"And you don't want me," she states plainly as if she already knows the answer.

"I don't want to want you." My honest answer lands with a stinging blow. "I don't trust easily, and I don't let people get close. It's a product of being a homeless foster kid."

She shifts in her seat. "I'm not sure that's the kind answer you meant to deliver, though I guess I should thank you for your honesty."

I drop a hand from the steering wheel and stroke her

fingers where they rest against her thigh. The skin is soft and smooth.

"I haven't dated since college. I tried to do what I thought was right. I was nearly finished with my degree and thought the next natural step was to get married, buy a house, and have a couple of kids. But as soon as she told me she loved me, it felt like I was suffocating. I became suspicious of everything. I don't do well with that word. It carries too much power. I'd once promised myself I'd never be that vulnerable again."

"What happened?"

I shrug and tighten the fingers still wrapped on the wheel. "I broke it off. She moved on, and so did I."

The words I keep hidden flow out with an ease I've never experienced. But here I am, spilling my guts along the Minnesota highway to a woman I barely know. Who the fuck is this guy?

"I'm not asking for marriage. Hell, I'm not even asking to be your girlfriend."

I recognize her defense for what it is—protection. The tactic is one I'm damn familiar with. I've already hurt her, and my admission puts me in the position to do it again.

"You haven't asked me for anything. You said we were friends." I run my finger over the ridges of her knuckles. "But I guess your words from the other day stuck. I've seen you cry. I've seen you half undressed. We've kissed. Those all feel like stepping stones on the way to a relationship I know I'm not interested in, and I didn't handle it well."

Along with other things. I still don't trust her answer about the bruises and that in itself makes me uneasy enough to halt any further developments that could or could not be happening between us. At least until I determine what's the truth.

"Nobody said you have to date me."

I grunt to disguise a laugh. If only she knew I might want to date her, but that's just not the kind of guy I am.

"Good, because I'm not trying to date you."

"So what are we doing then?"

"I'm saying sorry the way I know how. I'm not big on empty words. I prefer actions."

A small laugh leaves her mouth. "I guess I can't be mad at that. This is a big gesture. You didn't fuck up that badly."

My hand tightens around hers in warning. "Don't laugh at me, little girl."

Her swift intake of breath matches my own. Now why in the fuck did I say that? And by the tightening near my dick, why did I find that hot?

The sign for the boat launch saves me from further discussion. I turn into the lot, back the boat into the water, and leave her with it while I park, giving myself a few minutes to cool off. Suddenly, spending the day with her doesn't seem like such a great idea. We've touched upon unexplored territory, and the navigation could be dangerous.

Good thing I'm always up for a challenge.

* * *

SUNLIGHT GLITTERS off the navy waters ahead. The spray from the wakes on the side of the boat cools skin already flushed from the summer heat. It's still early, but the cloudless sky doesn't offer much protection from the direct morning sun. If we aren't careful, we'll be sporting sunburns by ten o'clock.

The wind whips Juniper's curly hair around her shoulders as she sits in front of me. Splashing water and the roar of the motor hinder our ability for conversation. I take the reprieve after the lengthy sharing I did on the drive over. There's plenty of time for chatter when our lines are in the water. And maybe this time, I can try not to embarrass myself and share even more of my entire life's story. She doesn't need to hear about some old guy's tragic upbringing. It's not even something I dwell on anymore. At forty years old, I've learned to leave the past where it belongs.

Finding my favorite spot off the edge of some weeds, I slow the boat and drop an anchor to keep us in place. A loon settles off to our left. The native bird releases its call around the unoccupied lake, serenading us just above the idle hum of the motor.

"I've never done this before," Juniper says, breaking the silence.

"Fishing?"

She shakes her head and looks out at the bird. "Being on a boat, on a lake. I've fished from shore a few times when I was younger."

My gaze rakes over the small vessel, wondering what she sees. The boat is a basic v-bottom with three bench seats that belonged to Terrance, which means it's probably older than she is.

"This was Terrance's boat. He used to take us kids out on Saturdays to give his wife a break from all the arguing. He had a rule. Nobody could talk until someone caught a fish, and our competitive little asses didn't catch on that he was just buying himself some quiet time. Sometimes, we'd be out here for hours without making a sound, but there was also that time Jude caught a little sunfish within the first five minutes."

Nancy gifted it to me when he passed away, and for the first few years, I'd come out on the lake just to feel close to him. I know it's not much in terms of luxury, but the emotional value is worth more than gold. My chest warms at the thought of sharing it with someone new.

"Come here."

Juniper cocks her head adorably, probably thinking about the fact we're only five feet apart in this small boat, but she complies without question and carefully moves to straddle the bench in front of me. The way her thighs innocently spread on either side sends my blood pumping in ways it has no business moving around her.

I swallow around the lump in my throat. "Ever bait your own hook?"

"Nope."

Grabbing a minnow from the bucket, I show her how to hook it on so it won't fall off.

"A little disgusting, but I want to try it." Her eagerness incites my own playfulness, and the need to touch her grows.

While she concentrates on hooking her minnow, I skim the back of my knuckles against her knee. Testing her reaction. Her gaze lifts to mine for half a second before she holds up her hook and proudly declares she did it.

"Good. Now drop it in."

"Here?" She gestures over the side.

"You can cast it out if you want, but there are fish under the boat too," I tease.

"Smart-ass." She complains with a smile and drops her line in the water. "Now what?"

I toss my own line in on the other side and lean forward. "Now we wait."

Juniper wrinkles her nose. "That's it? What do we do to kill time?"

"Well," I draw the word out, that self-preservation kicking in as alarm bells ring in my head.

Don't do it, asshole.

"When I'm alone, I relax. I watch the birds and enjoy the sun on my face. I soak in the peace and quiet."

Her body naturally shifts closer, as if she's afraid to miss a word coming from my mouth. "And when you're not alone?"

My voice drops lower. Husky. "I've never brought anyone out here before who wasn't family, but I can think of a lot of ways to spend the time with you." My gaze flits dangerously over her perfect, pink mouth. "There's one thing I can't stop thinking about."

"Wh-What is it?" Now she's focusing on my lips, snapping my remaining willpower in two.

"You kissed me." I engulf her hand in mine, tugging her to stand and guiding her between my knees. Even though I'm sitting and she's upright, we're nearly eye to eye, and I only have to tilt my head back slightly, squinting at the sun overhead. "If I had gotten the chance to kiss you first, it would have gone a little differently."

"You can show me on one condition."

Her bold declaration provokes a rumble from my chest. "What's that?" I rasp. My thumbs skate beneath the hem of her shorts, brushing against the smooth skin on the sides of her thighs.

At my touch, she closes her eyes. "You can't fall in love with me."

"I won't," I swear.

"You can't even fall in like with me."

With my left hand, I brush the hair from her cheek and tuck it behind her shoulder. "I find you repulsive." I provide enough humor in my voice to reveal the lie. "Physical only?"

She nods. "I can engage in a consensual adult sexual relationship."

I nearly groan. She's trying to sound confident and mature, but why does it just sound downright dirty?

"In that case…" I curl my fingertips around the back of her thigh and urge her closer yet so she has no choice but to lift and straddle my lap.

My cock surges to life.

"Our first kiss should have gone something like this."

My left hand grips her supple hip and the other settles around the back of her neck, supporting the base of her skull. I coax her to me, unhurried, as if I have all the time in the world until I need to meet her with my lips.

Her eyes flick between mine as the gap shrinks. Closer. Closer still. Before they finally flutter shut just as our mouths finally touch.

I give her one gentle press, one tempting brush like the kiss of a gentleman at your door after a first date before I part my lips and breathe her in, moving more deeply for a taste. She expertly responds, opening in time with me, allowing entrance to my seeking tongue.

I stroke velvet on velvet, consuming the bitter coffee

and sweet hazelnut cohabiting with her addictive taste. Swallowing her moan, I pull her hips forward, guiding her center up and down the length of my cock straining against my jeans. She moans again, and I entice her up and down, rocking her into me.

The gentle waves lap against the boat, smoothly pitching us, spurring us on. Juniper's wandering hands settle, one on my shoulder and the other holding on to the back of my neck. She uses them for leverage to speed up and take control, to rock herself harder against me, pressing her center more firmly along my bulge. The heat of her surrounds me until I don't just feel her on my cock. I feel her everywhere.

Burying my fingers in her hair, I tilt her neck to the side and kiss a line from the corner of her mouth, across her jaw, and to her ear.

"You're filthy, riding me on this boat where anybody could see. Be a good girl and make yourself come."

"Y-Yes, I want to come."

Fuck. She's grinding against me and panting, and I'm two seconds away from moving her off me so I can yank my pants down and shove my cock into her.

"Do it," I order, dangerously close to an orgasm myself. "I want your panties messy when you come on my lap."

She gasps, tilting her head back when I attach my lips to her neck. "I'm not wearing any."

"Fuck *me*," I growl.

"I would," she protests, picking up her pace and rocking the boat in earnest now. Jerky movements punctuate her loss of control as she reaches the peak.

"Next time," I grunt, revealing I already want more. She's easily woven me under her spell.

Her fingers tighten in my hair, and her head falls back, showcasing the slender column of her throat as she splinters apart and cries out loudly.

"Yeah, baby," I grunt, delirious with the sounds she makes. I crush her tightly against my chest, mindful of the bruises on her side, and hold her as our breathing returns to normal.

With a giggle, she eases back on my lap. "That was fun."

The rock-hard cock in my jeans disagrees, but I don't tell her that. Feeling her shudder and fall apart in my arms is more than worth the discomfort. I brush away the strands of hair sticking to her forehead. "You scared away the loon."

A red hue rises to her freckled cheeks, so I press a kiss to the tip of her nose.

"I fucking loved it. I can't wait to hear what other sounds you make when I'm pleasuring you."

She peers over the edge of the boat. "We probably scared away the fish, too."

"Grab your rod, and we'll see if you've had any luck." I pat her round ass as she climbs from my lap.

The cheeky grin she throws me over her shoulder does nothing to calm my aching cock, but we've played enough for one morning. I might have said I can't offer her anything but a physical relationship, but I don't want her to think it's the only reason I want her around.

Even if she is sinfully tempting, she has a stunning personality, too. And I can enjoy her body without treating her as if keeping my cock warm is her only use.

A sudden scream snaps my attention back to the present. I raise my head in time to see Juniper fall ass first out of the boat, horror etched on her pale face. Droplets of lake water splash my shirt with the force, the vessel rocking with the sudden shift in weight only made worse as I rush to my feet. I grip the edge for balance.

Adrenaline loops a circuit through my veins as I peer into the water, ripples and bubbles revealing where she disappeared. The depth is around fourteen feet in these parts, and I don't have a clue if she can swim.

Without a moment of hesitation, I throw my hands above my head and cut through the lake with ease. My heart pulses in my ears, louder beneath the surface. The water transforms from light blue to navy to amber the deeper I go, the sunlight rapidly diminishing.

Kicking feet propel me onward, arms circling wide and coming up empty. I swim in dizzying circles, searching helplessly.

Where is she?

I open my mouth, wanting to shout, knowing I can't. Even if I could, she wouldn't hear me. Panic returns from fear and lack of air, forcing me to return to the surface. The dirty water burns my eyes and blurs my vision, but sunlight draws me upward. Closer. When I'm about to breach, a pair of legs appear to my left, swirling to remain buoyant.

My hands span her waist when I crest the surface, a coughing gasp the first thing I hear. It takes a moment to realize the sound comes from me. Wiping a palm down my face, I blink the water from my eyes, and immediately return my touch to her body as if to assess she's really okay.

"Lee?" An uncertain note clouds her tone.

"You're okay." I fight to strengthen my voice to hide the breathlessness.

"I didn't intend to swim today, but here I am." She spreads her arms wide on the surface.

I must have drawn her in without noticing because her face is so close I can see dewy droplets clinging to her dark lashes. Apprehension hides behind her soft smile.

"Are you okay?" she asks me.

I rearrange my face into a neutral expression. "I haven't had a scare like that in a long time, not going to lie."

Her hands press into my shoulders and her legs circle my waist. "I was captain of the swim team in high school, and I swam weekly in college. I can handle getting wet."

A grunt passes my lips at the teasing innuendo. The feel of her in my arms calms the remnants of fear. "Next time tell me that before you decide to take a swim, little mermaid."

Her breath catches at the name I used when she fell into my lap. "I'll try to remember that next time I fall in."

"There won't be a next time," I mutter. Pinching her cheeks in one hand, I draw her close enough to take her lips in a close-mouthed kiss. What I intended to calm me down only makes my heart beat faster. I untangle her hands from behind my head and set them on the edge of the boat. "Now hold on so I can help you up."

I visually check her grip twice before hauling my ass over the side. Immediately, I lean back down, take her hands and lift her straight up and over to safety.

"There's a towel in the seat there. The lid flips up."

"Thanks."

I do my best to ring out the bottom of my shirt. Unfortunately, there's nothing I can do about the jeans sticking to my nuts unless I want to remove them.

But falling in a lake is one sure way to calm down a hard-on. Though, seeing her clothing plastered to her skin makes it unlikely it'll stay gone for long.

13

JUNIPER

I SPEND my shift at XO's Sunday night daydreaming about wallpaper. The rental company hasn't responded to my application yet, but it is the weekend, so the nerves remain minimal. That doesn't mean I can't start decorating my potential new place in my mind between serving tables and refilling drinks. More specifically, how weird would I be to put wallpaper with boats on it up in the bathroom. I'm leaning toward a nautical theme of navy blue and white with lighthouse décor for no particular reason.

The thoughts continue to assail me in the booth I occupy after my shift and that's exactly how Isla finds me when she wanders out from backstage after her set.

"I swear to god, Manny needs to uninstall his head from his ass. The tips I just earned are triple what I get during the day. I'm so fucking pissed."

Isla's tirade jolts me from the memory of the sun on my face while I rocked heavily in Lee's lap. "You should talk to him. Threaten to walk out if he won't give you what you want."

"And then what would I do?" She shakes her mass of blond curls. "He only had me fill in because he was desperate tonight, but he's made it clear he doesn't think I'm cut out for a prime slot."

"Go find another club that will actually take care of you! I hate to say it, because you're my best friend, but you're single and unattached here. I'm sure plenty of places around Minneapolis would love to have your sexy ass strutting their stage."

Isla snaps open a menu on the table in front of her face. "And leave your beautiful face to fend for yourself? I can't. Not until things have settled down for you."

"I have faith good things are about to happen."

"Are you hungry, or do you have to get back to your brother soon?"

I flip my own menu open. "I'm free for the night. He's staying at a friend's house." Thank god for Cortney and that I didn't blush too terribly hard while looking her in the face when I dropped him off. I'm not sure what she'd think if she knew I rode her brother's lap to orgasm just over twenty-four hours ago.

The smack of Isla's hand on the table startles me from the dirty thoughts. "Margs it is, then!"

Our friend Kira wanders over to take our order. We select an assortment of appetizers to go with our drinks, and a few minutes later, she's back with the alcoholic beverages.

Isla's shoulders shimmy with the hypnotic music while she sips her straw. "Maybe you're right."

I flick my balled straw wrapper at her. "I usually am, but what about this time?"

"I practically live here. Look at me. I get off work, and here I am, having a meal and drinks until I go home to sleep, only to return tomorrow. Maybe I should see what else is out there."

"Anywhere would be lucky to have you, but you need to be somewhere you're valued."

She wiggles her fingers in a "gimme" motion. "Keep hyping me up, girl, and I might just do it."

"And maybe your sweet Prince Charming is just waiting for you to leave this town."

"Or Princess Charming." She giggles and winks.

"Exactly." I nod with a serious face and gulp the tart concoction in front of me.

"Speaking of romance, have you sat in any laps lately?"

The mouthful of liquid nearly spews across the table. I force it down to save the front of Isla's shirt and end up inhaling half of it instead.

Isla's palm cracks against the wood separating us. "That's a damn sure yes ma'am. Spill! And I don't mean your margarita."

Without too much delay, I impart the sordid details of my little fishing trip. Before I'm even finished, Isla is draped half across the table and dramatically fanning her flushed face.

"I want to be you," she whines. "Granted, I give lap dances for a living but never to completion. How do you feel?"

I contemplate her question by swirling my margarita on my tongue. "My thighs are sore."

Isla bursts out laughing.

"Other than that, I'm good. It's a bit freeing not having to worry about feelings getting involved. I don't feel the need to spill every dark, hidden secret."

"Only the nasty, forbidden ones?" Isla blinks her false eyelashes with faux sweetness.

"I don't even have many of those. It's just sex, or it will be if we reach the point of actual penetration."

"What do you mean?" She digs into a nacho platter, unearthing a chip piled high with all the toppings. I snag my own bite.

"We didn't discuss anything further. Maybe he just needed to get it out of his system, but there are no rules here. I'll see him when I see him."

She holds her palm over her mouth while she chews. "I think you have plenty of opportunity what with him coaching your brother and showing up next door randomly. He's like a quasi-neighbor at this point."

"Maybe." I wave a hand between us. "But I don't want to think too much about it. If it happens again, great, and if not..." The rest of the sentence trails off.

"You should text him tonight. Get yourself a little something."

I flag down Kira for another drink. Once she whisks away the empty glass, I shake my finger in Isla's direction. "You are a bad influence."

"From my perspective, I'm a good one."

"We'll see. I don't want to make anything seem forced, but if I happen to hear from him, I'll go with it."

"That's my girl. Go with the motion of the ocean. Or, in your case, the boat."

"WILL YOU SHUT UP?" I hiss to Isla a few hours later where we lean against one another in a padded booth. A few hours after we began our girls' night, we had Benjamin drive us to another bar across town. Her drunken giggles ring in my ear while her warm breath wafts against my neck. "People might hear you talking about... that."

"So?" The volume of her reply signifies her lack of care. "This is a crowded bar. Nobody is listening to me. They're all too busy trying to hear their own friends."

"Maybe you should change the subject," I holler back, lifting the fruity cocktail she ordered the last round to my lips. Just as the black straw touches my tongue, the glass is tugged out of my hand. Curling my fingers around the straw left behind, I yank it out of my mouth with a "Hey, I was drinking that!"

Lee drains the rest of my glass in one solid gulp, grimacing as he sets the empty cup back on the table. "Tastes like college."

No response formulates through my drunken haze.

Isla, ever eager to stick her nose where it does not belong, leans across the table for a better look and exchanges a glance with Ben.

"Hi, I'm Isla!" Accusatory eyes burn holes in the side of my head.

"Lee, this is my best friend, Isla, and my coworker Ben. This is Lee." I ignore them further for the man standing in front of me. "What are you doing here?" I ask.

Lee turns his chin over his tense shoulder, drawing my gaze behind him toward the bar. I recognize his brothers from the baseball games. "Celebrating a birthday."

"Whose birthday?"

He hesitates and then mutters, "Mine."

Before I can fully grasp the conversation, Isla plants her hands on my back and eagerly shoves me out of the booth. My sputtering cry affords Lee only seconds in warning. A single arm slung beneath my torso in time saves me from a broken nose and two black eyes. The dirty scowl I send Isla's way doesn't even contain half the heat I wish it would in my drunken state.

Torn between telling her off and wishing Lee a happy birthday, the riddle is solved when his arm around me tightens, drawing me closer until his hardness surrounds me. Warmth from his body chases away a sudden chill. My fingertips dance along the muscles on his arms, ghosting gently to his biceps before coming to rest on his solid chest.

"Happy Birthday," I mumble, my voice weak with humiliation and desire. The alcohol crafts a continuous circuit between his touch and my very eager vagina that has started to produce its own heartbeat in time to the circles his thumb draws along my exposed lower back.

Cutting a glance through my tablemates, Lee pays them little attention and instead orders, "Come with me." Without waiting for my verbal response, he guides me ahead of him through the crowd with the arm at my back.

After the third stumble at his swift pace, I cry, "Lee!" in a bid for him to slow down.

Rather than relax the one-track path he's set us on, the determined man pauses only long enough to throw me onto his shoulder with a bounce before continuing his long strides across the room. His large hand secures me with a tight hold across my ass.

Just before the sea of bodies closes around us, I see Isla

standing on her seat, hands cupped around her mouth, but her cheer is drowned out by the crowd.

We burst through the entrance into the humid summer night, the air ripe with the hum of crickets. Lee rounds the corner and presses me back against the brick exterior of the bar. I'm nearly hidden beneath his big body. His forearm rests above my head, casting me in shadow.

Before I can utter a word in question, he twists his ballcap around backward, his chin dips, and his mouth settles over mine. His free hand cups my jaw. Four fingers fan against one cheek while his thumb rests against the other, the grip slightly pinching but not painful. Holding me where he wants me, he dips his tongue into my mouth with a groan.

The bite of some type of strong straight liquor on his tongue is something I savor. He shuffles impossibly closer, dropping the arm braced above my head to settle on my waist, engulfing my hip in his large grasp. His fingers dip beneath the fabric of my simple shirt, tracing along my naked skin. A full-body tremor answers his touch.

He can't seem to get enough, hands roaming my body, never venturing anywhere too indecent, but the effect on my panties is the same. By the time he rests his forehead against mine to catch his breath, I'm wet between the legs and ready to beg him to take me home to have his sinful way with me.

The lustful look in my eyes must catch his attention because he smirks and brushes his finger down my flushed, heated cheek. "I just wanted to say thank you."

"For what?" I pant, fighting to catch my breath from

his kiss, and the arousal still coursing through me. I want to kiss the bashful look from his face before using my lips to explore other parts of his body.

"I don't know the last time someone other than family wished me a happy birthday."

"Why not?"

"Mostly because I don't tell anyone."

I tangle my arms around his neck in an attempt to draw him back, and I zero in on his talented mouth. "I have a gift for you too."

But he remains upright, obstructing my advance.

"Oh, no. It's one thing to fool around with your sexy body sober. I am not taking advantage of you while you're drunk." With embarrassing ease, he unhooks my arms from around his neck and lowers them to my sides, but he doesn't drop my wrists.

"I consent, though," I pout, wrenching away.

He settles his hands on my hips again, the heat of them doing nothing to abate the steady throb between my legs. Lee flashes one of his rare smiles but shakes his head. "Not when you're drunk, you don't. Not with any man, including me."

Forget his chivalry. "If you aren't going to accept my gift, then the least you can do is watch me give it to you."

Wide, searching eyes find my hooded ones in the dim glow of the pub sign. Before I lose my nerve, I skate one hand down my soft abdomen, thankful this pair of jean shorts are a little loose. The stretchy fabric declines to hinder my trajectory beneath the band.

Lee snarls my name like a filthy curse word. "What are you doing?"

"What does it look like?" I answer breathily, dipping

my fingers into the wet arousal gathered between my legs. Even my own touch sends a tingle of electricity zapping beneath my skin with the knowledge Lee's watching with rapt attention as I pleasure myself. My head rolls against the wall behind me, the rough brick abrading the skin of my shoulders with my hurried movements. We could be caught at any moment, and I fully intend to finish.

He moves closer, rests his forehead on my shoulder, and gazes between our bodies to where my hand undulates unseen. My free hand loops the base of his skull, holding him there. Close and watching. My hips surge forward to meet my fingers as I circle my clit, and a soft moan escapes my mouth.

"You better hurry up. If my brothers come looking and see you like this, flushed and about to come, I'll lose my fucking mind," he growls, hurtling me closer to an orgasm.

My fingers twirl through my wet slit, bringing the lubrication to my swollen nub. I dance around my clit, faster and firmer, gasping and shuddering. Nearing the peak. Right when I'm about to splinter, Lee reaches out and pinches my nipple between the knuckles on his index and middle fingers through my shirt. The sudden pain blasts me straight to the point of no return and beyond, and I detonate, crying his name aloud to the starry night sky.

Our eyes lock as I slip my hand free. He snags my wrist in a bruising grip, stopping me from wiping the evidence of my orgasm on my shirt. Instead, he draws the dewy digits to his lips. My rapt attention refuses to move as he smears my fingers across his lower lip before throwing my hand to the side and crashing our mouths together so we both can taste the smoky essence from what we did.

This time, I pull away first, positioning my lips at his ear.

"Happy Birthday, Lee." My whisper remains husky with want.

Then I slip from his hold and back into the bar as if he didn't just help me rock my world again.

14

LEE

I'm fucked.

Totally, utterly, helplessly fucked.

And I can't even find it within myself to be upset about it. What type of guy would find a girl using him to get off as a negative? Not me, that's sure as shit, what with my unintentional dry spell finally ending.

I thought the number of times I replayed her hot little body riding my lap was obscene, but it has nothing on the image of her hand working beneath her shorts against a public brick wall. Not only that, but I've jerked off to the replay three times—just today.

Still, I stand by not accepting her offer to fool around while she was drunk. It would have been easy to take her home, to the back of my truck, or to the bathroom at the bar for a quick, drunken fuck. But I remember being her age, and fumbling around drunk was common for guys and girls, and that's just not the type of man I am. When I finally drive my cock between her sexy legs, it's an experience I want her to beg for and remember, not one she only retains pieces of the next day.

If only she knew I spent the last two days bumbling around my brother's house without much purpose, stealing glances at the covered window next door, wondering if she was inside, and cursing myself for hanging up that fucking sheet in the first place.

What in the hell is she doing to me?

My stubborn ass refused to let her know I was in such proximity since Sunday. Blame it on the fact she's younger than me, but texting her felt like a poorly veiled booty call. The theme to this liaison has been set, and I'm just following her lead.

She kissed me first and her orgasm count is 2-0. If she wants to sleep with me, I'll be a patient man until she's good and ready and one-hundred-percent sober.

A pang burns my chest when I climb into my truck Tuesday evening to head to baseball. Corjan will be home late tonight. As far as I know, he doesn't have any future trips planned, so this may very well be the end of our fun anyway. Maybe I shouldn't have kept myself hidden. Would inviting her over for a drink really have been so bad?

Yes, it would have. I don't want the first time I fuck her to be somewhere other than my own damn bed. The thought of her screaming inside my brother's four walls sends a ripple of jealousy through my gut.

The time for scrutiny is over.

I throw the truck into drive but hit the brakes when my phone buzzes incessantly from my pocket. The screen lights up with *Juniper Calling...*

Speak of the pretty redhead. A grin curls the edges of my lips, and I shove the truck back into park.

"Hello?"

"Hey." She sounds breathless. "I see you're about to leave."

"Nice of you to notice."

Rustling comes over the line. "The fence works two ways. So does the phone, for that matter."

"I'm teasing you."

"Anyway, I was working, which is why I'm calling. Can you take Lincoln to the game? I got called in to cover a shift."

"I'll be right over. Do you need me to bring him home after?"

A lengthy pause follows, so long I have time to ease the truck onto the road and pull into her driveway before she answers.

"That would be great if you could. Unless it's out of your way."

Is she testing my location without outright asking?

"I'll be back at my house tonight, but I can drop him off. It's no problem." *And pick you up*, I'd like to add, but I already vowed not to cross that line unless she asks.

The front door opens, and her brother jogs out with his bat bag slung over his shoulder and his hat on backward. She leans out after him, giving me a shy wave.

"Thank you. I owe you one."

"I think you owe me two," I mutter with a husky laugh.

"I haven't forgotten," she says sweetly. The tone conjures all sorts of images about what she could be planning. "Gotta run, but thank you again. I'll check in with you later."

"Bye."

The phone clatters in my cupholder where I deposit it just as her brother opens the door and climbs in.

"Hey," he says simply, reaching over his shoulder for the seat belt.

"Hey, kid."

Once his belt clicks into place, I set us on the road. Silence accompanies us, fragmented only by my fingers drumming against the steering wheel.

"Um, Coach?" His wary tone pulls my gaze from the road long enough to give him a quick once-over.

"You can call me Lee."

"Coach Lee?"

The formality almost makes me smile. "What's up?"

He pulls the ball cap from his head, twists it around, and fiddles with bringing the brim lower on his forehead. "I'm sorry for how I reacted during the last game. It won't happen again."

"Are you apologizing because you want to or because someone is making you?"

"I want to," he replies without hesitation. "Sometimes my temper gets away from me."

"You know, I know quite a lot of adults who can't manage their emotions, and somehow, we expect kids to have total control. As far as I'm concerned, you're doing just fine."

I can feel him inspecting me as I drive. "I hit my bat against the ground. I threw my helmet."

"You hit your bat once on the ground, and you threw your helmet in a corner where nobody was going to get hurt. When I was your age, I took off my catching gear after a humiliating loss and smacked it along the side of the fence a few times. You're just processing strong emotions."

"I think hiding them is a better option. I don't want people to see me angry."

"Why?"

"It's embarrassing."

"Why? Do you think other people don't get angry? Do you think your emotions are different than anyone else's?"

I catch his shrug from the corner of my eye. "I don't know. Yeah, maybe."

"When I was a little older than you, my parents took me to see a therapist because I was going through some stuff. Do you know what she told me when I told her I felt angry all the time?"

"What?" His attention expands, the energy filling the cab of the truck. He hangs on my every word.

I rub my palm across the rough stubble on my jaw. "She told me that processing emotions is a lot like eating. You have to chew them up and crap them out to get rid of them."

The kid laughs. "I'm telling Juniper that."

"What you're doing right now is processing. I'm proud of you for bringing it up. And you can come to me anytime."

The silence stretches on, broken only when we pull into the parking lot.

"Do you think anyone will look at me differently tonight?"

"Not in the slightest. They probably don't even remember." I'm not the type to betray someone's trust, but if only he knew just last week Ollie got a full day's grounding for throwing his video game controller when he got mad at his game. If only our society talked more about our problems without fear of judgment, we'd realize we aren't so different from one another and could stop feeling so alone in our shame.

That's one thing I appreciate the most about the big family Nancy and Terrance made. We're pretty close to one another without the judgment most of us grew up with, and being able to talk about shit has helped each of us heal in some way or another.

Speaking of my crazy family, they're all mostly assembled on their corner of the bleachers, hands waving as they talk animatedly to one another. On our way to the dugout, I steal the cardboard coffee cup from Cortney's hands.

"Hey, I thought that's supposed to be for—!" my sister shrieks to my back.

"She's not coming tonight," I call over my shoulder. Grinning against the plastic lid, my mouth twists into a pucker as the overly sweet hazelnut flavor hits my tongue.

How does she drink this shit?

And why am I smiling about it?

I adjust my hat and rearrange my face into a scowl. I need to get my head in the game. Sports. Baseball. Manly shit.

Not sweet tasting drinks and an equally sweet tasting woman.

I PUMP my fist at my shoulder. These boys pulled off a tough win. The crowd cheers, and I join them with a few thunderous claps of my own, greeting the team running off the field.

"Way to go, guys. Go shake hands."

We form a single file line to meet the other team. The smiles provide a satisfaction I never knew I'd receive when I was thrust into this coaching gig. Nestled in a post-game huddle with this great group of guys, I couldn't be more proud of the progress we've all made over the short couple of weeks since we started.

After a pep talk and some more thickly layered praise, we put our hands in for a team chant before I send them away to their patient guardians.

"See you on Thursday, boys. Bring this same energy."

Both Ollie and Lincoln linger behind. My nephew is a good kid. He could race off to his family, but he stays behind for his friend. Once the three of us are all packed up, we trek over to the group together.

And something beautiful happens.

The astute adults circle both boys to begin dishing out equal amounts of positivity, and right before my very eyes, Lincoln's hard shell cracks a little bit.

"Lincoln! That was a sweet line drive you had. Straight up the third baseline and two runs batted in. I'm impressed." Aiden taps knuckles with the glowing kid.

"Thank you."

"That inning you pitched was awesome," Jack throws in.

"I took a video to send to your sister," Cort adds. "And you had a great hit, Ollie."

He ducks when his mom tries to brush her fingers through his sweaty hair. "I hope you didn't take a video of me!"

She swats at his flailing hands and makes a face. "I took several."

Nancy tucks her shoulder against Jude's arm. "It's so fun to watch you two play together."

"Gramma, can Lincoln come over on Sunday for dinner?" Ollie stops running away from his mom long enough to ask his question.

"Of course he can."

Lincoln finishes chugging his water bottle and wipes his mouth with the back of his hand. "I'll have to ask my sister if it's okay."

Ollie leans in as if he's sharing a big secret. "It's Paintball Sunday."

"Aw, man. I'll call you tonight and let you know."

"Tell your sister she's invited too. Better yet, Lee, why don't you ask her tonight when you drop Lincoln off?" Cortney's sweet suggestion is anything but. The little meddler is sticking her nose exactly where it doesn't belong.

The sweat dotting my brow has nothing to do with the summer heat. "Sure," I grunt. Anything credible I could use to challenge her suggestion darts through my brain more slick than Slipper the uncatchable stray.

"Perfect. I'll see you all Sunday if I don't see you sooner." Nancy pats my cheek before replacing her wrinkled palm with a kiss.

"Drive home safe. Love you." I squeeze her hand.

Once she walks off with Jude, I turn to Lincoln. "Ready to go?"

He nods, and we start wandering up the path. "Do I need to have my own paintball gun?"

For the second time tonight, this kid nearly makes me

smile. "No. We have plenty. In fact, if you don't tell anyone, I'll let you use mine."

"Really? Why?" The awe in his voice sends warmth to my chest.

"Because it's unbeatable."

"Can you call Juniper right now? I want to make sure I can go," he pleads.

"I thought we could ask her when I drop you off at home."

"Oh." His expression falls. "She isn't going to be there."

Not wanting to disappoint the kid any further after a good evening playing ball, I dig my phone out of my pocket and type out a text.

ME

> You and Lincoln are invited to my family's dinner on Sunday. Wear running shoes and prepare to get dirty. It's a paintball war.

I hold out the screen to Lincoln. "Good?"

"Send it!"

With a tap of my thumb, the invite is out of my hands, and I'm not quite sure what I've just done.

Whatever it is, I did it for the kid.

15

JUNIPER

THE HAYWIRE HEARTBEATS at the sight of Lee's truck in my driveway on Sunday morning are new. I'm slightly alarmed that our distance may have something to do with the chaotic flutters. Besides the baseball game on Thursday, I haven't been able to spend time with my grumpy quasi-neighbor. Work and the fact he hasn't been staying next door hamper our opportunities for chance encounters. Though we did manage to squeeze in a few texts besides those needed to plan today's get-together.

To say I'm nervous is a massive understatement. My inclusion in today's event is a surprise, but not an unwelcome one. Though the territory is unchartered. Lee and I have an unconventional relationship so far, and it leaves me insecure about my place at his family's gathering.

I still don't even know what we are. Are we friends? Fuck buddies? I'd like to think he sees more in me than my generous ass. I know on my end he's more than just nice to look at. From gleaned information over the last couple of weeks, it's apparent he's a selfless man who takes care of those he loves without conditions or return with an undeniable protective streak.

Yet I get the feeling he finds himself lacking in some way. His mention of his failed relationships left an impression. A warning, perhaps?

I lock up behind us and Lincoln jogs off to the truck. His eagerness to spend time with his friend warms me, but I also think it has something to do with Lee. After the game on Tuesday, Lincoln hasn't been able to shut up about his coach. Lee this and Lee that and did you know Lee is letting me use his paintball gun? Yes, the reserved coach has definitely left his impression on this family.

"Morning." Lee taps his finger on the plastic lid of a coffee cup in greeting.

"Good morning," I answer brightly and reach for the cup after buckling in. "I made some cookies. I hope that's okay."

"Juniper's chocolate chip cookies are the best! She uses Mom's recipe, but somehow hers are just a little bit better than I remember."

"You're making me look bad. I never bring anything," Lee grumbles, backing us out of the driveway.

I drum my fingertips against the container in my lap. "I'm sure your mom is more than thrilled with your presence. She doesn't need anything else."

He shoves his head back into the headrest. "You sound just like her."

"I could teach you to make the cookies if you want to impress her next time."

"Deal."

The thought of teaching Lee how to bake does funny

things to my stomach. A sip of coffee obscures the electric feeling.

The trip returns us back into the main part of our small town. Cream-colored brick buildings pass by the window, shades of gray puffy clouds serving as a backdrop. The warmth of summer is in the air, but the sky looks like impending rain.

Lee drives us a few blocks off the main strip through an active neighborhood and pulls to the curb behind a line of cars in front of a single-story home. Unlike the rest of the houses we passed, this row butts up to a wooded area.

"Warning, it gets crowded in there."

"Is this your childhood home?"

Lee unsnaps his seat belt and takes the container from my lap. "No. We somehow managed to get Nancy into a more manageable place once all us kids were grown. Thank goodness because her arthritis acts up in her knee, and at times she can hardly walk."

"It looks like a lovely place." Colorful, vibrant garden beds on either side of the front porch catch my eye when I climb out. "Those flowers must take a lot of work."

"I help."

Just then, Oliver sticks his head out and waves Lincoln inside.

"What?" I grab Lee's wrist to stop his forward steps while my brother takes off toward his friend.

"When her knee's being funny, I help. Take care of the lawns and get down and pull some weeds."

Looking into his sea-green eyes, I wonder if he can tell how badly I want to kiss him. Instead, I release his wrist and head to the door. "You're a disgustingly good man,

Lee," I toss out as if it's a bad thing and not like it makes my heart sprout wings.

Before I can move inside, he threads his fingers through mine and pushes my back flush against the siding.

"Disgustingly good in bed."

His lips touch my cheek, and he walks inside.

THE INITIAL GREETINGS are cut short by two twelve-year-old boys eager to whoop some uncle ass at paintball. We don ridiculous white coveralls with hoods, Nancy's stipulation if anyone wants to return inside after the game, and as a group make the short trek to the edge of the woods behind the house. Corjan and Aiden divvy up paintballs and guns while the other siblings argue about teams.

"We're odd numbered." Cortney completes a second headcount for good measure, but she's right. There are seven adults and two kids.

"We could get Mom to play. She could hide in a bush or something," Jack adds, smirking at the matriarch relaxing on her deck.

"That's an unfair advantage. Nobody has the balls to shoot her," Jude says.

"How about one team takes both kids?" Lee's suggestion makes sense since the kids aren't skilled, but neither am I.

"Only if they also don't get both girls," Aiden adds with a wink at me, earning a punch in the shoulder from his sister.

"I'll take Juniper, the boys, and Jude on my team." Lee

moves to my side. I swear I feel his possessive fingertips brush against my lower back. A frisson of heat courses through me that has nothing to do with the summer weather.

Corjan crosses the small space and flings an arm around my shoulders, dragging me away from Lee's side. "Swap Juniper for Cortney, and game on."

Lee's expression turns stony. He bends to retrieve his gun at his feet, and when he's upright again, the look is wiped clean. "Fine. We'll still kick your asses."

"I think I just declared war," Corjan says wickedly, his gaze sweeping over my face with a flicker of interest. "And maybe secured our loss."

"Why?" I ask as he thrusts a colorful weapon in my hands. The unexploded balls roll around in the hopper.

"Because I know my brother, and I just took his shiny new toy away." Corjan hands me a mask and a purple armband. Lee's team dons green ones. The younger boys bounce around him with excitement, peppering him with questions.

"We're just friends." I laugh. I'm thankful for the mask shielding my face because my eyes flick over to Lee a few times. Even wearing a paint suit, he's ridiculously hot.

Corjan brushes into my side. "That's funny because I've never met one of Lee's friends. Not since college."

"I mean, I'm here as Lincoln's sister, too."

His mouth nears my ear. "Do you accompany your brother to all his playdates?"

Corjan flicks the barrel of his gun onto his shoulder and starts to march away. "Purple team, follow me."

Jack and I start to follow, and Aiden runs up to me from behind.

"Keep up, Juniper. Don't give Lee the opportunity to take a hostage. We're already outnumbered," the youngest Powell says.

We crash loudly through brush and sticks. Thank goodness Lee advised me on proper footwear and I chose to wear tennis shoes rather than flats. About fifty yards into the trees, Corjan as our unofficial leader instructs us into a small huddle.

"This is a simple elimination game. One hit, you're down for thirty seconds. Second hit, you're down for a minute. Three hits and you're out. You can't camp over a player who goes down. There's a lot of debris we've set up over the years you can use for cover. Any questions?"

"Is there a strategy here?" I ask.

"Yeah. Don't get shot," Jack answers. The sarcasm is strong with these Powell brothers.

"I say we sacrifice the girl. She's only going to weigh us down and might distract Lee long enough for us to get him and cripple their team. Sorry, Juniper," Aiden suggests with a grin that says he really isn't sorry. It's clear to me the youngest brothers are the biggest flirts.

I snort. "No sacrifices necessary. You don't know Lee if you don't think he's already planning on coming straight for me, probably with my brother as backup. I'm already screwed."

"Then I say we have our strategy. If Lee's looking for Juniper, then we hang back and wait for him," Jack says before pumping a few rounds into a nearby tree.

"Hands in! Team Sexy on three," Corjan yells.

Boys. I roll my eyes but toss in my right hand, participating with a smile.

After three, we disperse. Or at least I think we do. I

wander deeper into the trees and assume the boys are somewhere nearby, ready to tag Lee. My strategy involves not getting shot anywhere it might hurt and getting Lee before he tags me. And maybe taking a shot at Lincoln too. What else are big sisters for?

The farther I go the trees remain about the same, not too dense, but the brush provides some cover if I duck. I've already passed a couple of old barrels and a propped-up car door splattered with color from past battles.

Pop! Pop! Pop!

I duck behind an old weathered section of fence propped up on a tree trunk. Childish laughter echoes in the air. The sound isn't close enough for me to worry yet. But a crackling twig snapping beneath someone's shoe a moment later delivers enough warning for me to peek around the fence.

I snap the trigger three times, nailing Lee in the shoulder. Purple explodes all over his white suit. Darting to my feet, I scurry off with a laugh.

"I'll find you," he calls behind me. The low tenor sends a delicious shiver down my spine.

Wind picks up out of nowhere, fluttering old leaves and swishing tall grass. Once I'm far enough away, I make a wide arc and circle back. Now that Lee's seen me, he's not going to stop hunting until he explodes his own paintball somewhere on my body, and I have no doubt he'll see me straight to elimination.

Across the distance, Corjan pops up from behind a blue tarp strung between two maple trees. He points at a large oak and makes some gestures with his hands. I don't have a hope of reading the obscure sign language he for some reason thinks I'll be able to interpret.

Too late. A series of pops precede balls flying in his direction, a blue one exploding across his mask. Corjan falls dramatically to the forest floor, clutching his chest, and acting out a mortal wound to the amusement of two preteen boys who take off running in the other direction.

I send a few paintballs of my own at my brother's back. Either I miss or he pretends not to get hit as he scurries off.

A stinging pain on my left shoulder cuts my delight short. My fingers come away from the injury with pink paint. I lay the weapon down and count out thirty seconds in my head while scanning the trees for movement, but come up empty. My gut tells me Lee lurks nearby, ready to hit me again.

"I'm out!" I recognize the shout of defeat from Lincoln.

Drops of scattered rain fall from the gray sky. The summer sprinkling is welcome after running around in this warm attire. I start back in the direction of the house, trying to keep a wide distance from where I think the center is. Who am I kidding? The Powell's play frequently and probably know these woods in their sleep. I hold my gun at the ready and crunch through brittle leaves and sticks, making more noise than I probably should.

A paintball wizzes by my head and bursts into the tree at my right. Without thinking too much, I turn at the hip and pump the trigger. One after the other, paintballs fly from the barrel. A grunt sounds before I see Lee pop out from behind a tree, a splash of neon green over his forehead.

I take on damage to my right elbow and my left thigh, returning fire to his chest and abdomen. Neither of us stop. The rules of the game appear defunct as I take off running in the opposite direction with Lee hot on my heels. The rain picks up, a full summer storm in effect, soaking into the flimsy paper material covering me.

Stopping, I fire a few more rounds at Lee, but his bigger, longer legs eat up the distance between us. I spring from my crouch, fleeing on instinct, but only move a few steps. His thick forearm bands around my waist and drags me against his muscled chest.

"I think I win," he growls in my ear, then settles his lips against the sweat-dampened skin on my neck. He nips at the sensitive flesh.

"I hit you more than you hit me."

"But I have you as my hostage." As if to prove his point, he lifts me off my feet, pulls us behind a wide tree, and spins me around before pressing me into the trunk. The rough bark grounds me to this moment, pinned against it and Lee's hard body.

He gazes down on me, rain quickly dampening the strands of his dark hair and sticking them to his forehead, a serious expression on his face.

16

LEE

Fuck, she's pretty.

Drops of rain leave flecks of water across her protective mask. With a thick swallow, I feel my throat bob as I reach for the elastic wrapping around her head and hook my thumbs beneath. Gazing into her dark eyes, I slowly peel the plastic off, dropping it to the damp earth to join mine in the dirt at our feet.

Terrance used to warn me about what falling for someone would feel like, but I never believed him. I still don't. Even though Juniper easily embodies all things good and pure, she deserves a partner who can fulfill all her needs. This base-level attraction means we're both free to walk away when we're ready without either of us getting hurt. My thumb swipes across her supple cheek as I cradle her jaw, tipping her face. I want to lick the wetness from her skin.

My breath puffs against her lips with my exhale. The singular warning before my mouth settles firm and reckless against hers. A stolen groan rises from my throat to vanish between us.

Her lips part beneath mine, beckoning me to taste her forbidden sweetness. She's much too young for me to defile, but I plan to do it anyway. To take her willing offering and nothing more. She intoxicates me, siphoning my willpower until I'm firmly under her spell.

I thread my fingers through her thick hair at the base of her skull. My other hand grips her waist, fingers itching to graze her smooth skin, and my knee settles between her legs, pinning her against the tree. My hardened cock rests against her hip. With a flex, I press into her in an unveiled display of desire she can't miss.

Fuck, but I want her. I'd take her now on this dirty forest floor if my family wasn't dozens of yards away, probably wondering where we are.

Her teeth nip my bottom lip, and I groan again, so hard it fucking hurts. When I think I can't get any more turned on, she rests her forehead against mine and blows my entire world wide open.

"Touch me." The beg drips from her lips coated in desire.

"Tell me where." I kiss her jaw, her cheek, the corner of her sinful little mouth, ready to oblige her every request.

Those dark eyes lock on mine, the craving stark. Dainty fingers toy with the zipper holding her coveralls on. The sound of the teeth separating lures my gaze down to follow the path she draws. Like unwrapping a present, the open V down her torso gives a tantalizing glimpse of what's hiding underneath.

She snatches my hand from her waist and guides my fingertips beneath the material of her jean shorts.

"I want number three, and I want you to give it to me." Her confidence maintains this balance between us and keeps me from feeling like an old pervert.

I swear to god my cock fucking weeps, and an animalistic growl vibrates my chest.

Flicking open the button on her shorts, I lower the zipper for better access. As my fingers slip deeper into her lacy excuse for panties, I shift my mouth to her ear. "I think you meant to say you're going to give it to me."

I stroke her slit with one finger, causing her moan to float on a stilted gasp against my cheek. When I part the slick flesh between her legs, her breath hitches.

"I want them all, Juniper. Your orgasms are mine," I growl against her cheek.

Her next moan shoots straight to my dick as I tease her with slow strokes, gliding through the evidence of how fucking turned on she is. I want to draw her pleasure out until she's writhing on my hand and begging for more. I rub her clit, circling the little nub with small, teasing strokes. The way her hips punch forward to gain more pressure entrances me.

"Your little cunt is going to squeeze my fingers, and you're going to wish it was my cock inside you. And you're going to hold back your scream, or else all my brothers will come running and see what dirty things you're allowing me to do to you in the middle of a family gathering."

For a second, I wish I could take it back, showing her this side of me. But then her face contorts, and she whimpers. "Please."

Fuck yes. I drag my teeth along her neck with her

confirmation that she wants this as much as me. Goose bumps erupt before my eyes.

"Please what, my little darling?" I nudge her foot over with mine to widen her stance.

"Please, I need you inside me."

Her words are my undoing. My thumb takes over gently strumming her clit, and I thrust two fingers deep to feel her from the inside. "You are so fucking wet for me."

"Yes, for you," she pants.

"Are you going to come for me?"

"I'm so close already." She struggles to get the words out while holding back her cries. She buries her face in my neck, stifling the desperate noises.

She feels so fucking good in my arms, her body heat chasing away the chill from the rain. She licks at my pulse point. Her muscles tense as she nears the peak, and I plunge in deeper, curling my knuckles to hit the spot I know will drive her to ecstasy.

I cradle the back of her head just as she shudders and seal my lips over her mouth. Her climax tears through. A full body detonation pulses her cunt around my fingers as our kiss silences her scream. She squeezes me as if she's trying to keep me locked tight inside her body.

"God, you're a fucking dream," I pull away to mutter, diving back in for one more lingering kiss as I withdraw my fingers. I swallow her whimpers of protest and grin against her pouty lips. Despite wanting to lick them clean, I discreetly wipe the mess off on the inside of my coveralls. If I taste her again, I won't want to stop until I give her number four with my mouth.

"Are you even real?" she mumbles, going through the

motions of fastening her shorts. "Every time I'm around you, you make me come." She laughs in disbelief.

"I intend to keep it that way."

She stares at me a little dazed.

My lips compress to conceal a satisfied smirk. "You okay?"

"Oh, yeah. Fantastic, actually. Never been more relaxed."

She sounds a little drugged.

Lacing our fingers together, I grab the masks from the ground and tug her along behind me.

"Who do you think won the game?"

I look back at her with a small smirk. "We did." And I'm not talking about the green team.

Trampling back through the woods to the house only takes about five minutes. We were closer to my family than I realized. The recklessness carries a thrill at the very real possibility of being caught. At least my brothers are all grown idiots, so the worst that would come out of it is some gentle family ribbing, but I'm glad this time we can spare Juniper the embarrassment.

We clear the trees at the same time Jude walks out about two hundred feet to our left, wearing his usual serious expression. His eyes flick to our entwined hands, and a grin softens his face.

So maybe we didn't come out completely spared.

I don't release Juniper's hand until we reach the storage for our gear. The coveralls go in the garbage bin, and I store our weapons. Then we rejoin the rest of my family inside.

"Where did you two run off to?" Corjan raises his

eyebrows suggestively the moment we step foot through the door.

"This one got lost." I flick my thumb over my shoulder.

Juniper punches my bicep on her way around me. "I wouldn't have if you weren't chasing me like a lunatic. I felt like I was running from a poorly scripted Halloween movie serial killer."

"Lee! That's not very nice," Nancy scolds. She beckons Juniper over. "Come dry off and warm up, dear. We have coffee, hot chocolate, and tea."

Oh, she's plenty warm. Wet too.

Juniper fixes herself a hot drink, and I slink off to hide in the living room. Maybe if I'm out of sight, my family will stop trying to draw inaccurate conclusions about the two of us.

"There's creamer in the fridge," Cortney says.

"You guys have good taste. Hazelnut is my favorite." Juniper's remark causes my throat to tighten and that damn indigestion to return with a vengeance.

"Lee picked that up when he grabbed my groceries yesterday," Nancy replies. She rounds the corner with her own mug clutched in her hand and I make room next to me on the sofa.

"Lucky guess, then. It's even my favorite brand."

"He didn't guess." Lincoln pipes up from the corner where he and Ollie have their heads together over the Nintendo Switch. "He asked me what you liked that day you were sick and he took you home with him. When I called your phone, and he answered."

And there it is. Cue the record scratch. All my secrets blast out in the open. That kid is officially on my unofficial shit list. I'm about to take myself back out to the woods for the rest of the afternoon and spend some alone time throwing an ax around to release some of this fucking tension.

The unfolding silence reveals more than I'd like, stretching on what feels like entire minutes before Juniper laughs awkwardly. "Oh. That was really nice of you."

Nancy's eyeballs drill holes into the side of my skull.

"Juniper, come play a round of cards with us." Aiden shuffles the deck in his hands, his eyes flashing in her direction. Jack, Cortney, and Corjan sit with him at the same worn dining table I grew up eating meals at and bickering with my siblings over breakfast.

"Sure." She carries her hot drink ahead of her and sits down between my youngest brothers.

My body grows taut as they begin their game. So lost in my own head, I don't even know what they're playing. Only that the boys can't seem to keep their eyeballs to themselves. More than once, I've caught them each giving her a once-over while she plays with her cards or nibbles on an appetizer from the snack tray on the table. The only thing that keeps me seated is that it hasn't even been an hour since I had her coming around my fingers, and I know she isn't interested in them.

But maybe she should be. They're all closer in age than I am to her. Hell, Aiden's still in his twenties.

A wave of jealousy clutches my body and curls my fist in my lap. My teeth sink into my lower lip while I watch them laugh and joke around. The point of no returns hits like a shot going off when Corjan leans over and kisses her on the cheek playfully before taking a card from her hands. I explode out of my seat like someone lit a fire-cracker beneath my ass.

Without a word, I stalk to the door and mutter, "Taking a walk," before storming outside. The only other option is to cross the room to deck him, but I'd rather not get blood on Nancy's carpet.

Down the block, I drop into a crouch and rub my palms over my face only half intending to wipe away the raindrops clinging to my overheated skin. A well of emotion overflows inside me. The abandonment issues from my childhood resurface like an old wound that just won't heal no matter how much time has passed.

What the hell am I doing? She doesn't belong to me. My family invited her here as an extension of Lincoln, not because she's anything to me. But I'm too busy making a scene and running out like a coward because I can't stand to see anyone else making her smile like that.

And even though I have no business claiming them, her smiles are mine. Her laughs and even her orgasms belong to me too.

I thought touching her body would cleanse her from my system, but it seems she's only burrowed down impossibly deep.

The right solution evades me to the mess I've created. I can only blame myself for this uncomfortable situation.

The rain has lessened to a drizzle. Not wanting to give my siblings any more time to gossip, I lift myself from the ground and finish my walk, determined to get back in there. I'm ready for this get-together to wrap up so I can drop Juniper and Lincoln at home and leave this day behind.

But when I reach the open garage door, I find someone waiting like an answer to an unasked prayer, and the remainder of my willpower around her crumbles to dust.

Juniper's arms are crossed, more likely a defensive maneuver than protection from the weather. "Are you okay?"

I don't stop until my toes nearly touch hers and her arms brush my chest. Her sweet, tropical scent, stronger from her damp clothing and hair, surrounds me and I breathe her in like a soothing balm. Like the coward I am, I stare at our feet. "I needed a minute alone."

Her slender arms wrap around my torso, trapping my arms at my sides.

"What are you doing?" I mutter. I squeeze my eyes shut at the roaring blaze igniting in the left side of my chest.

"I'm hugging you."

I curl my fingers into fists, resisting. "Why?"

She's silent but her hold increases fractionally. "Because you looked like you needed one."

Long minutes pass while I let her hold me in her arms. I don't even lift mine to grip her back, and even though I don't know how to admit it out loud, most of my jealousy leaks away.

She loosens her embrace enough to lean back and move her palms to rest against my ribs. "Do you want to talk about it?"

"No."

"Do you want to go home?"

I nod. "Yes."

"Can I come with you?"

My lungs expand like I'm holding my breath. I quickly bring my gaze to search hers. "You want to come home with me?"

She traces my collarbone through my shirt with her index finger while looking up at me, and the wild inside me settles a little more. The angle makes her look so young. Younger than mid-twenties, reminding me that she should be with someone her own age. "Oliver asked if Lincoln could stay the night, so I thought maybe I could have a sleepover too."

Did I say someone her own age? I meant she should be with me. Right now. Because I'm fucking selfish when it comes to Juniper. I toss her up on my shoulder, banding a hand low over her ass. "Let's leave right now."

"Lee! You have to say goodbye to your mother," she squeals.

"I suppose." Sliding her down my body, I kiss her quickly.

17

JUNIPER

WE DON'T RETURN to Lee's house until evening. His mom barred the exit without us each polishing off at least one plate of the food she laid out buffet style on her kitchen island. And she hinted that she knew Lee's more than capable of clearing two, but let him off the hook in order to bring me home.

I didn't miss the twinkle in her eyes when she granted her permission or the way she hugged me extra-long to say goodbye.

Translation: His mom isn't a dummy and knows we want to have sex.

I'm just glad I won't be the one to break the news that her oldest isn't finally settling down with a nice girl. He's not settling down at all. If only she knew the dirty things we've been up to, she might not invite me over again.

And while I can pretend to ignore the tender looks he gives me sometimes or the way he let me hold him this afternoon, it's harder to overlook there's something brewing between us that might be deeper than physical touches.

The moment we walk through the door from his garage, I'm up and over Lee's shoulder. The man has a thing with carrying me and I can't deny it elicits a little thrill. I'm not small by anyone's standards, but I feel petite and weightless with the way he tosses me around.

I yelp and grip the sides of his tee shirt. Anticipation courses beneath my skin like a current zipping along.

He flips me over and I land on my back on his bed. The smell of his soap, that Big D Energy, and cologne surrounds me. He reaches back and fists the collar of his tee.

"I have a confession to make."

He suddenly yanks the shirt off, revealing his bare chest to me for the first time, and I almost forget to ask what he means.

Goodness gracious, sweet singing angels. My mouth dries at the smooth, tanned, chiseled skin. The dips and curves provide a roadmap to trace with my fingers and tongue.

"W-what?"

"I've accidentally fallen in like with you."

He picks up my foot and plants it in his chest, unhurriedly unties my tennis shoe, and peels it off with a slowness that dampens the place between my thighs.

Holy. Who knew removing a shoe could be foreplay?

"You weren't supposed to do that," I say quietly.

He switches to the other foot. "It was those damn chocolate chip cookies. You must have laced them with something."

Laughter sputters from me but dies an early death as

his fingers find the silver button on my shorts. My breath hitches. "Lee."

"Is this okay?"

I nod and he peels the zipper down. His fingers curl into the fabric and slides them off my hips and legs, and they join his shirt on the floor.

For a moment, he simply caresses my bared skin. His warm palms skate up and down the outside of my calves to my thighs before he tucks my legs around his hips and closes his eyes.

"I've wanted to feel you like this, bare and wrapped around me."

"I've wanted this too," I admit.

He groans, lowering into a push-up to kiss me. On his way back up, he guides my shirt over my head.

Never in a million years did I imagine I'd be lying on Lee Powell's bed in nothing but a black lace bra and panties, but here I am.

Conscious this time.

"You are a goddess."

I suck in a sharp breath as his fingers trail lightly over the yellowing bruise on my ribs, his brows creased with concern while he studies the mark. With a shake of his head, he seems to knock himself out of whatever place he's in. I tuck away the beat of sadness and return to the moment when he flattens his palm on my sternum and guides it in a gentle caress between my breasts. Dipping his head, he follows his hand, trailing feather-light kisses down the center of my chest. My nipples swell against the lace, begging for attention.

He drops to his knees and pushes my thighs up and

back. His heated stare settles on the remaining scrap of fabric over my center. "It's like unwrapping a present."

I prop myself up on my elbows. "Could you be a little more like a kid on Christmas morning and not like the grandma who saves the wrapping paper?"

Lee nips carefully at my inner thigh in reprimand. "Eager, little darling?"

"Yes." I flop back and run my fingers through my hair as he slips a calloused digit beneath the elastic at the crease of my thigh. "I want your mouth on me."

In the next second, my underwear vanishes, and Lee's tongue slides through my wetness. He slowly swirls my clit, tasting me with a gentle sweetness I didn't expect from him. He laps smoothly from my entrance to the aching nub, up and over and back down, as if he's savoring every last bite of his favorite meal.

The long-drawn-out strokes deliver me to the edge in minutes. I shudder and arch on the bed, lifting my hips to his mouth, silently begging him for more.

As if he knows, he drives two fingers into me. "You going to let me have number four?"

"Please," I beg. "Take it." With the next flick of his tongue, my fingers twist in his sheets.

He attacks my clit, swirling and sucking, and his fingers pump and curl against the spot, setting me off with a detonation that has me crying his name to his bedroom ceiling.

If I thought his fingers were skilled in orgasms, they have nothing on his tongue. He leisurely laps at me through the aftershocks. The rhythmic throb ebbs, but my legs continue to twitch around his ears.

"You're a hot little thing when you come." He rises to his feet, mouth glistening, and unbuckles his belt.

The visual has me sitting up and scooting to the edge of the bed before I'm even done panting, suddenly desperate to see him fall apart. "My turn."

He parts the edges of his jeans, exposing the black waistband to his underwear, but freezes with a serious expression on his face.

Like a light bulb flicking on, his hesitation becomes clear. "You feel wrong asking me to pleasure you?"

I knew he felt a little weird about our age difference, but he's been giving me orgasms like it's his job.

He rubs the back of his neck. "I just want you to be comfortable."

This isn't a discussion moment. No, this requires a demonstration. Wordlessly, I slip off the bed and kneel at his feet before grasping the edges of his jeans.

"Juniper. Wait."

"No. You don't get to do that. You don't get to sacrifice your pleasure for some misplaced moral bullshit. Maybe I don't want to make you feel good. Maybe I just want to taste your cock."

Lee merely grunts as I shove his jeans and boxer briefs down his thighs and take him in my hand.

God, he's big. His hard erection stands straight and long and thick. I should yell at him for hiding *this* from me. Penises aren't supposed to be pretty, but Lee has a beautiful cock. Hands down, the best I've ever seen. Licking my palm, I wrap my hand more firmly around him, give a few strokes, and bring him to my mouth. I lick around the crown before sliding him in.

With a guttural groan, Lee gathers my hair in a fist and holds it high on the back of my head. Little thrusts of his hips work him deeper into my mouth, sliding easily along my tongue until he touches the back of my throat.

I can tell he's holding back. The power surges through me along with the desire to make him lose control and fall to pieces by my hands. I work my fist around the base, stroking the part I can't quite fit through my lips, and wrap my other hand around the back of his thigh for balance.

"Fucking hell." His other hand grips my jaw and holds me still while he picks up his pace. "I've wanted these pretty lips wrapped around my cock. Look up at me," he orders, using his grip in my hair to tilt my head back.

I flick my watery gaze up to meet his heated stare and moan at the unbridled desire darkening his eyes. This is Lee unrestrained and tempted beyond measure, and I'm the one he's given over control to make him shatter.

"I want to fuck your pretty mouth. I want to feel you choke on my fat cock and gasp for air."

He can have my breath. He can take it all. I transfer my hand from his shaft to his other thigh and relax my throat, ready to give him exactly what he wants in vivid detail. With loud noises, I bob up and down his length, feeling him grow even thicker in my throat. Eager to please him, I ease him in deeper each time until he touches the place that makes me gag.

"So hot," he mutters, and the restraint cracks. He snaps his hips and fucks my mouth, bringing his fantasy to life. He reclaims the control he gave to me, plunging his cock deeper into my mouth until I can't breathe.

"I'm going to come," he pants. His warning provides me with a choice.

I hold onto his hips in answer, lips stretched wide, while he plunges deep into my throat until he emits a series of gritty curses as he comes.

I sit back on my heels and swallow down the remainder of his salty essence, gazing up at him while I catch my breath. I swipe a thumb beneath my eyes to clear the tears and black smudges of mascara.

"I like you like this. Lips swollen, your face ruined and eager for me." He drags his thumb across my mouth.

Lee hauls me upright by my armpits until I'm cradled against his sturdy chest, my feet dangling inches above the floor. He kisses me without restraint, not seeming to care that he might be able to taste himself.

Then he tosses me on my stomach on his bed and slaps my ass. "I'm not finished with you, but a man needs a second to recover."

I crawl up to the headboard and sink into the pillows with a sultry look on my face. "I'm a patient woman."

A predatory gleam flashes in his eyes. "I'm not that old. I said I needed seconds. And with that little maneuver you just pulled, putting your ass on display for me like that..." He grips my ankles and pries my legs apart until I'm spread eagle on his bed and my arousal leaks onto his duvet. "I'm already fucking hard again," he growls.

A gasp stutters free as his fingers find the wetness between my legs. With his hot gaze on mine, he slips two fingers inside. "You ready for me, my little darling?"

My head bobs, I pant, and arch my neck all at the same time. "Yes."

He props his head in his hand and looks to where his

fingers disappear inside my body. "I could stay here all night, doing this to you. Bringing you to the brink and letting you come down again until you were so hot and needy you'd climb on top and ride me entirely for your own pleasure, using my body to get yourself off."

A shudder forces my eyes closed. "I'm nearly there."

Hot breath fans against my exposed center. He swipes his tongue through my wetness, swirling around my clit, and climbs up my body.

I wrap my arm around his neck, dragging his mouth to mine as he slips his fingers free and replaces them with the tip of his hard cock. Inch by inch, he pushes inside me until he's fully seated.

He groans. I whimper from the fullness.

He wrenches from my mouth and rests his forehead on mine.

Our gazes roam down our bodies to watch where he glides out and back in.

"Are you okay?" he asks.

"I'm fantastic." In a desperate bid to get him to move, I score my fingernails down his back.

"Good. Because I'm going to take you, and I'm not going to be fucking nice about it."

A sudden scream flies from my mouth as he hooks an arm beneath my back and sits on his heels, sending me airborne and crashing into his chest. With his arm like a steel band behind me, he holds me upright and thrusts his hips, nearly splitting me into two.

Words fall rapid-fire from my lips.

"So big...

"You feel so good...

"Ohmygodyesthere...

"I'm going to come again…"

Powerful hips snap below me, driving inside, while I can't do much more than hang on and try to breathe. He hooks a finger into the lacy cup surrounding my breasts, yanking one down to lap at my aching nipple as it bounces in front of his face.

"Lee!" I scream, tightening around him as the orgasm hits me out of nowhere. I cry in his lap and bury my face in his neck, sinking my teeth into the corded muscle straining with his exertion.

"Fuck, fuck, fuck," he chants, rutting with jerky, irregular movements until he shoves upward and stills, throbbing deep inside. "You made me come," he grunts.

Wide-eyed, I pull my face from his neck and stare up at his sea-green eyes. "You can have a do-over if you'd like."

He snarls and captures my mouth. The kiss starts out frantic. I fall to my back, and Lee chases me down until we're lying side by side with our legs entwined, the coarse hairs covering his tickling my inner thigh.

Slowly, our kiss transforms into something more leisure and sweet until he pulls away with a final peck and tucks my hair behind my ear.

"I lost track of my orgasm count." I fake a pout.

"Two more for you and two for me, but you should always be ahead."

I roll my eyes with a grin. "I can't argue with that."

"Shit."

"What?"

"I forgot to use a condom."

"Oh. Is that all?" I settle back against the pillows.

"What do you mean is that all?" A hint of menace enters his voice.

I brush my palm over his solid pec muscles. "Accidents happen. We'll be more careful next time."

"I should be more responsible."

"Hold up there. My virtue isn't your responsibility. It's mine."

He watches his fingertips lightly trace a vein up my forearm. "Not when we're like this. I know it sounds like a total dude remark, but since the deed is already done, I haven't been with anyone for years."

"It's been a while for me too, and as far as pregnancy goes, my birth control is more effective than a condom."

"So no rubbers then?"

A blush hits my cheeks. "I like feeling you come."

He assaults my mouth with a bruising kiss. "You're going to make me fuck you again, but I think I should feed you."

My stomach releases a ferocious-sounding rumble.

With a grunt, he pushes off the bed. "Right. Food it is." He tugs me upright and into his arms where he shoves his tee over my head. The cotton falls to mid-thigh. After he tugs on a pair of sweats, he takes my hand in his. "Can I keep you like this all the time?"

"If you keep treating me the way you have been, you can do whatever you want."

"Deal."

18

JUNIPER

"THIS HAS to be the best grilled cheese of my entire life."

Lee lifts an eyebrow. He looks damn good in a pair of low-slung gray sweats, standing in front of the stove shirtless while holding a spatula at nine o'clock at night. With a cocky swagger, he crosses the kitchen and leans over the table. "You can thank the chef."

I swipe buttery crumbs from my lips and give him a kiss. "Thank you."

The way his tongue swipes across his lip sends dirty thoughts to the front of my mind. I'm afraid I won't be able to be around Lee without thinking of sex after this. Baseball games might be extra awkward from here on out if I can't stop picturing the head coach naked.

"Do you want a coffee?"

"Yes, please. I'm one of those weirdos who can drink caffeine at any hour and still fall right to sleep."

He passes me a filled mug. The cream color of the liquid indicates he added the perfect amount of hazelnut.

"Me too."

Holding his own mug by the handle at the center of his bare chest, he takes my hand with his empty one and leads me into the living room.

"Wait here." He deposits me on his soft brown couch and starts a fire in the fireplace.

I'm delighted to sip my sweet drink and watch the muscles ripple and flex in his back as he moves around the logs, allowing him to tend to both me and the flame without lifting my own finger. I'm a modern woman, but there's something undeniably sexy about letting a man take care of me, especially when he does so with all that smooth skin on display.

"Juniper." My name is a coarse growl.

"What?" Pure innocence fills my voice.

He stalks to where I recline, lifts my legs, and settles my feet in his lap when he sits. "I think you're trouble."

I lift my mug to my lips. "The sexy kind."

"Yes, the sexy kind, but trouble nonetheless."

He scowls without heat and digs his thumb into the sole of my foot. I groan around the rim of my cup.

"You're good at that."

"I'm good at a lot of things."

"What got you into dog rescue?" The opportunity to learn more about him is too good to pass up.

At first, he doesn't respond. We sit quietly with one another. Crackles and pops from the fire serenade us until he breaks the silence.

"I never wanted to be like my bio dad." The words are rusty, as if he isn't used to speaking them.

The quiet quality of his voice almost has me sitting up

to wrap my arms around him, but I sense he needs to say this without interruption, so I hold still and try to relax.

"Do you want to talk about it?" I tread carefully forward, wondering how this will tie together with what I thought was an innocent question.

He glides both his thumbs up the center of my foot. "He never took care of my mom. Not once. So it really wasn't a surprise when he walked out when I was ten. I vowed then I'd never be like him, so I stepped up. Did more chores. Helped run to the corner store for groceries. Took care of her the best I could. But it wasn't enough."

"What happened?"

A humorless grunt passes his lips. "She left too. I wasn't enough for her either. I learned people don't need a reason to leave. They'll go if they want to."

"I'm sorry that happened to you."

"I was too, for a while. She left a note saying I had a month before the landlord would evict, and that was that. I was fourteen. Had an older brother but he'd already been out on his own and cut ties with us. I spent about a year on the streets before Nancy found me. I always felt a little bit like a stray. I still do. I turned to animal work because humans, we can communicate and help one another. But animals are hurt by the people who are supposed to protect them. Like I was with my family. They need us to step up."

"Do you ever think about helping kids like you and your siblings?"

He nods, reaching for his mug from the coffee table. "We donate to youth charities and partner with them for fundraising galas throughout the year. There aren't many programs in Fairview Valley, and thankfully the need here is small. We run a coats for coats drive every fall. People bring their pets to the sanctuary for grooming, and if they donate a coat, the service is free. Then we donate the coats to the youth shelter. It's always a hit."

My heart flutters at the passion in his voice. "It sounds like you've made a good thing out of something that was out of your control."

"Yeah."

A lull prompts me to move to another topic.

"Did I tell you I should be moving out in the next couple of weeks?"

"Where to?"

I scoot into a sitting position and deposit my mug on the table, leaving my naked legs draped over his lap. "It's not far from your mom's, actually. I originally placed an application for a house on Main Street, but someone got in just before me. But the rental company called me the other day to say they have another house opening up in about two weeks if I'm interested."

A genuine grin splits his face. Warmth that has nothing to do with the fire suffuses me. "Congratulations. If you need help moving, I'm happy to lend a hand."

"Thank you. If the truck comes with the offer, I'll take you up on that."

He sets his mug beside mine. "I see how it is, using me for my body and now using me for my truck."

"Lee!" I playfully smack his bare chest. "I am not using you for your body or your truck."

He leans back against the couch and runs his thumbs teasingly beneath the waistband of his sweats. His abs flex, fully on display to my roaming gaze. "It's okay. I'm here for your pleasure."

Testing that remark sounds like an excellent plan. I rise up onto my knees and nod at his lap. "Take it out."

His darkened gaze flickers to mine, and he slowly lowers his pants, his hard erection springing free and bouncing against his solid abs.

"Now what?" he rasps.

"Stroke it." A rush of power infuses my veins with his instant compliance. "Harder. Get your hand wet."

Sea-green eyes lock on mine as he licks his palm and wraps it back around himself.

Suddenly feeling hot, I tear his tee over my head and unsnap my bra. The air immediately tightens my nipples before his hooded gaze. I climb onto his lap, spreading my thighs to the outsides of his, and wrap my palm around the back of his hand.

"Don't stop stroking."

Together, we glide along his length from base to tip. Every thrust tosses me in his lap, and my breasts bounce in front of his face. With a growl, he leans forward and latches onto a nipple, knocking me off balance.

"Oh, god." Our joined hands nearly separate. I manage to brace myself on the back of the couch and lock my thighs before toppling off him. I twist my fingers in his dark hair to hold him to me.

I watch us work his thick length, the purple crown leaking clear fluid. Every few strokes, the tip smears against my pale stomach. My mouth floods, remembering his salty flavor, and arousal drips down my thigh at the thought of tasting him again. A flush covers my chest as he switches to the other breast and strokes that nipple with his velvet tongue.

Feeling the first clench below, I cry out. His fingers dig into my ass, pulling me flush against him and dislodging our hands.

"This is for you," I whine, pushing my palms flat against his solid chest.

"Not without you," he grits through clenched teeth. He yanks my underwear to the side and slams into me from below.

My head falls back with a gasp as he bottoms out. "I'm so full."

Dragging my hips forward and back along his lap, I ride him.

Brows snapped together in concentration, his face twists in ecstasy. He sinks his teeth into his lip and clutches my hip, coaxing me. Urging me to take all of him. His torso twists, and then I'm flat on my back with him on top of me, driving back in deep and hard and fast.

"Gonna come inside you again." His hand clutches my belly where it shakes beneath his powerful thrusts. "I'm going to fill you up until I'm leaking out of you."

Normally, I'd shy away from someone touching that place during intimacy, but with his forceful hips nailing me blissfully into the couch, I can't find it within my brain to care. The only thing I can focus on is the twisting in my lower abdomen as I clench rhythmically around him.

He shoves my thigh up and into my chest, the position tilting my hips and opening me for better access.

"Lee! Ah, yes!" I cry out. My eyes slam shut, and my head rolls back into the cushion as the powerful waves crash over me.

A string of curses falls from his lips as he chases me over the edge, his cock throbbing so hard I feel his release deep inside.

"I can't last when you squeeze my dick like that."

A bubble of laughter bursts out, sounding weak and breathless. "Consider it my superpower."

"Or a curse. I think I'm addicted." With a groan, he collapses on top of me, careful not to crush me beneath his solid weight. An arm slips between my back and the couch, and he rolls us to our sides while he's still lodged inside me.

Strands of hair tickle my cheek. I brush them away and rest my palms flat against his hard chest.

"You're going to have to carry me to bed." I yawn. My limbs are liquid and heavy, loosened from the sex and the heat of the fire.

"You can sleep here. I'll keep you safe." His arms tighten around my back, caging me in.

I think he meant it jokingly, but the sentiment rings true. I do feel safe here. I don't think anything could hurt me when I'm with him. He wouldn't let it.

THE FOLLOWING MORNING, after filling a travel mug with my favorite coffee and making out on his back patio, Lee drops me off at the end of my driveway. I have a shift at the diner this morning before I pick up Lincoln in the afternoon.

"Will I see you at the game tomorrow?" he asks as I unbuckle my seat belt.

I appraise the man beside me. One wrist rests on the

top of the black steering wheel. The sun shines through the window and across his face, highlighting the scruff on his jaw that left a tingling burn on my neck when he woke me with his lips this morning. Remembering the feel of his mouth in sensitive places sends a delicious shiver across my skin.

"I'll be there."

His attention runs down my body, returning to my face with molten irises. "I'll look forward to it."

The extra bounce in my step can't be helped, though I hope it isn't too obvious as I walk to my door while wishing I could crawl back into Lee's arms instead.

Grown-up sleepovers are my new favorite thing. Right up there with hazelnut coffee creamer and being carried by a certain someone as if I weigh nothing.

A soft creak accompanies the front door opening. I shut it behind me with an unobtrusive click and rest my back against the wood, taking a moment to soak in the past twenty-four hours. I can't remember the last time I enjoyed myself so freely. Like a heavy load's been lifted. Whether temporary or not remains to be seen.

From running around in the woods shooting at one another to joking around with his siblings. All the freaking glorious sex and Lee working over my body as if he'd been in charge of it for years. When I left this morning, the official orgasm count was eleven for me and five for him. Between the legs, I throb just thinking about the way he stretched and filled me.

The sound of soft sobs blankets the joy in an instant with a heavy fog. A cloud settles over me. I should just go to my room. Walk through the hallway and disappear behind the closed bedroom door and get ready for work. My father's beyond help when he's like this.

The easy instructions are dashed the moment I round the corner.

He sits on the floor clutching a framed photo with a bottle of Belvedere open at his side. My heart cracks at the pitiful image of someone who was once the strongest person I knew now drowning in grief without a way to get help.

The sight is nothing new, and I try to sneak by with my face slightly turned in the other direction.

"What the fuck are you doing here?" He spits the dark question, immediately rising unsteadily to his feet.

I press my lips together and continue with a little more urgency.

"Can't a man grieve peacefully in the privacy of his own home?" The volume intensifies with each word out of his mouth until he's screaming at the end of his rhetorical question. "What's the fucking matter with you?"

"I'll just go." With a steadying breath, I open the door to my bedroom.

The hallway isn't big enough for us, and he stumbles roughly past, his shoulder checking into mine.

I fall into my open door, the knob catching onto my side and stealing my breath. My palms slap against the hardwood floor, and I cough as I try to breathe against the new ache in my ribs.

"Get out of my fucking way," he mutters and slams the door to his bedroom closed behind him.

Tears sting my eyes as I drag myself into a sitting position and lean against the wall, kicking the door shut with my foot. A tremor courses down my spine, and I bring my knees to my chest to tuck myself into a tight ball.

This is how it always is. This abuse that isn't abuse. These accidental injuries that only happen when he's drunk that he conveniently forgets about when he sobers up.

I used to look up to the man with stars in my eyes, but all I see now is a black cloud of hatred. No matter how many times I've picked him up from the floor and tried to get him help, he still can't stand being near me without reminding me that I'm at fault. Without reminding me that while he lost his wife, I lost my mom. And that without his constant accusations, I already blame myself.

The urge to call Lee hits abrupt. I should have him come back to pick me up and take me to work. I should tell him everything. But as my fingers itch to find his contact in my phone and initiate the call, I can't bring myself to tap his name. Just remembering the dark look on his face when he saw the bruises left from the last time has me completely dismissing the idea. I can't trust him to help me rationally and not go all caveman and kick my father's ass. No matter how badly he deserves it.

Allowing a man as good as Lee Powell to serve time in jail helps no one, especially not on my behalf.

But I do file away his offer to help me move. Maybe having a bigger guy around will keep my father at bay if he happens to show up before I finish hauling out my meager possessions.

Two weeks, I remind myself and start to gently change into the uniform I wear at the diner. I suck in a sharp breath. My side screams in pain when I lift my shirt over my head. Around two weeks and I can finally get Lincoln and I out of here.

Just before I pull on my clean shirt, I snap a photo of the red mark blooming on my side. I'll take another one later once the bruise forms. That unsettled feeling returns as I document yet another piece of proof, but it's my insurance. Either my father lets Lincoln leave and be safe with me or all the evidence goes to the police. A real-life Uno Reverse card I hope I don't have to play.

19

LEE

TUESDAY EVENING, I clock her presence before she notices me standing near the dugout. The first pitch is still fifteen minutes away. The assistant coach, Rob, has the players running drills in the outfield while I adjust the lineup so I have a moment to discreetly admire her without looking like a creep.

Her beautiful red hair is secured in a ponytail. Curled, escaped tendrils lay loose around her face and neck. A gold chain glints in the hot summer sun against her lightly tanned skin. The navy tank top she wears is a little loose-fitting and flutters in the breeze, and her short shorts with the jagged hem are downright unacceptable with other male eyes around. Her smile is wide and genuine as she laughs at something my sister says.

My heart speeds up a little as I trace the length of her delicate neck.

As if she can feel me undressing her with my eyes, she glances over, and if possible, her smile grows. She says something to Cort before heading my way.

As much as I fight to keep the signature scowl on my face, my lips tip up in the corners.

She stops close. Not as close as I'd like when my dick demands I take her in my arms and kiss the shit out of those pouty lips, but close enough when there's an inquisitive audience. She tilts her head, her attention flickering down to my hand.

"Hi," she says.

"Ask your question," I order and run my tongue over my lower lip.

"Is that for me?"

I raise an eyebrow and extend the paper cup. "You can try it and see for yourself."

Her wary gaze finds mine over the plastic lid.

"What are you scared of?"

"That you hide whiskey in here in order to handle these rowdy kids." She sniffs the lid. "It smells like coffee."

"Can you not be so damn adorable when I can't do anything about it?"

Finally, she sips the drink and lets out a little sigh. "What would you like to do?"

I scan the sea of nearby faces. "I don't think it's appropriate to even tell you." My voice is growly and deep as a running list scrolls through my head.

Touch you

Taste you

Lick you

Spank you

Fuck you

A pink flush hits her cheeks. "I should go before you get us both into trouble."

"You are trouble," I mumble.

"The sexy kind," she whispers.

"Find me after the game."

A bashful look crosses her face before she spins and returns to her seat.

I'll be damned if I can get through a night of coaching knowing she's in the stands behind me with that sassy mouth and that sweet little outfit that makes me want to take her out to my truck for a dirty quickie.

Corjan catches me staring, halting my thoughts. He slips into the spot beside Juniper with a grin designed to piss me off. I pull my ball cap off to run my fingers through my hair before straightening the hat and stalking off. The tenuous hold on my control slips, tempting me to do something stupid, like stomp over there and lay my claim in front of the crowd of parents.

Get your head in the fucking game, Powell.

"You win some, you lose some, boys. This was a hard loss, but take it for what it is and know where you can do better next time."

The sea of young faces stares back at me as if I have the power to take their disappointment away. A few even shed tears. We break apart with our team chant, and with shoulders rounded and drooped, the boys walk off. Ollie throws his arm around Lincoln's shoulders. His friend had a rough time pitching tonight and is taking the loss extra hard.

After making sure all the litter is picked up from the dugout, I pack up my coaching bag, ready to get out of the dust and heat.

"Tough loss, Coach." Juniper stands at the entrance, her fingers curled into the chain-link fence. She's as pretty as she was an hour and a half ago. A beautiful sight to a man in a low mood.

"They played a good game. It just wasn't in the cards tonight."

Her gaze shifts beyond my head, and she moves in closer. We're both silent except for the sound of the zipper on my bag closing. When I stand, her line of sight is blocked by my chest.

"Can I make it better?" she asks in a hushed tone.

I agree to her silly game with a nod, looking down at her, eager to see what she has in mind. I grasp my ball cap and spin the hat backward on my head.

Her eyes sparkle at the move.

You like that, do you?

She must be around five foot six to my six foot one. Taller for a woman but still dwarfed by my size. She links her fingers around my neck and rises on tiptoe. I wrap an arm around her low back, pulling her flush as our lips meet for a brief kiss. She starts to pull away, but I'm not ready to give her up.

I nip her bottom lip, using her gasp to slip my tongue into her mouth.

She tastes sweet, like her coffee, and minty, as if she tried to mask the bitterness. Not that I give a fuck when I can have her like this. I smile against her mouth and press my hips flush to hers so she can feel what she does to me.

All too soon, we break apart. I curl my shoulders and rest my forehead against hers, not ready to put space between us. "Thank you."

She lowers down to flat feet. "I wish I could give you more."

"Spend time with me?" How is it she makes me feel like a teenager asking her to stay out late without her parents' permission? I just know I don't want to be away from her. I swallow hard, steeling myself for her rejection, and readjust my hat back the way it was. "If you want. We can go back to my place, or I can take you out for a bit."

Indecision creeps into her features, making me want to retreat with regret. "I want to, but Lincoln…" She trails off.

"You can take him home first, or I can drop him off." I shove my hands in my pockets, trying to appear casual.

As if she can see through my vulnerability, she reaches up and brushes her thumb along my jaw. My eyes drift closed at her touch. "Let me tell him."

She treats me with a softness I'm unaccustomed to. As if she can see inside every little crack of vulnerability and seals them with her goodness.

"We should probably get over there before someone comes looking for us."

Her eyes widen. "I forgot your entire family is sitting there." She groans. "How many minutes has it been?"

"We're so busted." A rare chuckle slips free.

"Okay, well I'll go first and then you wait like a minute before following."

But I'm already trailing her and staring at her ass.

"You're not following the plan," she grouses.

All I can do is shake my head. Leaning close, I put my mouth near her ear. "You better get over there before I find a reason to keep you even longer."

The hitch in her breath makes the teasing all worth it

as does the glare she sends my way. I try to pretend I don't see the knowing looks my family exchanges with one another. The nosy fuckers probably placed bets on how long we'd be tied up with each other.

Can't say I blame them when the six of us siblings are all single with no signs of settling down. Me spending time with a woman is a novel idea.

I clear my throat, and my family disperses, having already said the majority of their goodbyes.

We start for the parking lot while Juniper speaks to her brother.

"Will you be okay if I drop you off at home and leave again?"

The astute kid looks back and forth between the two of us. "What's in it for me?"

"What do you mean?" she asks with a furrowed brow.

"I was going to ask you to play a video game with me tonight." He's totally full of shit. He adopts a pair of puppy dog eyes while biting back a grin.

She's going to fall for his scheme because that's just the type of person she is. Sweet down to the core. She'd give Lincoln the moon if he made the request.

She shifts her weight to her other foot. "If you really need me, I can stay home."

"Just promise you'll play with me tomorrow and it's a deal."

With a radiant smile, she holds out her hand. "Deal. As long as you stay out of trouble tonight. Not too much junk food and don't stay up too late or make too much noise." Her gaze swipes through me before settling back on her brother. "Dad needs his sleep."

"I know, you don't have to remind me."

"And have your cell phone in case you need to reach me."

"You're so annoying," he grumbles and climbs into her car, slamming the door.

She looks at me and cocks her head. "I guess that's settled. Where am I meeting you?"

Resisting the urge to brush a strand off her cheek, I palm my keys instead. "I'll follow you to drop him off."

"Okay. See you in a few minutes."

The drive is more like ten, but I don't complain. My heart beats increase the closer we get to her house. I spend the ride contemplating where to take her that isn't lame but doesn't scream this is a date because it isn't.

By the time she's settled in my passenger seat, I've come to a decision.

"Where are we?" she asks, watching out her window as I turn off the main road onto the private driveway.

I can admit the view is a tad creepy in the dark, considering how far we are from the main part of town.

"My Sanctuary."

Her audible inhale breaks through the quiet cab of the truck. After getting out to punch in the code and closing the gate behind us, an enthusiastic chorus of barks and howls sing in the distance. From only the glow of the headlights, I see her wide-eyed expression turn to me. "Are those your dogs?"

"Yes," I respond, mildly cautious.

"Can I meet them?" Her barely contained excitement fizzes through the cab.

"That is the plan." My shoulders relax, and I bite back a grin at her enthusiasm. While we were dropping her brother off, I sent a text to tell Jude not to come investigating when we showed up.

She turns back to the shadows passing in the dark out the window. I could kick my own ass for not bringing her here during the day when she can see everything clearly, and I can observe her reactions.

"There's so much land. Do they get to roam around?"

"Yep. Jude takes the entire pack on a daily hike. They also freely run the pasture and swim in a small lake on the property. If you watch up ahead, you'll see them in a minute. They're probably waiting on the porch."

Her gaze remains glued to the windshield the rest of the drive. Sure enough, the pack vies for the front of the gate to see who's here to visit.

"I've always wanted a dog. My dad is allergic, though, so we couldn't get one."

"If I had a dollar every time an animal lover told me they were allergic to their pet but kept them anyway, I'd be a rich man."

She laughs, holding me prisoner to the throaty sound. All I can do is throw the truck into park and stare.

This is casual, I remind myself. But damn. A man could fall in love with a laugh like that.

"What?"

"Nothing," I grunt, shrugging off the impossible notion. "Let's go play with the dogs."

Juniper hops out and beats me to the front, nearly bouncing on her toes. My long strides eat up the distance between us. I imprison her palm against mine and lead her through the gate blocking the front porch.

"All right, you pack of mutts. Back up and let the lady through."

As expected, the dogs descend in defiance. Most have enough manners not to jump all over us, but one leaps and puts his paws directly on her chest.

"Oh, hello." She laughs and strokes the short fur on the black lab's head.

"That's Grizz. He's only ten months old, so he's still learning how to behave."

"He's sweet." The pup jumps down, and she starts scratching Winnie beneath the chin.

"That's Winnie. She's Jude's favorite, so don't get too attached."

Everywhere she turns, a new dog takes the place of another. "How many are there?"

"Fourteen currently."

Her smile lights up the darkness around us. "Are you guys hiring because this seems like the best job ever."

I rest my ass against the wooden railing and cross my arms. "It really is. We run a pretty efficient team. Jude puts in the most hands-on work day-to-day. Cortney is our resident veterinarian and brings along her technician, Bridgette. Corjan runs marketing and events and other networking tasks. Jack and Aiden work other jobs but help on rescue calls when we need more people. And I have my hands in everything, but mostly do all the back-end boring crap when I'm not here. Budgeting, scheduling, stakeholder meetings with donors."

Juniper rises from her crouch and wipes her hands on her shorts. "It's incredible. They all look so healthy and happy."

I rub the back of my neck. "That's the goal."

"Now I have to ask, why don't you have a dog?"

"Ah, I was waiting for that question." I uncross my

arms and lean back against my hands. "I did. Her name was Pumpkin because we found her abandoned in a pumpkin patch. She was my very first rescue, an Australian shepherd mix. She passed away a few months ago at the age of thirteen. I only ever had the one. She didn't get along with the rest of the pack, so I kept her at home. Great fucking dog."

"You loved her."

"I love them all, but she was special. I don't know when I'll be ready for another."

"I've never lost a pet before, but I'm sure there's no rule for how much time should pass."

I suck in a fresh breath of humid summer air. "I'll know when someone special comes along."

She settles into my side, her body heat warming my skin through my cotton tee.

Dogs prance around our legs, and occasionally, we reach down and pet whoever is neediest. Our gazes tip to the heavens. Out here, the stars are innumerous pinpoints of light against a sea of blackness. Without light pollution, the sky is magnificent.

"I like this. This peaceful quiet," she says softly as if she's worried about disturbing the very thing she admires.

"Sometimes I envy my brother. Jude, that is. This life he's built for himself on the ranch is exactly how he wants it."

Her hand strokes softly down my stomach. "Yours isn't?"

A pulse rockets straight to my cock. I shrug with indifference. "I don't know. I'm content with my life. But at times, it feels like something is missing."

Some*thing* or some*one*?

"I understand the feeling," she says but doesn't elaborate. "It's so beautiful out here. Can we take them for a walk?"

"You want to take the dogs on a walk?" I don't know why I find her request surprising, but I do. Her sense of adventure thrills a restless guy like me who's constantly on the move.

"Sure. I don't want to leave yet, and they seem to have a bit of extra energy."

"All right. But we'll only take a couple of the bigger ones. I don't think you want to know what it's like to bathe fourteen dogs at midnight if they decide to roll around in the mud." I leave her side to grab a couple of headlamps from the cabinet beside the front door.

"Oh, I don't know about that. But you're the boss, so I'll default to you."

I puff out my chest. "That's right. I am the boss."

She pokes my pec. "So tough and scary. Lead the way, *boss*. Before I get bored with this date."

The word hangs between us like a physical thing, but if she's uncomfortable with the slip, she doesn't let on. I'm not uncomfortable, *per se*, but the word feels foreign. A line we both agreed not to cross that feels perilously close to snapping. The problem is I find it hard to keep her at a distance when she doesn't show any signs she's getting ready to walk away.

I shove the thoughts aside to dissect later and call Winnie, Grizz, Roxy, and Toyota beyond the gate, leaving the rest of the dogs behind. We switch on our lights and set off on a brisk walk on one of the trails Jude designed.

We're mostly quiet. I think she's enjoying the experience for what it is. I like that she doesn't need to fill every moment with mindless chatter. Sometimes just the presence of another person is enough to chase away the loneliness. That and something about the sound of paws on uneven terrain soothes the soul.

We reach a clearing near the lake. The panting dogs take off to the edge. A silvery moon hangs overhead and casts a glow across the rippling water. A summer breeze brings the scent of fresh water and mud, and the sound of croaking frogs cuts through the silence.

Juniper turns to face me but breaks into laughter and throws her arm over her eyes. "Your light is blinding me."

With a click, the lamp extinguishes, and I reach over to darken hers too. The move closes the distance between us until I can feel her full breasts brushing against my chest.

"Better?" I whisper. Dark night surrounds us now that we removed our light source, and my eyes haven't adjusted. I can just make out her features in the glow of the moon.

Her fingertips brush my cheeks. Tentative and maybe a little searching. She strokes the five o'clock shadow along my jaw, down my neck and back up, where she threads them into my hair.

She nods. "I'm not afraid of the dark, Lee. Besides I can think of a few ways you can light me up." The words float across my lips at the same time she tugs.

A rumble from my chest is the sweet sound of surrender. The need to feel her again too strong to resist. I band my arms around her.

She fits perfectly against me, her torso flush with mine while my tongue probes the seam of her lips. Without protest, she lets me in and strokes her tongue gently against mine. Slow and unhurried under the moonlight, we kiss as if time doesn't exist.

"We really like the outdoors." She laughs gently. At some point, she shoved her hands beneath my tee, caressing my bare chest, and I have one hand planted firmly on her ass. If we rely on our history, I'm probably thirty seconds away from trying to fuck her against a tree or bent over a large boulder.

I force myself to take a step back. "I'm not opposed, but I don't think you'd appreciate the places mosquitoes can find when you're naked."

"Oh god, I can imagine." Her nose crinkles adorably.

"Come on, my little darling. Before I decide the itch would be worth it." I flick on our headlamps one at a time and slot our fingers together, resuming our late-night walk.

"I have to tell you something."

She sounds so serious that I almost stop. "What's that?"

"I had to remove the sheet from my window. I figured it might lead to awkward questions when my dad discovered it."

If only she could see my scowl in the moonlight.

"I promise to keep my curtains closed at night. Unless you're the one next door spying on me."

"I'm tempted to tack one up over my brother's window just in case you forget."

"Now that would definitely lead to awkward questions."

Toyota nudges my hand on her way up the trail, the other dogs rustling leaves off to the sides. Juniper's deep breath is loud in the quiet night.

"Nighttime makes me think of my mom."

"Why's that?" I prod gently.

"We used to spend a lot of time together at night. She'd pull weeds in her garden, and we'd take midnight walks. Whenever I couldn't sleep, she'd drag me outside just to sit in the fresh air until I got tired."

"Are you a night owl like her?" I want to keep her talking. Grief like this isn't meant to be kept inside to fester.

"Sometimes." Her hand flexes in mine. "Night is too lonely without her, though, so it mostly makes me sad."

"I'm sorry."

"Her accident was at night." She tips her face to the sky, the beam from the headlamp disappearing into the atmosphere. "She was coming to pick me up from a party. We had a rule that if I ever felt unsafe, I could text her and drop a pin, and she'd show up at my location without any questions. So I did. I took her up on it a few times, but this time when I dropped the pin, she never made it."

I sense where this is going and squeeze her hand tighter, hanging on, reminding her she's in the company of someone who understands loss.

"The sirens could be heard from the field we were in. Everyone took off running away, but I knew something was wrong, and I ran toward them." Her voice cracks.

My stomach twists at the raw words spilling from her sweet lips. "I know sorry isn't enough, but dammit, Juniper, I don't know what else to say. I'm so fucking sorry."

A small, sad smile plays on her lips. "I've been through a lot of therapy. It's okay. I didn't mean to drag down the evening. I just felt like sharing her with you is all."

"Anytime. You can bring her up anytime and I will listen. Happy, sad, or in-between, you hear?"

"Thank you."

I drag our hands to my mouth and kiss her knuckles, wishing I could do more. "You're welcome. Besides, you just reminded me you owe me a baking lesson. I need to learn how to make your mom's famous chocolate chip cookies."

Her smile sucker punches me in the soul. "She'd love to hear you call them that. She was so proud of those cookies."

"They really were a hit." I pat my stomach. "I might be in trouble if I can make them myself."

"All the more reason for you to keep me around. So I can make them for you."

Making cookies for me doesn't even reach number ten on my list of reasons.

But I keep that information to myself.

20

JUNIPER

"YOU'RE TERRIBLE AT THIS!" Lincoln sniggers.

My fingers cramp as I mash the buttons on the controller to flee the debris the video game boss shoots our way.

"You're the one who wanted me to play. I never said I was any good."

My character spasms and becomes transparent as I lose another life. Our laughter breaks loose at how terrible I am, but the sound of the front door crashing open cuts it short.

"Dad's home," I whisper. We both toss our controllers to the floor and stand.

"Why do you think he's early?" he asks, a tremor in the voice he fights to keep steady.

"I don't know."

What I do know is anytime he deviates from the norm, trouble follows. I'm supposed to be heading to work in a few minutes, and Lincoln was going to make sure he was in his room when Dad got home after his shift at eight thirty. It's only four in the afternoon.

Our father rounds the corner into the living room, a wrinkled brown paper bag clutched in his hand. He leans heavily against the doorframe and aims his glassy eyes at the two of us. I'm instantly appalled he drove in this condition. Risking not only his life but those around him.

"What're you doing here?" He drinks deeply from his bottle.

I step slightly in front of my brother. "I'm about to go to work."

Dad snorts. "Yeah, right. Why don't I ever see any of that fucking money? My boss Kyle said he seen you over at that strip club. That has to be some good tips."

"Go to your room," I mutter to Lincoln, but he doesn't move.

"Hey, I asked you a question." Dad stumbles into the room.

The hair on my neck stands on end. I feel locked in this unwinnable battle, and Lincoln has a front-row seat to something I never want him to witness. Our unpredictable father with a bottle in his hand.

"Dad, just let it go."

He takes a step closer.

I skirt around the side, pulling Lincoln along by his wrist.

"I can't." Dad throws his head back and closes his eyes. "You just keep taking from me, you ungrateful little bitch."

"I'm going to go, right now. I'm leaving, and I'll even bring Lincoln to a friend's house so you can have some time to yourself."

His fist cracking the plaster in the wall startles me, and

I jump. "I know what you're doing here!" He points an accusatory finger at me. "Leave my son and get out."

Trembling fingers tighten reflexively on Lincoln's wrist. "I'm going," I respond coldly.

"For good."

"What?"

Lincoln frees himself from my loosened grip, and the shock coursing through me prevents me from stopping him.

"Pack a bag. I'm sick of your shit. I want you out of my house right now."

My mind races with the demand. The list of reasons I can't. How to stall his drunken tirade long enough to get Lincoln and me out safely.

But it's like a dam broke, and he keeps on screaming, well past the point of reason.

"You killed my wife! It's your fault she's dead, and now you're trying to turn my son against me while you live in this house I paid for and eat the food I bring home. You're selfish and ungrateful. You've only ever thought of yourself! I want you gone. I don't want to look at you ever again."

I need supplies. I need Lincoln's stuff. I should have had a bag ready. I should have planned better for this moment instead of naïvely thinking I could make it until I found a place to live.

"Lincoln, come on," I whisper and tug on the back of his shirt.

"Leave my son and get the fuck out of here!" Dad moves forward threateningly, a nasty smirk on his face. "You think you can just take him from me? I've never laid a hand on him."

"Please," I start, not sure what I'm even asking him. Please let us go. Please stop forcing me to confront you like this.

"Juniper, just go!"

My entire world completely halts.

Lincoln extracts himself from my grip and calmly approaches our father, stopping a few paces away to face me. "Please, just leave. You're making this worse."

The smirk on Dad's face plunges a knife straight into my heart, but Lincoln's words wound me deeper.

"You heard the kid. Even he's smart enough to know you're good for nothing. Thought you could take him from me, eh? Well, look at that. He doesn't want to go."

I flick my gaze between father and son, feeling like all the air has been sucked from the room. "Lincoln…"

But he simply shakes his head.

I'll get you out of here, I silently promise as my worst fears come true. Leaving him here feels like leaving a piece of my heart behind, but what more can I do? What I need is time and a little distance to come up with a plan. Lee will help me. He'll know what to do.

Woodenly, I turn my back on my remaining family members and walk out the front door, not sure if I'll be able to return. Not sure what will happen to my stuff. Not even sure if Lincoln will be safe. I could call the cops for a well check, but given what just went down, it might only add fuel to the flames. Something tells me Lincoln will be okay. For now. But I don't plan to leave him here indefinitely. I just need time to figure out what to do.

My heart shatters as I climb into my car alone. I twist my fingers around the steering wheel until they're white from my grip. A helplessness I've only felt once before—

the night Mom died—resurfaces and steals my breath. Before I force myself to drive away, I send Lee a text.

ME

I need to talk to you after work. Can I come over to your place? I'll leave XO's around 10.

Once I send the message off, I force my shallow breathing back to normal and drive to work. More than ever, I need the money and the distraction.

Even though my heart is with my brother, I chase away the sadness with a steely determination. This might not have been in my plans, but I'm not going to let it delay my forward momentum. If I can find somewhere to stay until my new rental is ready, I can have Lincoln out soon. We just have to make it a little bit longer.

I tie my apron around my waist, feeling my phone vibrate in the pocket. Digging it out, I find a response from Lee.

LEE

Is everything okay?

ME

Everything's fine. I just need to see you.

LEE

I'll be waiting for you to get here

ME

Thank you

So many things I want to say flood my brain, but I pocket my phone instead. It won't do either of us any good for me to sound the alarm when I'm not in a position to talk right now. Instead, I throw myself into work. The place is fairly busy. Full tables keep me running back and forth from the kitchen to the dining area most of the night. It's not until my last table leaves at 9:45 that I have a moment to breathe.

I'm just about finished rolling silverware when Isla bustles up to the bar in a tight leather skirt, knee-high boots, a satiny top with a bow on the shoulder, and a pink dessert box.

"Yay, you're still here! Come with me." She snags my hand and leads me into the back, not stopping until we reach the dry goods storage.

"I only have a few minutes." I glance behind me at the main doors as they disappear from view.

She sets her box down on a shelf. "That's all I need. Wait here."

She breezes past me only to return a moment later, dragging Benjamin in much the same way she manhandled me.

"What's going on?" He wipes his hands off on a white towel. He slings it over his shoulder before crossing his arms and leaning against a shelving unit.

"Ta-da!" Isla flicks open the box and holds it out to him. "Happy Birthday, Ben! And Happy You're Finally Getting Laid, Juniper! And I'm celebrating a solo trip to see what else this state has to offer."

"What does that mean?" I ask, eyeing her bright face with suspicion.

"I have a hotel booked in Minneapolis tonight. I'm taking your advice and a few days off on a solo road trip to check out some clubs. And maybe I might also find a beautiful stranger to fall on top of."

I snort, instantly feeling lighter than I have all night. "Good. I'm proud of you."

My best friend dishes out cupcakes. Ben's is chocolate with white frosting and a plastic Happy Birthday ring stuck in it, while mine is white cake with bright pink frosting and a plastic penis jutting from the middle. The one she chooses for herself looks just like mine, but it has a set of plastic boobs with protruding nipples.

"I added the party favor to ours." She beams.

"This is just what I needed." My spirits lift a little. I pluck the flesh-colored plastic from my dessert and lick the frosting off the base.

"Could you be a little less obscene about it?" Benjamin's frown changes to laughter when I punch him in the arm.

"Stop being such a pervert."

"I'm not the one who brought a dick to this party." His critical gaze flicks over to Isla, but he's too late to catch on. Laughter bursts from us.

"No? Should I check?" she giggles, wiggling her fingers in his direction.

"I meant a plastic dick. Mine is au naturel." He sends us both a middle finger.

"Well, thank you for this. My night has been a little shitty, so the timing was perfect." I sink my teeth into the sugary sweet cake.

"You're welcome."

"I'd love to stay, but I have somewhere I need to be, so I should get going. I'll fill you in later, Isla." I toss my wrapper in the trash.

"Fill me in too. I want to hear about how hard and long—ow!"

Isla's elbow lands perfectly in his ribs, cutting off his mockery.

"You two have a good night." I toss the strap to my crossbody over my head and wave behind me.

Just before I reach the exit to the main floor, my boss Manny walks out of his office. His dark eyes flash as he gives me a silent once-over. More than once he's asked me if I'd ever consider the stage, but he doesn't push the subject when I tell him no. With a shove, he parts the double doors ahead of us.

"You have something on the corner of your mouth," he says over his shoulder before straightening the lapels of his black suit jacket.

Embarrassment sweeps through me, carrying a flush to my cheeks. I guiltily swipe the corner of my lip with my thumb and push the cupcake crumbs into my mouth, staring at the back of his jacket as he walks off. I straighten my shirt for good measure. God, I can't wait for this night to be over, ideally spent falling asleep in Lee's arms and in his bed with a plan in place for moving forward. Optimism drives a bounce to my step, and I start off for my car.

Only, when I look up, I meet Lee's eyes for half a second. Hurt flashes across his features before he storms out through the main entrance.

I have no choice but to chase after him.

21

LEE

I CHECK my phone for what feels like the hundredth time this evening to find the screen blank. Again. Juniper's text earlier left me unsettled, and I find myself counting down the minutes until her shift is done.

I've spent the evening helping Jude settle in our new rescue, Penny, a beautiful Bernese mountain dog who came to us from neglectful conditions. The poor thing is about twenty pounds underweight and skittish. She'll take a little while to warm up to the humans, but we've already seen her showing interest in the pack.

The water source cuts off with a flick of the handle, and I gently dry off her newly cleaned coat. Her frozen stature breaks my fucking heart.

"I know, sweetheart. Now you're all clean, and I can give you a nice big bed to sleep on until you're ready to hang out with us."

I toss the towel into a laundry bin, and she gives a hearty shake, followed by a yawn. I glance down at my splattered shirt with a small smile. I hope I have a spare in my truck or I'm going to fucking stink.

The minute I received Juniper's text, I decided I wasn't going to wait at home for her. As soon as I'm finished with Penny, I'm driving straight to the club she works at to assess with my own eyes that she's all right.

Then I'm taking her back to my place.

The sentiment delivers warmth to my chest, and not the kind that needs a strong antacid. The kind that says I might just be in deep shit and not from the dogs. The kind that wraps me around dainty little fingers and has me buying stock in coffee creamer. The kind that has me wanting to fall asleep only to wake up beside her.

Brushing aside the unfamiliar feelings, I lead our newest member through a door into a holding area. We have six individual dog runs to allow for decompression, though we've had at most three dogs here at a time. Tonight, Penny will have the place to herself.

I dress up her cot with a blanket for comfort and softness, adding in a couple of toys, and turn on the spigot for fresh water to fill her bowl. Once she curls up on her new bed, I slip a bowl of food just inside the door and shut it behind me.

The poor baby. I bet Juniper would love to come see her. One day too late. Hopefully soon she'll want a return visit.

As late as it is, I could use a pick-me-up, not sure what waits for me when Juniper is off her shift. I plod up the hill into Jude's kitchen before taking off.

"All finished?" Jude asks, walking into the room wearing a pair of sweats and scratching his stomach.

"She's all clean and settled. Sweet thing. I wish I could

find the owners myself," I mutter while pouring fresh coffee into a travel mug.

"She had to be tied up to that stake for months, left outside in all the elements. People don't fucking deserve dogs."

"Agreed. Anyway, I'm out of here. I'd ask if you had a fresh shirt, but I'm guessing the answer is no since you aren't wearing one."

Jude flips me off. "Seeing your girl tonight?"

The sip I take delays my expected response. But since he's my brother, I give it to him. "Yeah."

He nods once. "Happy for you. Later." With a flick of his hand, he walks back out.

If I were a different man, I'd tell him that I'm happy too.

I strike gold when I find a clean, albeit slightly wrinkled black tee in my truck. While standing outside, I switch it out, swatting a few thirsty mosquitoes in the process. Once changed, I spritz on cologne and set off to meet Juniper.

I entertain myself on the drive with thoughts about other activities we might partake in later. After I determine she's okay, that is. The sex is fun, but it comes second to her well-being. The direction of my feelings is a welcome surprise. This isn't a position I imagined being in, but Juniper slid quietly into my life, and it's not hard to admit I like having her there.

I joked that I was falling in like with her, but I might be falling in other ways too. Despite only knowing one another for a handful of weeks, this feels anything but casual.

The light feeling in my chest doesn't stop when I pull

into the parking lot and spot her Mazda near the back. The clock on the dash reads 10:05. She should be walking out those doors any minute. I back my truck into the space beside hers and wait, drumming my fingers on the steering wheel to pass the time.

By ten fifteen, I'm a little restless. She probably has a lingering table. It wouldn't hurt to sit at the bar and wait for her to finish. Not to mention a glimpse of her working would be a sweet, simple form of torture. To look, but not touch. To watch all the male eyes follow her around wishing they could take her home to bed and knowing she'll be coming back to mine.

The engine cuts abruptly and the next second I'm striding across the pavement.

I like that image in my head a hell of a lot. Too much to pass up the opportunity.

The dark atmosphere inside cloaks the finer details. Intense lights illuminate the stage where a woman twirls on a silver pole. On the dining side, small flickering centerpieces brighten the tables. A strip of pendants hangs above the bar. The room smells like sex, even though I don't think it's that type of establishment. My brothers and I have been here a time or two, but it's been at least a decade since I've stepped foot inside. Corjan's twenty-first birthday was probably the last time.

A woman walks by wearing an apron. I flag her down.

"Can you tell me if Juniper's done waitressing? I'm a friend."

Her face twists with confusion. "I'm sorry, I don't know who that is."

"Are you sure?" Some unnamed emotion forces me to straighten. Frisson of uncertainty mixed with shame.

"Yeah. I don't know anyone with that name." She scampers off, and I don't bother calling her back.

A slithering feeling twists in my gut. Did she lie? I glance around the room and spot two other waitresses milling around. My eyes flicker over to the woman dancing.

The doors to the right of the stage fly open and that feeling in my gut intensifies until a red haze eclipses my vision.

A well-dressed man walks out, speaking over his shoulder and twisting back to survey the room with a smirk playing on his lips. And behind him is Juniper, her face flushed, fixing her lipstick and clothing, looking guilty as fuck.

Suddenly, a barrage of images and memories fills my head.

The way she didn't mind showing off her nearly naked body through the window and her reluctance to explain the bruises. They weren't from the fall and they sure as fuck weren't from my brother. The pieces fall into place.

My nostrils flare with the force of an exhale that does fuck all to calm me down. Not waiting to confirm she saw me, I storm back out to the parking lot. The desire to shut down keeps me moving to my truck. Even when I hear her call my name and the slap of her feet across the pavement. I don't care if she chases after me and tries to talk. I ignore her and keep moving.

But when her small hand wraps around my bicep, I nearly lose the final thread on my restraint. I fucking hate that she did this to me. That I let her get close enough to tear me apart.

"Don't touch me." I rip my arm from her grasp and head back in my original direction.

"Lee." Her voice is barely a whisper through the hand covering her mouth. Her eyebrows crease in concern over eyes clouded with worry.

But I know what it is. She won't fool me again.

It's all a fucking lie. Just like her.

"I can explain." She reaches for me again, but my legs are longer. Two strides widen the gap separating us.

"I don't need you to explain. I know what I saw. I can put it all together. If you want to be a stripper, fine, be a stripper. It's not my business. But I'm not going to let you lie to me about it." My voice comes out steady despite the storm building inside.

She shakes her head, confusion dipping her brows. "I don't strip. I'm just a server."

But I'm beyond hearing her spin another tale to keep me tangled in her web. "I know what I saw!" I tear a hand through my hair.

She flinches back, and for a second, my anger douses. Just a little. Scaring her isn't my intention. I'm not that type of fucking guy. But the pain I feel doesn't know what else to do. It beats a wild drum against my ribs, begging to be unleashed. Doesn't she see my heart is fucking bleeding in her hands?

I keep my eyes pinned to her like one would watch a stalking predator. I put my heart in her control, and she did exactly what I expected. "I learned from a young age that what someone shows you is more important than what they say. And what I see is a pretty girl who has no issues flashing her body through a window. I see bruises that come from sliding up and down a pole for cash. And I see you coming out of the back like you just got done earning some extra tips for the evening."

Tears glisten in her eyes below the streetlight, but she doesn't refute me. She doesn't fucking say anything.

I inch closer, hands clenched at my sides. "Fight for me, Juniper. Tell me I'm wrong."

She straightens her shoulders and lifts her chin. Her demeanor shows her strength while at the same time shredding me to pieces. Ruined mascara colors the skin beneath her eyes, and for a second, I fight the desire to wipe it off.

"I don't have it left in me to fight for you when I'm fighting for myself."

I scoff. "I thought you were different, but you're just like everyone else." I move a step closer to my truck but think better of it and turn back. "Say something," I demand, hands fisted at my sides, the young boy inside me begging her to show me I'm worth fighting for. But just like everyone else who's come across my path, she fails me.

Once again, I'm the fifteen-year-old boy walking the cold winter streets all alone.

"Sometimes we only see what we want to see." Tears break free and slip down her cheeks.

"I'd say goodbye, but there's nothing good about this."

This time, I don't look back. This time, I climb into my truck and peel out of the parking lot without watching her in the rearview. Even though I know in what's left of my heart that she just stood there and watched me go.

I didn't just fall in like with her. My stupid ass went and fell in love.

And I'm the one paying the price.

22

JUNIPER

FIVE MINUTES.

Five minutes of tears streaming unchecked down my cheeks leaving hot trails behind. Five minutes of feeling the anguish coursing through me without trying to stem the ache. I give myself five minutes because when I leave this spot, I need to have my head on straight.

With my heart still bruised and bleeding, I dry my cheeks with the scratchy sleeve of my shirt, and drive to the nearest fast food joint for an ice cream shake.

Cupcakes and chocolate shakes—the post-breakup dinner.

Sitting in my car in the parking lot, I stuff my feelings down my throat with frozen bites of chocolate and check in on my brother.

ME

Are you okay?

LINCOLN

I'm fine. Dad fell asleep on the couch after you left, and I've been playing video games with Ollie.

For all the griping parents do about kids and technology, I'm so thankful at this moment that he has a way to connect with me and his friend without leaving the house.

ME

Promise to call me if something happens? I'm worried about you.

LINCOLN

What about you? Where will you sleep? Are you with Lee?

Even the twelve-year-old hasn't missed the budding relationship between his coach and me. I hope he isn't crushed too much when he learns of our untimely demise.

I sniffle and respond even though it'd be easier to ignore him.

ME

I'm going to stay at the motel. I'm okay. Don't worry about me.

LINCOLN

I think you should ask Lee to help you. He has good advice.

The accusations burn too bright to even consider and will for some time. Going to Lee no longer remains a viable option. My lips tremble around another bite while slippery, cold fingers slide across my phone screen.

ME

I'm a capable adult, little brother. I'll be fine :)

The smiley face is solely for his benefit. Those muscles won't be working for a while. Not while my heart is cracked and broken.

I roll my shoulders and shove one more bite in my mouth. I can't stay here all night, and I need to pick myself up and get settled. With Isla off on her solo adventure, there's only one place in this town I can go. What I said to Lincoln is true. I'm capable of taking care of this myself.

A short distance away, on the side of the highway leading out of town, sits a quaint little motel. A white light shines on the sign near the road. Jack's Inn. The clean white exterior is cute in the daytime, but nearly impossible to see in the dark. Only two windows glow on this side of the rectangular building this late at night.

Dainty chimes ring through the reception area when I step over the threshold. The wooden desk to my left is empty. Tourist pamphlets are stacked on one side and a laptop stands open in the center of the counter. Bold of the owner considering how greasy some people's fingers can be. To my right, a quiet fire flickers in a brick fireplace and navy blue armchairs beckon me to sit on either side. An open staircase leads to the second floor.

"Hello." A deep voice rouses me from examining the comfortable space. But when I turn, I wish I could keep walking straight out the front door.

I press the heel of my hand to my forehead. "Of course. I should have put it together."

Lee's brother Jack leans one tattooed arm on the desk, a warm smile on his handsome face. A lock of brown hair falls in the center of his forehead. "Put what together?"

I wave a hand between us. "This. You. I didn't realize you were the owner."

"Name's on the sign." He chuckles. His other arm braces with the first until he leans fully into the desk. His gray eyes settle inquisitively on my face. "That would be a problem because…?"

"Can you not tell Lee that I'm here?" I grip my cross-body strap with both hands.

"I can't agree to that."

My feet carry me across the rug toward the door. "Then I can't stay."

"Wait." He skirts around the desk as if he's considering a chase. "It's late. You're obviously here for a bed. What I mean is that I won't go running off to call him the second I give you a key. But if not knowing where you are causes him concern, I will at least tell him you're somewhere safe." He's not unkind in his explanation, only clarifying where his loyalties lie. I can't argue with knowing Lee has good people around who care about him. "Deal?" he presses.

I force my chin to remain high. "Deal." Not that I anticipate this to be a problem. Lee feels so betrayed by me he probably wouldn't care if I left the entire state.

Emotion wells up like a balloon in my chest, so I step closer to the desk and slap my credit card down. The sooner I get checked in, the sooner I can attempt to sleep this disaster away.

"Is everything all right?" Jack asks while keying in my information.

"It's not, but it will be." Determination infuses my tone.

Jack slides my card back and holds out a room key. "Room 7. It's upstairs at the end of the hallway. You should have a little more privacy there."

"Thank you."

He settles the plastic key in my palm. "If you need anything, don't hesitate to ask."

"This is all I need." The words get pinched on their way out. "Good night."

Does he have a magical cure for a broken heart? Because I'd take one of those, stat.

The key card opens to a small, clean room. The smell of fresh linen and lemon provides a temporary reprieve. This situation isn't going to last forever. In a short week or two, I'll be moving into my own place, and I can start fresh. As new of a beginning I can get while still sharing this same small town with Lee Powell and his entire family that I'm bound to run into again.

Wetness gathers in the corner of my eyes, and I swipe it away with a huff. Not for the first time in the last two years, I wish I had my mom, but if I had her, then I wouldn't have been in this situation. Not with Lee. Not with my dad. Not with Lincoln. None of it would have happened if we hadn't lost her.

I put myself through intense therapy after her tragic death, but for the first time in a while, I feel the inkling of blame festering beneath my skin. Tears pour thickly from my eyes and without even removing my purse, I flop face-first into the bed and cry into the pillow to muffle my sobs.

THE SOUND of my phone ringing wakes me Thursday. I called out of work early and spent the rest of the morning in bed. I moved once to accept a food order I placed and checked in with my brother, but otherwise, the curtains remained closed and the door locked with the television loud enough to drown out my intermittent crying. My sick and twisting stomach held me hostage. Regret at not forcing Lee to listen to me. Frustration that he doubted me in the first place. I fell asleep with half a Reese's cup in my hand while watching *A Little Princess* on a streaming service.

Checking the time, I find it a little before one in the afternoon. The number to the rental office has me sitting up straight and slapping the device to my ear.

"Hello?" I answer, my voice clogged like I have a head cold.

"Hi, Juniper. This is Catherine. I have some good news. The property you were interested in will be ready next week if you still want it."

Almost falling from the bed in relief, I stagger to my wallet to get her the card for the deposit.

Once we hang up, a laugh bubbles free. The hysterical kind that sounds a little crazy. What am I doing crying in bed? My phone clatters against the nightstand. With newfound determination, I head to the shower to clean up. I have a couple of hours to plan. I was going to hide out except for work, but I need to go to Lincoln's game and talk to him. If I can get us into a new place next week, he needs to be ready to come with me and avoid Dad as much as he can.

I send him a text to remind him I'll pick him up at four, then jump in the shower. I wash up with the motel soap and dress in my dirty wrinkled clothes. Okay, so before I do anything, I need to buy a few clean spares. Or I could sneak over to the house and pack a bag.

The thought entices me, but I set it aside. If my father notices I came back before I'm ready to get most of Lincoln's and my stuff out, I don't know how he'd react. He might have already changed the locks.

I'm safer picking up a few necessities until I have a place to store all my possessions.

Summer sun beats down when I step out of the nearest department store after stocking up on essentials and clean outfits. I went for the cheap, plain tee shirts and jean shorts and a few basic toiletries. My optimism says this is temporary, but if I have to start out with nothing, then I'll make do.

After a quick change into fresh clothing and running a brush through my hair, I throw on some sunglasses from my purse and pick up Lincoln. My dad's truck isn't in the driveway when I pull up, but I still give an urgent wave when Lincoln emerges from the house.

No matter how desperate I am to punch the car in reverse, it has to wait. My little brother dives across the console and throws his arms around me.

"Whoa, hey there, buddy. You all right?" I squeeze him back before pushing him at arm's length for inspection.

"Yeah." He adopts a tough scowl, looking far too old for his age. "Are you?"

The worry in his voice chases away some of the chill inside.

"I'm good." I back us out and drive to the baseball field.

"I'm staying at a motel, and I just got a call this morning that my new house will be ready next week."

"Really? He won't be able to hurt you anymore?"

I breathe my way through a rush of tears. My fingers curl tight around the steering wheel. "Not anymore."

"And I can come too?"

"I won't leave you behind. I'm going to ask if you can stay at Ollie's for a few nights. I don't like you being alone with him."

"He's rarely around. I sleep in, and he's gone to work by the time I wake up, and I try to be in my room before he gets home."

"Keep doing that," I urge. The less time he has to spend around our father, the better.

The minute we arrive at the field, I send Lincoln out to meet his team. I hang back an extra twenty minutes until I know the game has started. Cowardly? Yes. This way, I can sneak in unnoticed. I straighten my ponytail and dab the mascara smears from beneath my eyes. After swiping on a coat of lip gloss, I decide I can't stall any longer.

I fortify my heart against the battering it's about to receive seeing the hardheaded coach.

The crack of a ball hitting a bat precedes the parents screaming in the stands. The first inning is well underway. Lee's voice carries just above the ruckus as he hollers at his guys to get their heads in the game. I try not to look, but I find myself seeking him out anyway.

Hands secured on his hips, he stands just in my line of sight with his back to me. Jeans molded to his backside. His brown hair peeks out beneath the edges of his forward-facing hat. He looks as tall and imposing as ever. I can even imagine the scowl on his face. The memory of his hard body pressed against mine invades my defenses and a crack forms in the shield around my heart. A dagger twists deep beneath my ribs.

I knew seeing him would hurt after his accusations, but not this much. Like someone cranked all my organs in a vise. I shouldn't be in this much pain after letting him walk away. Because that's the truth. I let him go. He was just a hookup after all. A friend with extra benefits. A fun way to pass the time. But somewhere along the way, I began to feel cherished and cared for in a way I'd been missing. He broke through my defenses, then tossed me aside at the first sign of trouble.

The truth is, he wasn't wrong. I didn't fight for him the way an innocent person would. But I'm not innocent. I have lied. I lied about the bruises, just not in the way he thinks. And somewhere in the back of my mind I recognized it would be easier to let him go, hurt and hating me, than explain to him what was happening with my dad.

I decide then and there that I can't let him close to me. He hasn't reached out, not that I expected him to, but I haven't either. This thing between us is done. Aching and awful as it feels admitted in the privacy of my thoughts.

So I proceed as if I never knew him, as if I never fell into his lap, as if I've never had him buried inside me making me come. I approach the bleachers and seek out his sister, a friendship that predates he and I, and I climb into the empty spot on her right.

The sight of a paper coffee cup on the step directly below where I sit sours my gut.

Someone else left it behind. I can't even consider the alternative.

"Hey!" Cortney's happy greeting startles me. The lack

of warmth I expected doesn't come. The smile she aims my way is as bright as ever. "I didn't know if you were coming."

"A little delay but I'm here for a while."

"Oh, do you have to go somewhere?"

Actually, yes. Anywhere that doesn't have your brother. Rather than admit to the shambles my life has become, I tuck a stray lock of hair behind my ear and shake my head. "Just preparing for a move."

"You got the place?"

"I did."

Cortney turns more fully to me, her brows dipped over her eyes. "You don't seem excited."

I am one-hundred-percent failing at this whole I'm fine thing. "I am. I'm just a little tired is all."

Her hand lands on my forearm, friendly and comforting. "Let me help. Can I take Lincoln for you?"

"Actually, I was thinking of asking you, but I, well, you do too much."

She tips her head back with a laugh. Her long obsidian hair falls neatly down her back. "Are you kidding? Do you know how much it saves me having a friend over for Ollie to play with? I'm totally up for an extended sleepover at any time."

I elbow her arm. "Don't lie. I know there's work involved. And feeding two preteen boys is not cheap."

"I grew up with five brothers. I'm well equipped to handle those bottomless pits."

As if she summoned one of those brothers, I feel Lee's eyes. And I can't quite resist the urge to seek him out and read his expression for myself.

The glare piercing the distance between us is severe

enough I immediately look away and suck in a sharp breath as pain slices through my gut. That's just his face, remember? That grumpy, stormy, angry, kind of hot, pinched eyebrows and frown. He can't suddenly hate me this much.

"I know this is nosy, but did something happen between you and my brother?"

If she weren't so gentle, I'd probably tell her to mind her own business. I bite my bottom lip and direct my focus to my palms pressed between my knees. "You could say that."

"He can be a tough one to crack."

"We had a misunderstanding, and I'm just trying to move on from that." I clap along with the parents as our team scores a run, but the game lost my attention long ago.

"He feels deep, and if he even senses he's about to be hurt, he'll cut you loose to protect himself."

"Cortney…" I warn.

She raises her palms in defense. "I'll stay out of it. After one more thing. I think you're great for him, and I know my brother could be great for you too."

Any response would further the discussion, so I let it drop. Instead, I rise and wipe my palms against my thighs. "I'm going to head out if you're okay to take Lincoln."

"Of course. I'll plan to bring him home Sunday unless something else changes."

"Thank you."

I twist to climb down, but she stops me with her hand on my arm.

"He may be my brother, but I care about you too. And

I give you full permission to call him out on his shit if it's what you need to do. Our friendship will last."

"He thinks I cheated, even though we weren't anything," I blurt.

"Did you?" Her neutral tone surprises me.

I shake my head, ignoring the way my lungs cinch tight. "Of course not."

"Then it's my brother doing what he does best. He pushes away people who get too close."

"I wish that made me feel better, but it doesn't."

"I know," she says and lets me go.

23

LEE

Four days after I left Juniper crying in a dark parking lot, I'm still a mess. Everything bothers me. Every sound burrows beneath my skin until I'm more pissed off than I usually am. I've reached the point that even when my phone rings, I want to throw the thing against the fucking wall. Seeing Jude's name on the screen gives my twitching fingers pause, and I put it to my ear.

"Hello?"

"You still a cranky motherfucker?" he says by way of greeting.

"What do you want?" I answer back, not in the mood for fucking games.

He mumbles something beneath his breath. "We have a lead on that dog. She's on the corner of Pineridge and Watercress."

Already locating my keys, I pinch the bridge of my nose. "Which dog are you talking about?"

"That white one. The husky, Slipper." Rustling wind

sounds through the speaker, indicating he's likely already on the move.

My heart contracts like a vise at the mention of Slipper and the last time I saw her rushes forward in my mind as if begging me to retain the memory. When I think of that day, it's not the dog I remember. My favorite part is Juniper lying across my thighs. "I'll meet you there."

The door slams behind me harder than necessary, and I lock up my house, grateful for something distracting to occupy my thoughts. Sitting in my idling truck, I hold my phone, and before I can talk myself out of something I've thought about since I saw Juniper at the baseball game, my fingers fly over the keys and type out a quick text.

ME

Can we please talk?

Instead of waiting for a response that probably won't come, I pocket my phone. The drive takes ten minutes. Ten minutes of distracting thoughts swirling around my head. The regret lies thick and heavy, blanketing everything else. The righteousness I claimed for catching her cheating. The pain I felt realizing she wouldn't fight for me. As the days tick on between the time I last saw her face, I find it doesn't matter as much. Not until I can talk to her and hear her side of things.

The pain remains strong. Every so often, it flares beneath my heart as if to remind me that things went to hell between us. I snort and run a hand over my face. As if I could fucking forget. Her tearstained image haunts my consciousness and swims behind closed eyelids.

My anger still lingers, though it's waned. Now that I've

cooled off, she deserves a chance to explain her side of things. Selfishly I want to know why. Was I just a convenient fuck? A fun summer distraction? Did she not feel anything more between us?

How could she not?

Jude's black utility van is easy to spot idling in the driveway of a single-story blue house. I park behind him, grab a spare leash and catchpole, and lock the doors. He's probably prepared, but just in case, I don't want to have to run back for supplies.

Not spotting anyone out front, I circle the garage into the backyard, appreciating the subtle breeze across my face. Jude's crouched down at a gap between a fence and the shed with a McDonald's cheeseburger in his hand.

I sidle up but not too close. Near enough to hear him talk to her. Jude tosses a wrapped burger behind his back that lands at my feet. "Take that to the other side," he says and moves an inch closer.

"This is your high-value treat? I thought we used freeze-dried liver. Since when do we feed the dogs fast food burgers?"

"No, this is my fucking lunch. I was in a hurry and didn't want to miss her."

A muffled whine tugs at my heartstrings. Or what's left of them. I do as he says, lowering myself carefully to peer into the crack.

The dog appears thinner than my last encounter with her. Her hips are more pronounced, and I bet I could see most of her ribs. She doesn't seem to be hurt, just scared of humans like a lot of the dogs we rescue.

I follow Jude's lead in unwrapping the cheeseburger

and tear off pieces to toss near her. After a few minutes, she cautiously backs up and eats the food near her feet.

"Come here, baby. We won't hurt you." I coax the husky in a tone meant to soothe her, and with each piece I pass her way, she inches in my direction. There isn't enough space for her to turn around, but each step back brings her closer until there's room to loop the leash around her neck and ease her out from her hiding place.

"I've got her," I tell Jude. With a little more coaxing, I'm able to bring her around the front of the shed. My brother meets us there and gives her another bite of the burger in his hand.

"She's gorgeous," he remarks.

"Can't wait to get her home and healthy."

We lead her across the grassy lawn. He moves to get her into one of the cages in the back of his van, and I pause.

"I'm going to take her," I announce. For some reason, I don't want to say goodbye to this elusive stray just yet.

His impassive face gives nothing away. "Suit yourself."

I keep a kennel in the back of my truck in case I come across a dog in need, so we settle her there instead. He gives her the rest of the food to eat if she gets hungry.

He slams the doors on the back of his van and leans against them. "You look like shit," he says seriously, surveying my wrinkled jeans and disheveled shirt. My hair is a mess from running my fingers through it, and dark purple circles under my eyes reveal I haven't slept.

"I'm fine," I snap.

"How's your girlfriend?" he throws back, smirking like he knows things aren't going well and that I fucked everything up.

"She's not my girlfriend."

"Sure looked like it to me when the two of you walked out of the trees holding hands."

"Fuck you, Jude." Curling my fingers in the front of his shirt, I push him against the side of his van.

He shows a toothy smile, something we rarely see from him. He acts like this is exactly what he wanted. "What are you gonna do? Are you gonna kick my ass like we're kids again? Think I could take you, old man."

I shove him away from me. "Leave me alone, jackass."

He just laughs and shakes his head. "Whatever you did, I'm sure you can still fix it."

"It's not mine to fix. She broke it, not me," I snarl.

"Did she say why?"

"Did she say why she cheated on me? No, I didn't give her the chance."

His mouth drops open in surprise.

Yeah, exactly my reaction too, asshole. I didn't expect that from her either. "There's no fixing this."

"I think you should go talk to someone. Keeping all this inside isn't going to do you any favors."

"Yeah, and who would like to play therapist with me?"

He shrugs, one hand on the door to his van. "Maybe start with Mom."

I DON'T SEE NANCY, and I don't go stalk Juniper as much as I want to force her to talk. I need to give her the same space I asked for, and if she's never ready? Well, I don't want to think about that.

Slipper is surprisingly easy to coax out at home. She

climbs from the kennel in my truck with a mighty stretch once her feet hit the pavement. Her nose immediately goes to work sniffing the areas she can reach while attached to the leash in my hand.

"That's it, girl. Go potty."

My cell rings, and my heart slaps my ribs. But the screen says *Corjan calling...*

"Hey, I'm a little busy right now."

Translation: I don't want to fucking talk to any more of my nosy family members.

"I heard about the new mutt. How's she doing?"

I admire the newest rescue sniffing around on a loose leash in my backyard. "I just got her home a few minutes ago. So far, so good."

"That's great. I was calling to see if you could come by and watch the dogs, but I see that might be a problem if you're busy getting her acclimated."

I rub the back of my neck. "Yeah, that's tough. She needs some time to decompress before I bring her around other dogs."

"Do you think you could ask your friend Juniper to stop by since she lives next door?"

The problem with having so many siblings meet the girl you're sleeping with is they all fucking talk about her. But the reminder of her next door has me mentally adjusting my plans.

"You know, I could swing by and give them bathroom breaks and feed them a couple of times through the day. It shouldn't be a problem."

"You have to play with them too. Otherwise, Friskee will eat my shoes."

"I'll make sure your shoes are safe, little brother. When

do you need me?"

"Starting tomorrow, if you don't mind."

"I don't mind at all."

We hang up, and just as I go to tuck my phone in my pocket, it pings with a text. Corjan must have forgotten something.

But it's Juniper's name in the text bubble, and I fumble the device in my haste to unlock the screen.

JUNIPER

If you still want to talk, I'm at Jack's inn

I look down at the dog and back at my phone.

"It had to be today you finally let us catch you, didn't it, girl?"

The sweet husky just cocks her head.

24

JUNIPER

THE URGE TO vomit lingers long after I send the text.

I've torn down the cuticle on my right thumb, and Jack probably thinks I'm a crazy person standing outside the door to his motel. Thank god it's summer and not the middle of a Minnesota winter or else my ass would be frozen.

Lee texts back almost immediately he was on his way, but half an hour has passed. I wouldn't blame him for changing his mind. Even though I know he's wrong about this whole thing, he's the one who feels betrayed, and that gives him the power to walk away, or in this case, stay away. He could refuse to ever hear me out, and that would be that.

I only want him to listen to my side. The pain in my chest demands we don't leave things between us unfinished and cold.

The crunch of tires on gravel snaps up my head. Lee pulls his big truck in the lot and stops at the curb in front of me. He hops out and rounds the hood.

My mouth goes dry, and I begin to catalog all of him for my memories. The wrinkled gray shirt and the dirty jeans. His disheveled hair and the tired look on his face. Apparently, I'm not the only one getting poor sleep, but I don't think that's a good thing. I physically ache at the evidence of his stress. The knowledge I did this to him.

His face is wary as he completes his own scan. Mouth a compressed line. Shoulders tense and arms crossed.

For a split second, I'm not sure I can go through with this. Whatever is about to happen. The muscles in my legs tense in preparation to bolt.

"Are you staying here?" His squinted gaze scans the building.

I mimic his position and cross my arms over my chest. "Yeah, for a bit. Lincoln is with your sister, and there was an issue at home."

His eyes narrow on my face, but he doesn't question me further. "Do you want to go up to your room or..."

"This is fine," I rush to answer. I don't think I could handle being alone with him right now.

His hands curl into fists at his sides, almost like he doesn't know what to do with them. "I just want to know why."

"I didn't cheat on you." I keep my voice even despite wanting to cry.

He appears to struggle before he says, "Can you tell me what I saw, then?"

I relax a little that he didn't jump straight back into the painful accusations.

"I don't know exactly what you saw. My friend Isla brought cupcakes, and I stayed after a few minutes to have one. When I walked out, that man in front of me was my boss. I never have, and never would, fool around with him. Whatever it looked like, I can promise you I was never with anyone else. I know it's not much, but it's the truth. I can give you Isla's phone number or let you talk to any one of my coworkers."

"They didn't seem to know who you were when I asked about you."

"That's a safety rule, Lee. Some men can get a little weird about the dancers, so if anyone asks for someone by name, we pretend they don't work there."

His green eyes search mine. A little of the tension around the outer corners fades. "I should have let you explain," he says in a quiet voice.

"I kind of understand why you didn't even though it hurt me."

"I took my hurt out on you."

I nod. "You did."

"I didn't want to lose you, but then I pushed you away."

My throat constricts. "Yes."

He thrusts his hands in his pockets and rocks back on his heels. "Can we fix this?"

"I don't think that's a good idea right now."

Lee looks over my head, and a muscle in his jaw jumps. When his gaze returns to mine the intensity almost forces me a step back. "I think I've fallen in love with you."

"Lee," I whisper, my hands covering my mouth as a tear finally breaks free. The first sign of my crumbling strength.

"I know I wasn't supposed to, but you made it so damn easy." His rigid stance looks like he's physically keeping himself in check.

"I think now would be a good time to look after yourself."

"Juniper," he tries to cut me off, but I hold my palm out.

"Stop. Please listen to me. If I've learned one thing about you over the past few weeks, it's that you're always taking care of everybody else. Your siblings, your mom, the dogs, me, even Lincoln and the baseball team. People call on you and you're always there, and while it's not a bad thing, I think you treat it like a duty. Or a punishment. You don't have to earn your keep with those who love you. I think it might do you some good to stop shouldering the responsibility of everyone else's happiness."

"You're the missing thing. You make me happy." The grit in his voice nearly makes me cave.

"I'm not enough. Not right now."

I almost tell him the truth about my dad—what I wanted to tell him a few days ago before everything fell apart—but it wouldn't do us any good now. I don't want him to be with me out of some misplaced obligation to keep me safe when I can take care of myself.

"You're more than enough to me."

"Someday, I think you'll thank me." I step back toward the motel on shaky legs. I said what I needed, and I cleared my name. But until this thing is over with my dad, it's best we keep our distance before I just become one more person in a long list that depends on him.

Hurt flashes across his face. Just when I think he's about to keep arguing, he simply nods. The acid crawls back up my throat at the realization this thing between us is done. I couldn't fight for him, and he's done fighting for me.

I run back into the building, not even able to watch him get into his truck. I watched him drive away from me once. I'm not sure I'd survive it a second time when I'm the one pushing him away.

Even if it's for his own good.

25

LEE

I DON'T KNOW why I'm doing this. I tell myself it's because I feel all itchy inside that I'm standing outside this house a few hours after leaving the motel. I've never done this before. Showed up at Nancy's unannounced without a task to complete, without grass to mow or groceries to pick up, or siding to paint. But the more I sit at home, the more I feel like my chest might actually cave in.

I rap my knuckles hard against the familiar wooden door. I knock three times before I hear the lock slide out of place. It swings open to reveal Nancy with her gray hair tied at her nape.

"What are you doing standing out there knocking on my door like a stranger?" Her kind eyes narrow, and her brows crease. She swings the door open wider and gestures me inside, but I'm frozen, staring at the woman who single-handedly saved my life.

"Mom." The word scrapes painfully up my dry throat. The last bit of my heart splinters into pieces. I've never done this part before. The fixing. Not as a kid and never as an adult. I usually shove the broken parts back together as best as I can and carry on, ignoring the way they jab my skin and don't quite fit right.

She covers her mouth with her hand, lowering it moments later to grab my wrist. She gathers me into her arms. "What in the hell is the matter?"

I rear back from her at the curse word. I think the only time I ever heard her swear was when Jude and Jack were new to our family and they put a frog in her lukewarm coffee as a prank.

She ushers me inside and immediately pours me a cup of coffee, sliding the mug across the weathered table.

"I was hoping for something stronger, like bourbon."

"I don't need you sleeping off a hangover on my couch, son. Tell me what's going on."

I trace a grain in the wood with my finger while coming up with the words to say. Do I really want to spill my guts to the woman who raised me? I rest my elbows on the table and drop my head into my hands, jamming the heel of my palm into my eyes.

"I think I messed up, and I don't know how to fix it."

Mom takes a seat beside me and pats my elbow with her wrinkled hand. "It's about that girl? Juniper?"

"I thought I caught her cheating on me, and I lashed out." I relay some of the shameful details. The stillness between us does nothing to settle the storm inside.

"I'm not going to ask you what you did or what you said. That's none of my business. I am going to ask you, if she had done this to you, would you hear her out? Would you forgive her?"

Turning the tables twists my gut. If I'm really honest with myself, I know the truth. "I'm not sure I would," I answer out loud. "I tend to expect the worst, and I didn't hear her out."

"Well, there's your answer." She slaps her hand on the table as if everything is done and finished and rises to her feet. She's speaking in riddles.

I look up at the woman who selflessly gave me a home and a loving family.

A soft smile plays on her lips.

"Could you spell it out?" I snap, unintentionally terse.

"Does she know anything about your childhood?"

"I've shared a few things."

Mom shrugs. "I think if you can get her to sit down, she'll understand where you were coming from."

"That's the problem." I rise from my chair and dump the remainder of my coffee down the sink. My fingers tap against the silver basin. "I tried talking to her, but she's done with me."

Mom steps in close, her five-foot-three frame shadowed by my mass. She reaches up and pats my cheek. "You're not trying hard enough. You have to make her listen."

"She's stubborn."

"So are you. Goodness, it wouldn't kill you to be a little vulnerable."

"What the hell do you think I'm doing?" I don't usually speak to her like this, but she knows just how to push my buttons.

She tsks and wears that stupid smile again. "Words are nothing without action. Isn't that what you've always said? So you told her you loved her. But have you shown her?"

"I think so? I don't know. I'm not a grand gesture kind of guy. I'm not even a fall in love kind of guy."

Now I'm pacing across the kitchen. When I lift my head, I find her looking at me with that dumb grin again.

"Will you stop looking at me like that? Jesus, I don't even know why I came over here."

"If I rile you up enough, maybe you'll decide to fight for her."

"Haven't you been listening? She wants me to leave her alone."

Mom laughs. This was a stupid idea.

"Never mind," I grumble. "I have to go let out Corjan's dogs."

THE FIRST THING I do the next morning is deliver a coffee to her door. Technically, I drop it off with Jack and make him deliver it, but she'll know it came from me. When I arrive back home, I release Slipper from her pen and coax her with treats to sit on the floor in front of the fireplace.

She tucks her long limbs beneath her and rests her head on her front paws with her ears flat while she looks at me.

"Don't be mad. I have to bring Cortney over so we can check you out."

When we take in a new rescue, Cort normally drives to the ranch, but since I have Slipper here, she and the boys are coming to my place in a few minutes to complete an exam.

Extending my hand, she sniffs it curiously, so I ease my finger beneath her chin for a scratch.

She lets out a long yawn, and her ears relax.

"There you go, baby."

Dogs, I understand. I've won the affection of some feisty little pups over the years. If only I could win over Juniper with some snacks and a well-placed rub. The direction of my own thoughts makes me smile to myself. Snacks and well-placed rubs might actually be the key to keeping a good woman and making the world a happier place.

Only a few days have passed and I miss my woman like crazy. A nearly constant, unbearable ache. Like my skin is suddenly too tight and my heart's off a few beats. I miss her sass and her laughs. I miss her sweet scent and the way her hair tickles my face when I kiss her. I miss her confidence and her sense of adventure.

Her love for the outdoors.

Her disgustingly sweet coffee and providing them for her.

Her little gasps when she rocks against my lap.

My thoughts take a turn I don't have time to entertain. I move my attention back to the dog before I end up with my jeans around my thighs and my fist around my cock.

A knock sounds before my front door slowly opens.

"Knock, knock," Cortney says in a gentle voice, her attention flickering to Slipper.

The boys follow. Ollie moves to the couch, but Lincoln seems rooted to the spot just inside the door.

"Come on in, guys. Make yourselves comfortable. Ollie, you know where the snacks are. Why don't you get something for you two?"

"I'll show you," Ollie pipes in and hops up. "Uncle Lee keeps the best snacks around."

Cort scowls. "I force him to eat vegetables once a day on top of all the garbage he eats. You'd think I never let him have anything fun."

But my attention rests on the kid at the door. His worried expression triggers something deep in my gut.

A moment later, he blinks and it clears, and he follows my nephew to the other room.

Cortney, ever the observant Mom, doesn't miss my interest, but mistakes it for something else. She runs a microchip scanner over the dog's back.

"How are you? Juniper told me a little about what happened."

I shrug and stroke Slipper's fur. "I fucked up, and I'm trying to fix it."

She pulls out her stethoscope. "Good. She doesn't deserve to be hurt but neither do you."

My shoulders sag when she doesn't pry further. A first for the Powells, and I assume it's only because she's already heard Juniper's side.

"Have you decided to keep this one?" She sets the stethoscope aside and starts palpating Slipper's spine and hips.

"I'm thinking about it."

Nobody but Corjan knows about the incident with Slipper, and I doubt he'd even guess the reason I want to keep her. She was the catalyst for some of the best weeks of my entire life. And she might end up being the only tangible thing I have left after all this is over.

I help my sister finish up her assessment and we're even able to get a blood draw done and clip Slipper's nails.

"The only other thing she needs is a bath. Once she puts on a bit of weight, she'll be perfect." Cortney beams at the dog who's moved into my side. "She looks to be around two, two and a half."

Loud whispers come from the kitchen. I open my mouth to tease Cortney about the bickering boys when it sounds like a full-blown argument breaks out. Something clatters loudly to the floor, sending us both to our feet.

"Boys, what's going on?" Cortney takes point, and I'm hot on her heels to the kitchen.

Ollie wears a genuine look of concern, and Lincoln's bright-red face is wrought with guilt.

"Tell them what you told me," my nephew orders.

"Ollie," Lincoln hisses and takes a step back.

"You have to tell them. They're adults. They can help," Ollie says.

Instantly on high alert, I step closer to Lincoln. A tense moment of silence passes between the four of us.

"He asked me if he can keep staying over because his dad is mean," Ollie announces.

Lincoln's breath hitches, the sound urging me to him where I drop down on a knee. "Hey, tell me what's going on."

He studies the collar of my shirt. "I didn't protect her."

The hair on my neck stands on end. "It's okay. Whatever happened, it isn't your fault."

"Juniper isn't safe, and I tried to protect her, but now she's gone, and I'm afraid of being there alone when she's not."

My heart trips over itself to beat twice as fast. "Does your dad yell at her?"

"He hurts her," Lincoln mumbles, and for a second, I swear I black out from the rage.

The bruises.

She lied.

And after she cleared the air yesterday I didn't even fucking think to ask. I was too worried about a second chance that I missed it.

With the way I feel right at this moment, she probably saved me from going to jail. If she would have told me the truth the morning I confronted her about the marks, there's no doubt I would have driven straight to her house and kicked her father's fucking ass.

For the sake of the kids, I control the fury rolling through me. "How does he hurt her, Lincoln?"

He twists his fingers together. "He gets drunk a lot since our mom died, and he yells. And when she tries to help him, he pushes her around, and sometimes he just pushes her for no reason."

I could throw up.

I yelled at her in that parking lot, and she flinched away from me. The pieces all make sense. Her working two jobs and extra shifts. The way she acts like Lincoln's mom. Her crying in her backyard after a fight with her dad. Did he hurt her that evening? Was I sitting outside enjoying a beer while he left bruises on her skin?

I don't have it left in me to fight for you when I'm fighting for myself.

Fuck, I'm an idiot. I focus back on the kid. "You did the right thing by telling us."

He starts to cry, loud bursting sobs as if he was trying to hold it back and just can't any longer. Without thinking too much about it, I yank him into my arms. Holding him in a way I wish I had someone to hug me when I was a kid.

"H-He was screaming at her to g-get out, and sh-she

wanted me to go with her-er, but I wanted her to be s-safe, so I told her that she was making things worse and to j-just go."

The fragmented words slip into old cracks from my own broken childhood.

"Where is she?" Cort's strained voice comes from behind me.

"She's at Jack's Inn," I answer.

"Do we call the police?"

"No!" Lincoln thrashes in my hold. "You can't. If you go to the police, then I can't go with her, and she'll have to leave me behind."

I stroke my hand over his sandy-blond hair. "Shh. Let's calm down now, hey? You told me, and I'm not going to let anything bad happen to either of you."

He hiccups, and his shaking shoulders settle down some. When we pull apart, Ollie is there, tucking his friend beneath an arm.

"Here." He thrusts one of the ice cream bars I keep in the freezer into his friend's hand. "I won't tell anyone you cried. It happens to me too sometimes."

"Thanks," Lincoln mutters, red eyes cast downward, clearly embarrassed at his breakdown.

"Why don't you two eat those in the other room while we talk," Cortney instructs, and without argument, the pair walks off.

I drag my fingers through my hair and pull my palms down my face, still crouched in my kitchen. "Fuck."

My sister's hand lands on my shoulder. "Should I call Jack?"

"Not yet. She's safe there, and I don't know what her

reaction will be when she knows that Lincoln told her secret."

She releases a heavy sigh. "I feel awful for her. What are you going to do?"

The alarm on my phone rings, reminding me I need to check on the dogs. "I'm not sure yet."

"She's going to be okay. Last I heard, she got a new place. Hopefully, this is all over for them in a few days."

"I have to stop by Corjan's."

Cortney's expression switches from sad to worried in an instant. "Do you think that's a good idea? Maybe I should go instead."

I give her a look that says abso-fucking-lutely not. "I'm not going to go off half-cocked and knock on his door."

"I'm more worried what your reaction will be if you see him outside."

Yeah, I am too.

I snag my keys from the kitchen table. "You can stay here with the boys or lock up Slipper if you take off."

"Where are you going?" She follows me down the short hall to the door leading to the garage.

"I'm going to convince Juniper to call the cops. I'm going to warn her dad to keep his fucking hands off her. And I'm going to get back the woman I love. Not in that particular order."

"Lee!" she calls after me, but I shut the door and climb into my truck.

But first, I have to feed some geriatric dogs.

26

JUNIPER

ME

It's signing and keys day!

ISLA

No freaking way! I'm so proud of you, bestie

ME

You're in charge of housewarming snacks because I'm now broke :(

ISLA

I'm off on Friday. I'll bring the stuff for margs!

THIS IS PERFECT.

I walk out of the private bath, with a separate clawfoot tub and standing shower, and enter the main bedroom. The space isn't huge, but it's more than enough for what I'll be bringing over. I'll need to start fresh with new beds for me and Lincoln, but the closets are huge so we won't need extra storage for our clothes.

The light gray walls and white trim are clean. The hardwood floors mean I don't have to worry about him damaging the carpet with spills and other childish experiments. Add in an area rug or two when I have extra money for decorating. Isla already offered me her couch since she's planning to buy a new one anyway. If I can find a kitchen table at the thrift store, we'll have a place to eat, sleep, and relax.

Excitement I haven't felt in a long time chases away some of the darkness over the last few days. This fresh start can't come at a better time.

"What do you think?" the property manager asks where she waits in the recently updated kitchen. They added in new stainless steel appliances, and the color scheme carries on from the rest of the house.

We just finished the final walk-through.

"I feel like this should be way out of my budget, but I'm not complaining."

She claps her hands together. "I'm so glad you're happy with it. Here are your keys. It's all yours once you sign the paperwork."

I've already produced a pen from my purse before she's even finished talking.

She shows herself out with her folder and leaves a copy of the documents for me. I close the door and look around the empty space, and a pang fills my heart.

I wish I could call my mom. I know she'd be so proud of me.

My fingers find the gold chain around my neck and twist the rose-shaped pendant she gave me for my twenty-first birthday.

"I miss you."

The first thing I'm going to do after the basic furnishings is plant a few flowers below the front window. I'd pack her entire garden box from the backyard if I wasn't afraid of giving my dad a reason to come after us, but he loves looking at those flowers almost as much as she loved planting them. I wonder if he'll let them die once I leave.

He's supposed to be at work today, so the timing is perfect. I can zip over and fill a bag of Lincoln's and my things and be ready to take my brother with me when Cortney drops him off in about an hour.

After a week of feeling like my life is falling apart, this is a welcome step in the right direction.

I idle in the driveway for a moment, sipping the remainder of the hazelnut coffee that was delivered to my door this morning by someone I'm attempting not to think about, and admire the cute houses next door. Memories resurface of the grump who hammered a sheet to my window, and I feel a little sad about leaving.

Certain elements of my life might be falling into place, but there's still a lie hanging over my head. A big lie. One I don't see him accepting and sweeping under the rug. The more time apart, the more it gnaws at me to tell him. To inflict the pain on us both if we want to have any chance to possibly heal.

Because I'm trying to be strong for all of us, but each day that passes I'm breaking little by little. Missing him. Wanting him. I know I'm doing what's best for me and my brother, but is it possible Lee can be part of the equation? Isn't he good for me too?

If I'm honest with myself, I know the answer is yes.

He breaks up the rigid schedule and the responsibilities. The fun I've had with him is something I haven't had in years, not since before I lost my mom. He ignites this sense of adventure in me I let lie dormant while I took the world upon my shoulders.

And I told him not to fall in love with me, but I think I've been falling all along.

I blink back hot tears before they can fall and reverse out of the driveway. I'm done crying over my circumstances. Besides, there's much to do now that I have the keys to my new house.

On the way to my childhood home, I blast Taylor Swift's *Reputation,* and the tension fades just a little.

My hands shake when I insert my key into the lock, and I sigh in relief when the knob turns. The air inside is stagnant. Take-out containers litter the counter, and more trash collects in the overflowing bin in the corner. I wouldn't be shocked to see a rodent skitter across the dirty floor.

Less than a week has passed since he kicked me out and already filth covers most surfaces.

The desire to implement my simple plan sends me straight down the hall to my bedroom after grabbing a couple of trash bags from beneath the kitchen sink. Nostalgia for my childhood home can wait for another day. I shove open the door and flip on the light. I set out to work, starting with the most important things first.

Most of my clothes fit in a single bag. I deposit it near the door and move on to other replaceable necessities like makeup and jewelry. I empty my pillows from their cloth cases and fold up the flowery quilt Mom gave me one year for Christmas.

The last thing I need is the photograph of my mom

and me that I keep beside my bed. My fingers brush the smooth wooden frame.

I sit heavily on my mattress and stare at the image of us at the county fair riding a merry-go-round. I grasped the pole rising from the decorated unicorn with an exaggerated smile on my face while Mom stood proudly behind me with a hand on my back. The colors are a little aged and muted, the red hat I wore appearing pink with time.

This is how I always remember her. Happy and involved in her children's lives. She'd drop anything to be there for us, which is exactly how I lost her.

The front door creaks open, and the picture slips from my hands. I catch it on my knees just as heavy steps walk inside the house.

"Shit," I mutter and bury the picture frame inside the bag beside me. My heart thunders in my chest. My muscles freeze. I don't even think I fully breathe while I listen.

His keys clatter against the table. Something thuds close behind.

I close my eyes and will my heart to slow, to keep my breaths even.

The sound of him moving closer makes those things nearly impossible.

Why did I turn my light on and leave my door open? None of it matters because he would have seen my car in the driveway when he pulled in.

I shoulder one bag and move to the other.

His fist slams against my ajar door. I withdraw my head just in time for the door to crash against the wall.

"The fuck are you doing here in my house?" His ominous tone sends warning bells ringing in my ears.

I nearly gasp at the state of him. Greasy hair sticks out in several directions, and his face is ashen, the lines more pronounced. Brown splatters stain his white tee shirt.

I straighten and hold my chin high, meeting his glassy eyes. "I'm getting some clothes. But I'm done now so if you could move, I'll leave you alone."

"I thought I told you to get out." He steps closer, forcing me back in to my room.

My features harden. "Don't worry. I won't be back after this."

"Oh yeah? Figured it all out now did you?"

His big body blocks my escape. The slim options present themselves. Stay and wait for him to tire himself out or press by and hope he doesn't retaliate.

"You wanted me gone. Get out of my way."

"You think you can order me around after all you took from me?"

He's been strumming this tune so frequently, the words barely land.

And like a taut string, my control snaps.

"I didn't take anything from you!"

Wham.

The back of his hand contacts my face and forces my head to the side. Pain radiates, a hot pulse in my cheekbone.

"Stop!" I sob, throwing my arm instinctively to shield my face.

He hauls me up and shoves my back against the wall in the room I've slept in since I graduated from the crib in my parents' bedroom. Memorabilia from my high school achievements bears sole witness to my father's violence.

The bags slip from my grip and land soundlessly at our feet.

"She died because of you, you little bitch." Spittle lands on my face.

I flinch.

The world around us blurs. Flight or fight kicks in and for the first time, I do more than put up my hands in defense. I slam my knee into his gut.

He grunts and tangles my hair in his fist, wrenching my head back until a scream tears up my throat.

Terror grips me. I slap at his face. This is so much worse than the other times he's left a bruise. Drunken pushes and shoves that knocked me into doorknobs and stairwells.

This is different.

This is intentional.

He's trying to hurt me, and he's succeeding.

He yanks me forward before slamming me back, glancing my head off the wall. Stars erupt in my vision, and the breath leaves my lungs. I cough and gasp, fighting through pain and disbelief that this is really happening right now.

And nobody knows I'm here to stop it.

"Please," I beg, tasting blood in my mouth from biting my tongue. "Just let me go," I sob.

"I should fucking kill you."

And that's when I start to scream.

27

LEE

THE COFFEE in my hand heats my palm for the second time today. Jack clocks me the moment I cross the threshold to the motel even before the stupid chime dings. I keep telling him that thing is obnoxious, but he likes to not be constantly chained to his front desk.

With an eyebrow raised, he returns his attention to his laptop screen. "She isn't here."

"Any idea where she is?"

"All I know is she left a couple of hours ago."

"Shit," I mutter and plunk the cup down on his desk.

"Problem?"

I rub the back of my neck. "You could say that. I might need you for an hour or so, but I have to talk to Juniper first."

"I can let you know when she's back, but she's not going to like that." He grins as if the idea of a little drama excites him.

"Yeah." The flecks of dirt on my boots suddenly interest me.

"What's going on?"

"Found out her dad likes to get drunk and rough her up."

His face darkens. "Come again?"

Hearing it was one thing, but saying it out loud churns my empty stomach. "I need to talk to her, and then I'm planning on getting her out of there. I thought maybe having a few extra guys, showing him he's outnumbered, might hurry along the process."

"She's so fucking sweet." The softer of my twin brothers just looks sad. "Let me know when and I'll be there. Hunter is around here somewhere and can watch the front so I can take off."

I rap my fist against the wood. "Will do. And thanks."

"You forgot your coffee."

But I've already opened the door. "Keep it for when she shows up."

On the way across the parking lot, I let Cortney know that Juniper wasn't at the motel.

CORTNEY

I'm supposed to drop Lincoln off at home in an hour

ME

Can it wait until after I talk to Juniper?

CORTNEY

I can't exactly kidnap him, but I can stall until you find her

ME

I'm on it. Give me a little longer

Not for the first time, I'm grateful to be helping out

Corjan. If he didn't spend so much time away from home, I wouldn't have an excuse to be close by next door. Not that I expect anything to happen. I meant what I said to my sister. Going rogue on Juniper's dad would only land us both in jail.

And that'll fuck up my intentions of getting her back. Conjugal visits aren't really my thing.

The neighbor's house appears quiet when I pull into Corjan's driveway. The daylight obscures any lights in the windows, but there aren't any cars in the driveway to indicate someone might be home. A squirrel runs along the fence separating the two properties, and the sun beats down hot on the back of my neck.

I let myself inside to a chorus of yips and yaps, the little ankle biters scratching at my calves in greeting. Pickle stares up at me, tongue hanging out his mouth, and Friskee attacks the laces on my boot.

I hold one beneath each arm and trek out to the patio. "Do your business, kids."

While they sniff the grass, my thoughts return to Juniper.

The motel was a bust, but there are plenty of places to search. The diner and the club are obvious locations. Maybe I'd run into her friend Isla.

She could be shopping for her new place. Or with someone I haven't met.

And if the desperation mounts to unbearable levels, I could ask Lincoln to check in with her. I'm not above using the kid when her safety is a concern.

The dogs trail me inside where I feed them with puzzle toys to keep them busy so they don't eat Corjan's shoes. I open a few of the blinds to let in some natural light. The space is chronically dark, and the bachelor pad style doesn't provide a lot of warmth. His ex left the personal touches when she walked out on their marriage, and Corjan made several trips to the local dump not long after, leaving the walls achingly bare.

Not that I'm one to talk about decorations when I have none either.

I rinse a few dishes my sloppy younger brother left in the sink and load them in the dishwasher for later, then raid his fridge for a quick snack. I slap together a turkey sandwich and stand over the sink to let the crumbs fall in the basin.

Memories of that night weeks ago, standing in this place and watching Juniper undress for the first time, flit through my head. I pop the last bite in my mouth and glance at the bedroom across the way, my blood running cold and the food turning to sawdust in my mouth.

Without the glare from the sun, I can see straight into the bedroom. And there's no mistaking that burgundy hair against the white wall or the wide shoulders of the man holding her there.

Fuck!

The dogs bark and chase me to the door. Damp fingers slide on the bronze handle, but I wrench it open and manage to shut them inside. Blood roars in my ears as I sprint around the stupid fucking decorative fence separating the properties. My strides eat up the expanse of overgrown grass on the other side. I notice her car and a truck in the driveway that weren't there when I first arrived. I probably beat her here by a handful of minutes.

A blood-curdling scream reaches my ears still some

hundred feet away from the front door. I almost black out in rage.

This goddamn motherfucker.

So much for not going in half-cocked because I have a feeling this ends with both of us in jail or one of us dead, and it isn't going to be me on the floor when this is over.

But if I fly in there in a blind rage and beat him within an inch of his life, I can't keep her or Lincoln protected if I'm the one in prison and he's the one walking free. I didn't have a chance to talk with her. I don't even know if she has evidence of her abuse, and if it's her word against his? I can't guarantee he'll be found guilty. We've all heard stories of our justice system letting a perpetrator walk free.

My heart hammers so hard I swear I can hear it punching against my rib cage as I climb the steps. I shove away the whispers in my ear warning me about what I might find.

I swallow hard, open the screen door, and test the handle. Twisting it with ease, it glides open with a small creak. The muted words of a distant argument reach my position in the kitchen. A strangled, "Please."

"Sweetheart, you ready?" I call out in the steadiest voice I can manage with my blood boiling in my veins, putting into place an impromptu plan that might completely fail or it might be the brightest idea I've had in my entire life.

"Who the fuck is that?" Footsteps stomp down the hall, her father appearing in the living room. Glassy eyes narrow and sweat dampens his lined brow. A snarl curls his upper lip.

I don't breathe. Not until I see her.

Juniper steps out from her bedroom. A hand held up to her tearstained cheek, terror-filled eyes find mine. My heart fucking breaks at the sight of her damp face creased with pain.

But I keep playing the part. Especially now that I can see she's physically standing in front of me and my interruption forced him to remove his hands from her.

With a tilt of my head, I glance between the two of them. "Baby, I thought we were exclusive. Who's this guy?" I ask casually. The irony from the week before burns through me, along with the familiar pang. Pretend scenario or not, the idea still cleaves me into two.

Maroon cheeks, his wasted eyes bug out, and he says, "I'm her fucking father!" He moves a threatening step forward, increasing the distance between him and Juniper.

"That's funny." I disguise my fury with a chuckle. My voice drops to a threatening level. "She calls me Daddy too."

"You sick fuck!" he roars. "You fucking touched my daughter!"

He's just drunk enough to forget moments ago he was abusing the very daughter he now wants to protect.

A sloppy fist flies at my face with uncoordinated movements. I take the brunt of it in the cheek, sucking air through my teeth as stars explode behind my eyelids. Juniper screams, but the sound is muffled, like someone cranked the volume down as the room tilts around me.

"Look at me," I order her. Dropping down to one knee, I brace my hand on the floor beside my foot. "Don't look at him. Look at me."

"Lee!" she sobs, frozen in the hallway, stuck in freeze mode as chaos erupts. Her fearful eyes meet mine.

"Go call the police."

Hit number two forces my lips into my teeth, the lower one splitting on impact. Blood drips down my face and onto my knee.

"Go!" I shout at her, throwing a hand up instinctually when he grunts. The block misses his fist, and pain explodes in my left eye.

She finally runs past her father's back and around me. Close enough for me to see the trickle of dark red blood leaking from the end of her nose.

My control snaps and pretenses splinter around me to join the dust motes in the air. The door creaking open serves as enough indication of her safety for me to drop the act.

"You. Made. Her. Bleed." The punctuated words fall from my mouth like a curse, but he's too far gone to notice.

My teeth clench so hard in my bruised jaw it feels like they all might crumble beneath the force. With a burst of adrenaline, I surge upward, blocking his next advance. I flex my fingers around his flimsy windpipe and shove him up against the nearest wall.

A modicum of fear enters his cool blue eyes, chasing away some of the drunkenness, as if he instinctively knows how easily I could kill him. A wheeze puttering from his papery mouth gives me a sick sense of satisfaction.

"Take a good look at the damage you inflicted. Memorize it, you stupid, drunk son of a bitch. She might be too afraid to press assault charges, but I'm not. What kind of weak-ass man beats up his own daughter?"

With my thumb, I swipe at the blood dripping down my chin and spit a mouthful onto his floor.

"Let me go." He coughs. "I didn't mean to... lose control."

I test my grip on his windpipe, not wanting to leave any bruises. Even though my head swims, I bring my face close. Close enough my nose nearly touches his. My brows dip over slit, bruised eyes.

"The only place you're going is jail, motherfucker."

When I remove my hand, he sucks in a dramatic breath and crumples down the wall to land on his ass.

"Try to run before the cops come, and my brothers and I will find you. You'll never lay your hands on her again."

I stalk from the room. A man on a fucking mission.

The reason my heart beats stands outside in the middle of the driveway, one hand on the handle to her car as if she isn't sure a quick getaway is needed. The stupid organ responsible for falling in love slams against my ribs as I near her.

Tangles of red hair blow around her shoulders, wrapping around the hand held up to her ear. She's speaking, but I can't make out a sound. My focus is singular.

Get to her.

She's hardly within reach before I yank her into my chest. Tucking her as close as two people can get. It's only with my arms banded tight around her that I feel the sobs wracking her frame over and over, making it hard for her to catch her breath. The hand holding the phone falls limply to her side.

"Breathe, my little darling. Just breathe." I press my cheek to the crown of her head, feeling some of the tension fade now that she's safe in my arms.

The urge to bury my face in her neck is strong, but I don't want to taint her with my blood. She's been through enough without the reminder smeared across her lightly freckled skin.

"I thought you were going to let him kill you." She hiccups.

"Now what would be the purpose of that?"

My thumbs stroke along her jaw and tilt her face.

"Lincoln told me everything." I brush my knuckles over her swollen, red cheek, flooded with rage anew.

Guilty eyes flicker away from mine.

"Hey. Don't do that. I'm not here to scold you for doing what you thought was best."

"I lied to you. About the bruises and why I was staying at the motel." I can see the force of her swallow bob her throat before she says, "You were wrong about me cheating on you, but your gut was right about me not being honest."

"My gut told me that because I'm used to people walking away. Because when it comes to you, I feel jealous. I want you badly, and I was protecting myself from being hurt again."

"I still lied."

"And I still forgive you."

The whoop of sirens approaching interrupts our discussion. Two squads and an ambulance pull up. I immediately recognize the first cop out and breathe a quiet sigh at the familiar sight.

"Lee Powell. Quite the face you have there." Sutton Stone's brows dip behind his dark, tinted sunglasses.

My arm flexes around Juniper, whose fingers curl into the sides of my shirt, hanging on. "I need to press assault charges."

"On who?"

"Tom Kelly."

Sutton nods, his hand resting on his hip. "Is he here?"

"I left him in the house."

Juniper sucks in a sharp breath, and I draw her in closer.

Sutton's mouth compresses into a tight line. "Jesus, do I need to bring the medics?"

"I didn't lay a finger on him." Not exactly the truth, but hopefully, they don't find that out or this might become a bigger mess.

"Don't go anywhere. I'll need statements." He grabs his partner, and together, they enter the house.

"Are you okay?" I scan her face, looking to catalog every scratch. When she looks toward the house, I see a long bruise forming on the side of her throat. "I should go back, and fucking kill him," I seethe.

Her palm settles on my chest. "I'm fine."

"Bullshit. You're not fine."

"I'm not as hurt as you." Gentle fingertips prod the split in my lip. "You took those hits for me."

I press my fingers into her spine. "I'd do anything for you. I even contemplated going to prison."

"That's not funny," she snaps, her temper flaring.

"Honey, I'm not trying to be funny," I murmur and nip at her fingertips.

Her body melts into mine as some of the tension releases. "What happens now?"

Over her head, I observe the scene. The paramedics walk toward us with a medical bag, and the front door opens to the officers leading Juniper's dad outside in a pair of cuffs. The instinct to hide her blazes. I nearly force her into the car away from her father's searching gaze, but she's a capable woman able to handle seeing her father taken away by the cops.

"We have to give statements. They're taking your dad to jail, and these paramedics are going to look us both over while I fight them off me, and you sit still like a good girl."

Her glare contains enough heat to incinerate me on the spot. "If *you* don't sit still, Lee Powell, I swear to god… You took at least three hits to the head. You probably have a concussion."

"Kiss me and I will," I order, my voice husky. With the waning adrenaline, a new desperation sets in.

"Lee," she says, exasperated, but wraps her hands around the back of my neck. Her mouth gently touches mine as if she's afraid of hurting me. I breathe her in, settling into the fact she's here, and she's whole, and she's protected.

"What the hell happened?"

We break apart at the sound of my sister screeching. A scowl settles into place, and I aim it her way as she rushes across the yard with Ollie and Lincoln trailing her.

"Oh my god, Lee, you're bleeding!"

I catch my sister's hand when she goes to touch my face. "I'm fine."

Her face crumples. "You big dumb idiot!"

"Jesus, Cort." I pull her into my arms.

"You could have been killed." She sniffles.

Juniper snorts on my other side. "Wait until you hear what he did."

I shoot her a glare as Cortney pulls out of my arms to direct her own dirty look at me. "What did you do?"

"Later," I mutter. Over the top of my sister's head, I catch sight of a certain twelve-year-old who looks like he's moments away from breaking. Extracting myself from my sister, I twist to the side. "She's okay, Lincoln."

"Is she mad at me for tellin'?" he yells back, standing his ground.

Juniper moves around me. If her dad wasn't already cuffed in the back of Sutton's car, I'd stick to her side like superglue until he was no longer a threat.

"I'm not mad at you, buddy."

Red cheeks give away his emotion, but he curbs the tears, forcefully nodding his head. "Okay. That's good because I'm not even sorry."

"Whoo, the emotions are strong today." Cortney fans her face and moves closer to Juniper's side as if she, too, needs to assess her friend is okay.

While the two women talk, I dig out my phone and find Jack's contact.

"Everything still good?" he answers

"A little complicated, but fine now."

"Complicated how?" he asks, and I can hear movement in the background.

"Juniper's father, Tom Kelly, is currently in the back of Sutton Stone's cruiser."

"Shit." A pause follows before he says, "What do you need?"

I kick a rock with the toe of my boot. "You, Aiden, Jude. Corjan is out of town, but I want to get their stuff moved out of this damn house ASAP. I also need someone to take over Corjan's dogs."

"You got it. Where are we taking it?"

"I'll get the key to her new place, and you can take it there for now." I lift my head to find Juniper. She faces the other direction, but even the back of her head brings a sense of peace.

"What do you mean for now?"

"Mind your business." Sutton flags me down with a wave. "I've got to go give a statement, so I'll let you go. See you later."

"You got it. Bye."

As I pass, I rest a hand on each woman's shoulder. "You got her?" I ask Cortney.

She links her arm through Juniper's at the elbow. "Yep. We decided I'm going to take the boys back to my place once you two are done to give you guys a chance to unwind."

I give her a nod and press a soft kiss to Juniper's temple. She looks at me with so much hope in her eyes, I nearly fall to my knees in front of all these strangers and beg her to love me back.

28

JUNIPER

ROLLING MY SHOULDERS, I rock my head from side to side and rub the back of my neck. A tap on my window prompts me to turn off my car and open the door. "Sorry. I got distracted for a minute."

"You're in pain," Lee retorts venomously. "You should have let the paramedics take you in."

I poke a finger into his chest to back him up so I can stand. "No, you should have let them take *you*."

"I grew up with four brothers. I can take a few hits."

"And I'm fine, so you can quit looking at me like that."

"Like what?" he asks defensively, moving for me to shut the car door before stepping back into my space.

"Like I'm going to break."

His toes touch mine where we stand in the driveway to my new place, and he gazes down at me with such ferocious love in his eyes, I nearly step back.

"You are breakable, my little darling, but nobody will ever touch you again." He slips his hand in mine and tugs me toward the door. "Besides, you're in pain and don't even lie about it. You keep rubbing the back of your neck."

I bite my lip to keep from arguing. He isn't wrong. "Okay, fine. My muscles are sore."

He inserts the key in my lock but glances back at me with a frown. Holy hotness. Combine the frown with the bruises and split lip, and I think my panties just combusted. "What's that look?"

"What look?" I return innocently and move ahead of him through the door. When I stop suddenly, he walks right into my back.

"Juniper?"

"What have you done?" Awe replaces the innocence in my voice from a second ago.

Heavy palms land on my shoulders, soothing circles rubbed into my skin by his thumbs. "I enlisted some help," he murmurs in my ear.

The door opens into the front room. I knew his brothers would be bringing over a few bags of my stuff while Lee took me out for food, but I didn't expect it to look like this.

A brown sofa I've never seen before sits along the wall beneath the window facing the street with a gray-washed coffee table in front of it. A colorful bouquet rests inside a navy-blue vase in the center. Across from the couch, a matching gray-washed TV stand holds what has to be at least a forty-inch flat-screen television.

My gaze darts to the entrance to the kitchen, where I can see a small square table and four chairs. Another squat bouquet acts as a centerpiece.

"Where did this come from?"

"The Powells are very resourceful." Lee takes my hand

and leads me down the hall to the bedrooms. He flicks on the light to the main suite and with a solid palm on my back, he guides me inside. "Extra odds and ends lying around. The TV was a spare from Jack's motel. The couch came from Aiden's den. Don't worry, it's clean. He never spent time in there." Lee laughs, the warm chuckle like a soothing summer breeze.

"The flowers came from Mom."

I turn so quickly I nearly bump into his chest. He steadies me by my elbows. "You called her Mom."

Lee licks his lips, a nervous energy pulsing between us. "I should have realized a long time ago that she earned that title from me. I'm just glad it wasn't too late for me to fix it."

The parallel isn't lost on me. Before I can address that he's already fixed things between us, he grasps my shoulders and turns me back around. "The bed and dresser are yours, but the rug is new."

"Thank you doesn't seem adequate."

He wraps his arms around my stomach and rests his chin on my shoulder.

"Thanks aren't necessary. I wanted this chapter closed as quickly as possible so you can put it behind you. Living in an empty space while working two jobs to scrape together enough money for a TV for your brother wouldn't have allowed you to do that as fast as I'd like."

I reach back to cradle the back of his head and run my fingers through his hair. He presses his lips to the side of my neck, leaving a light dew against my skin. Shivers force goose bumps to the surface.

"You're a good man, Lee."

"You make me want to be better."

The vulnerable confession sends me twirling around, dislodging his head from my shoulder so I can face him head-on. Words to express how I feel fail to fall passed my lips. With gentle fingertips, I prod his brows, around the side of his eyes, and his lids flutter closed at my exploring touch.

A rumbled groan sounds from his chest, tearing up his throat as I trace his bruised cheek and gently nudge his split lip.

I grasp his chin between my finger and thumb, urging him to tilt his neck until he's low enough for me to surround his injured lip between mine.

"Can I touch you?" he rasps against my mouth, his shoulders rigid.

I take his hands in mine, placing one on my breast and the other on my hip where the hem of my shirt gives way to bare skin. "Yes."

With a groan, he dives in to take my lips, not seeming to care for his bruises as he tastes me fully for the first time in a week. The pad of his thumb strokes my rigid nipple beneath my simple tee, bringing a surge of arousal to the taut flesh. His other hand dips beneath my clothes and up, stroking the skin of my hip and back. He pulls me flush as if he's trying to burrow beneath my skin and even that wouldn't be close enough.

I grip the hem of his shirt and yank it up. We break apart long enough for the fabric to clear his head before he's on me again. I drop the shirt to flutter to the floor.

His mouth hits the corner of mine, and he peppers his way over my jaw, to my ear, before skating down along the darkening bruise across my throat.

A hitch steals my breath from his gentle touch.

He drops to his knees before me, hands braced on my hips, and rough thumbs stroking beneath the hem of my shirt on my sensitive skin. His face is open and pure when he looks up at me and presses an open-mouthed kiss on the fabric covering my navel. Those sea-green eyes shine bright in the yellow glow of the overhead light.

"Lee," I whisper, not even sure what I'm asking for as I bury my fingers in his thick, dark hair and hold him to me.

Deft fingers flick open the button of my jean shorts before curling into the edges to peel them down my legs. He slips off my shoes and socks, discarding everything on the floor. I gasp in surprise when he surges to his feet, hooking his hands around my thighs in one fluid motion to hitch me up in his arms and circle my legs around his back.

He cups my ass, but not lasciviously; this is different from the other times we've been together. The dirty words are gentle kisses, and the rough display of desire transforms to something tender.

He sits on the edge of my bed cradling me in his lap, my legs spread to accommodate his hips. He pauses the gentle assault on my mouth long enough to watch himself guide my shirt up, slowly exposing my torso inch by inch. Left only in my purple lace bra and underwear, he places his palm flat between my breasts.

"You're so beautiful," he says reverently, almost like a disbelieving prayer.

Tears tingle the corners of my eyes. "So are you."

His head dips, wearing almost a bashful look as he bites his lip before running his hand over the top of my head and down my curly strands. Twisting at his torso, he brings me beneath him and drops my back on the pillows. With eyes locked on mine, he twists our fingers together, planting our joined hands near my head while he unsnaps the button on his jeans with his other.

"I'm going to make love to you."

My chest seizes at his gentle declaration and the fire in his eyes.

"But first I'm going to make you come."

He looks between my legs, at the panties covering the place he seeks, and drops a tender kiss on the center right above my slit.

A wanton moan falls from my mouth. My legs press together, blocked by the width of his shoulders wedged between them.

He releases my hand to hook his fingertips between the flimsy straps and the crease at my hips and tugs, slipping the fabric down my legs.

I know he can see the wetness pooling at my center, but I don't feel the least bit of shame. I want him to know what he does to me. I want him to see and revel in the desire only he's responsible for.

Without preamble, he flattens his tongue and strokes my clit while he eases one finger between my slickened flesh.

I immediately tense and arch against the pillows, a moan slipping free at the sparks of arousal.

Where I'm used to hard and fast with Lee, a race to the finish, he sets a leisurely pace. His tongue laps and licks and draws with purpose, knowing exactly where to touch to get me hot. To make me whine and beg, but not enough to push me over the edge.

He adds a second finger to the first, curling them

against the front wall of my pussy, coaxing me toward the edge like we're rowing down an indolent river.

Slow, unhurried, lazy.

Tremors begin in my thighs, the muscles shaking around his ears, and my hips undulate under his talented tongue. With a languorous stroke over my clit, he drives his fingers deep and curls, finally pushing me into a rapturous orgasm, and I come.

Lee kisses up my soft stomach, over stretch marks from puberty. A hand snakes around my back to unsnap my bra, freeing my breasts. His mouth lands there next where his tongue swirls around a pale-pink peak before he sucks hard.

"Please," I whine, rubbing my thighs against his hips.

"Tell me what you need." He gently scrapes his teeth against my other nipple.

"I need to feel you inside me."

In one thrust, he's deep, filling me until I'm stretched around him. His hand discovers mine at my side, and he laces our fingers tight as if he's afraid I might disappear from beneath him. The other tucks around the side of my neck, thumb brushing my pulse point.

And then he moves. Languorous strokes that have him almost withdrawing fully. His pelvis rubs against my clit, and his cock grazes the spot inside that has my neck arching and a gasp falling from my lips.

He buries his face in my throat, just below my ear, licking the dampness from my skin.

"I love you, Juniper. I'm in love with you. And I'm not even a little sorry for breaking my promise." He pulls back to gaze down at me, a pink tinge to his lightly stubbled cheeks, brows drawn downward. "I'm forty years old, and if I'm lucky, I have forty more to spend with you."

I squeeze his hand tightly in mine, feeling my heart speed up as if it's trying to answer for me.

"I'm in love with you too."

"Really?" The hesitance in his question hurts my soul. This man has gone so long feeling like he's unworthy of love.

I hold him tightly to me, his naked chest crushing my breasts. "Yes. I love you, Lee, and not just because of today. Because you're a good, honorable man, and you showed me what it feels like to be safe."

"You're mine," he murmurs, hips punching downward and the speed picks up, just a little bit. Grunts punctuate the air around us. The muscles of his shoulders bunch beneath my hand.

"I'm yours." Anything else I might say is lost when his lips take mine as if he's trying to seal the words between us. The promises we say and the ones we speak with our bodies.

His groans increase, and his hands roam my naked skin as if he can't touch me enough. And when his strokes become erratic and his muscles taut, I clench around him, and we fall apart together.

Collapsed against me, he rolls us to our sides without losing our connection. Our combined release leaks out around him, and I relish the feel of him softening inside. Tucked close, Lee stroking my hair, surrounded by him with my nightmare coming to an end, hope chases away the darkness I've felt for so long.

Sleep loosens my muscles, whisking me away to

another place, but the feeling of the bed shifting forces an eyelid open.

"What are you doing?"

Lee holds out his hand. "Come on, sleepyhead."

I flop back onto the pillow for a second, regaining my bearings. I must have drifted off for a few moments. The sound of running water entices me enough to place my hand in his. Though if I'm being honest, I'd follow him just about anywhere, without questions.

At some point, he fully shucked his jeans. I watch the muscles in his hard ass shift with admiration on our way into the adjoined bathroom. Steam curls from the claw-footed tub, a heap of iridescent bubbles rising above the rim.

"Get in."

He helps me step over the edge like a gentleman, and my heart literally swoons right there in my chest. The hot water laps at aching muscles. A sigh bubbles free.

"Move forward, my little darling."

I grip the lip of the tub and lean into my knees.

Lee slips in behind me. Holding my shoulders, he eases me back against his wide chest. Producing a cloth from somewhere, he begins soaping my skin. "Just relax while I get you clean."

The sex, the feel of him, and the hot water lapping around us cause the remaining tension from the day to drift away. Once I'm clean, he digs his thumbs into my neck muscles. I'm so relaxed, I could fall asleep and be comforted that he'd never let me drown.

When his hands switch from kneading to stroking along my damp skin, I carefully rise onto my knees and turn around. Water sloshes over the side of the tub. Lee grips my slippery waist to steady me as I sink back down, straddling his lap.

"What are you doing?"

With wet fingers, I brush off the damp, dark waves sticking to his forehead. "I'm taking care of you."

He watches me with interest as I give him a similar treatment. Starting at his neck, I dig my fingers into the corded muscles. His head drops back on a throaty groan that settles deep in my abdomen.

"That feels good." His fingers tighten on my waist.

Steam curls around us and clouds the mirrors and windows while I work. The open air cools my skin as I massage from his neck to his shoulders, down each arm, and to his hands. When I reach his fingers, I kiss each individual one before rolling them one at a time from the big knuckle to the very tip.

When I'm done, I curl into his chest, and his arms band around me. We soak in the silence until the water starts to cool. Lee wraps me in a towel before securing one around his hips. Scooping me into his arms, he carries me into the bedroom. After shedding the towels on the floor with the rest of our clothing, we climb between the sheets naked, and he arranges me across his chest with my thigh wedged between his.

29

LEE

THE NEXT MORNING, with Juniper's hand firmly in mine, we follow Sutton back to the cell holding her father at the Fairview Valley jail. She begged me to let her talk to him, and since I'm wrapped around her finger like a tourniquet, here we are even though I'd rather still be in bed with my gorgeous, naked girlfriend.

"You have five minutes," Sutton says and moves off to the corner.

Tom Kelly looks up from his slouched position on the lone bench against the concrete blocks of his chamber, still in the clothes from yesterday, greasy hair slicked up on one side, and a surprised look on his craggy face.

"You're going to listen to what she has to say without a word," I snap. Standing in the same room as the guy simmers my blood all over again.

The look on his face lets me know exactly what he thinks of me, and it isn't much, but I don't give a shit. He can rot in hell for all I care.

Juniper steps slightly in front of me, her shoulders

back and chin held high. Her strength sends a bolt of pride through me. "I wanted to let you know I'm submitting papers with the county to become Lincoln's sole guardian."

Tom bares his teeth like he has something to say to that but thinks better of it.

"It'll make the process a lot smoother if you could sign your rights over without a fight. Even if you hate me, Lincoln's already lost his mom and you aren't doing him any good with your drinking. Let me take care of him."

When he doesn't say anything, she steps closer, her voice lowering until nearly a whisper. "If you make this hard for Lincoln, I will turn in all the evidence of your abuse over the past two years. Every photograph and date of every bruise is impossible to deny. You'll be locked up for a very long time."

"I'm sorry," her father says, but it sounds more like a swear word, his voice rough. "I didn't mean for things to get that far. I was drunk."

"You said you wanted to kill me." Juniper's voice cracks, and she pauses. In a comforting gesture, I cup her hip while I turn my stony glare on her father. "There's no coming back from that, not for me, but if you want to try, this would be the start."

Tom nods, a flash of guilt in his eyes. "Tell him I'm sorry too."

Juniper doesn't confirm or deny his request. She flicks her gaze to Sutton before returning them to her father.

"Do yourself a favor and sober up. Before the rest of your life is ruined. Your children hate you and your wife is gone, but you might be able to still find something to live for. And if you don't, I no longer care. You aren't my problem anymore."

She twists her fingers in mine, and together, we walk to the door to wait for Sutton to lead us out.

She doesn't give him the satisfaction of looking back.

"Do you mind if we stop by my house?" I ask once we're back in the truck. Technically, I'm already driving back to my place, but I needed to break the silence. I worry she's getting sucked into her pretty little head after what just happened with her father.

But when she turns to me with a serene smile on her lips, all that worry disappears.

"Not at all. Cortney just said to let her know when we're ready for Lincoln, so we have time." She knocks the visor down to shadow her eyes from the blinding sunrays.

"She's giving us space." I reach over and engulf her hand where it rests in her lap.

"I think she knows we're having sex."

"That too." I chuckle and brush her knuckles against my lips.

Several minutes later, we arrive. For some reason, nerves attack all over again. One more action to show her, but I have no idea how she'll react.

I let her lead, and seeing her in my boring space, it's immediately apparent I no longer want to be here. This house suited me for most of my adulthood, but now I want to be somewhere else. That somewhere else is wherever she is.

A howling yap sounds from the laundry room

followed by the rattling of metal. Juniper freezes in the center of my kitchen, turning toward the noise. "Is that…" She trails off and moves toward the sound. "Did you get a dog?"

I flip the light switch. Slipper bats at the door to her kennel and wags her tail back and forth. "Not just any dog," I reply and slide open the lever to release the young pup. The sweetheart walks right to Juniper and bows with her front legs stretched out and her butt high in the air, her tail sweeping side to side.

"This is the dog from the day we met."

Juniper's eyes widen, and she moves to stroke her hand over the husky's head. "Are you keeping her?"

I lean against the doorframe and cross my arms. Tension ripples through my body, and I exhale more forcefully than I mean to. "That depends."

"On what?" She smiles and crouches to scratch the dog's belly.

"On if your rental accepts pets."

Her hopeful gaze snaps to mine. "You're giving me the dog?"

"I thought I could come too."

"Are you presuming I want you to move in with me, Lee Powell?"

Restless fingers move to the back of my neck. "I'm actually asking. If you'll have me. I no longer want to be anywhere you're not, and this house hasn't ever felt like a home to me."

"And the dog comes too?" A teasing lilt enters her voice.

"Are you saying it's a deal breaker if she doesn't?"

Juniper nods. "I'm afraid so."

"Well, then, you're in luck." I help her to her feet and hold her close. "We're a packaged deal. Unless you want to come live here."

She looks around the underwhelming space, a sparkle in her dark eyes. "I have some incredible memories here."

She rises on tiptoe and kisses me hard. "But I'm ready to make some new ones with you somewhere else. What is it you're always saying? Love is an action word. Let me show you how much I love you."

EPILOGUE

JUNIPER

One Year Later

"LOOK AT YOUR BEAUTIFUL FACE! You're positively glowing!" Isla appears on my cell phone screen with a wide smile. Her blond hair frames her face messily as if she just crawled out of bed.

I roll my eyes. "You say that every time. Once a week for the last six months."

"Excuse me for missing you. I'm used to seeing you multiple times a week, not just once on a cell phone screen."

"I miss you too, babe. How's the club?"

Six months ago, Isla finally had enough and told Manny to kiss her ass. One of the clubs she visited during her solo road trip hired her, and Lee and I helped her move an hour and a half away. Close enough for us to do lunch about once a month, but far enough I miss her like crazy.

She throws her hair into a messy bun. "It's amazing.

Really. But you know me, I won't be satisfied until I'm headlining Saturday nights."

"Manifest that shit. I have faith in you."

"Oh, have no doubt, my friend, I am. The tips are already triple what I was making at XO's. I can only imagine what I could rake in as a main event." She waves her hand in front of the camera. "But enough about me dancing naked. That's old news. How's the job working out for you? Resident dog trainer, huh?"

"It's been amazing getting to work with the dogs every day. I feel like I'm really making a difference."

Two weeks after Lee moved in, I quit both my waitressing jobs. He argued I no longer needed to support myself alone and offered me work at the sanctuary. That quickly progressed to me becoming a dog trainer to help some of our fosters with behavioral issues. A picture of my future became clear, and I returned to school and started working toward my dog behaviorist certification.

She beams. "I'm so happy for you."

"Me too," I reply.

"Have you heard from Tom lately?"

His name sets firecrackers off in my stomach. "Another email arrived just the other day. This is only the second one. He's still in jail. He says he's sober and that he misses us, but it doesn't matter." I run my nail across my cuticle. "He has another few years before he's out, and by then, Lincoln will almost be an adult. Whether he wants to see him or not will be up to my brother."

My best friend gives a solemn nod. "Thank goodness for that."

I flick away a crumb on the table. I'm more than content with the end result of that chapter of my life, but thoughts of my father will never fill me with warm fuzzy feelings.

"Anyway, I'm thinking of making a trip up there next week. Can I see you?"

I set down the iced coffee Lee got me when I left the ranch earlier this afternoon. "Of course. Maybe you can catch one of Lincoln's baseball games and we can have a girls' night after."

"Oh, I like that idea. Maybe I can scope out a Powell brother for myself."

"Honey, you should have tried that before you moved away."

"Gives me a reason to come back." She wiggles her eyebrows and grins.

"I'd almost pay money to see one of them try to handle you."

Footsteps nearby have me turning in my chair just as Lincoln wanders into the kitchen in his baseball gear. "Are you ready to go?" he asks me.

I nod and turn back to my phone. "I've got to run. Let me know when you're coming and I'll get the couch ready for you."

"Don't you even. I have plenty of friends I can stay with that don't require me to intrude on their happy little family."

I bite my lip to hide my grin. The thing is, I like hearing us referred to as a family. I like it a lot. "Okay, see you soon. Love you."

"Love you too."

I pocket my phone and slip on my shoes while Lincoln waits impatiently by the door. He's changed so much in the past year, and I don't just mean physically. His outbursts have grown further apart and now they are a rare occurrence.

"Lee said we should bring Slipper."

"Sure. Hand me her leash."

He passes over the six-foot leather lead, and the sound alone has the bouncy husky prancing into the room.

She sits near the door and serenades us with a chorus of excited howls. Lincoln buries his fingers in her long fur while I clip on the leash.

"Got everything?" I scan him head to toe. Baseball cleats, pants, jersey, and a bag slung over one shoulder.

He rolls his eyes. "You don't have to ask every time."

I give him a playful shove out the door. "Except every time I don't check, you seem to leave something behind."

"I'm not a little kid anymore." He throws his shoulders back and puffs his chest before climbing in my car with Slipper happily in the back.

"I'm well aware." More than he'd ever realize. He'll always be my kid brother, but becoming his guardian has shifted my side of the relationship. Even though some moments have been tough, the payoff has been incredible to witness.

"You're not going to cry, are you?"

"No," I croak, my tight throat exposing my secrets. My emotions run a little freer these days now that I don't have to worry about appearing so strong.

"Stop," he groans.

"What?" I rapidly blink back the sting in my eyes.

"You better not tell Lee it's my fault you're crying, or he'll make me run laps around the bases."

I laugh. "He will not."

Lincoln and I exchange a glance at a stop sign. My

eyebrows are raised, and his clearly says *are you that stupid?* We burst out laughing.

"I won't tell him a thing." I hold out my pinky, and he wraps his around it.

"Thank you." He shoves my hand away.

As I approach the parking lot, one lone truck is parked in the sea of blacktop. "You did have practice today, right?"

"That's what Lee said." His voice holds as much confusion as I feel.

"He said nine o'clock?"

"Yep."

An inkling of curiosity has me parking beside his empty truck. "I suppose we should track him down."

"Do you want to take Slipper or should I?"

His helpful question nearly reignites the tears. He's such a thoughtful kid. "I can take her."

Lincoln hands over the leash, and together, we walk the darkening path to the field. The stadium lights aren't even on, and the sunset slowly withdraws the final rays from the day.

"This is weird." Lincoln shatters our silence.

The baseball diamond comes into view, along with the coach standing clear on the pitcher's mound. A confident air surrounds his posture.

A frisson of something exciting races beneath my skin.

"Hey, what's the hurry?" my brother calls a few steps behind me.

Without even realizing it, I kicked my pace up a few notches. I try to slow down, but the smile on Lee's face takes my breath away. Even from a distance, I can see the love he wears only for me.

Lincoln catches up to me and groans. "Lee!"

"What?" he calls back.

"If she's crying, it's not my damn fault!"

"No worries, bud, it'll be mine!" Lee yells, returning that devastating grin to me.

"What are you doing?" I ask as I enter the fence near home plate. This close, I finally slow my trot to a walk.

"Waiting for you," he says.

"Did I make you wait long?" My question comes out a little breathless.

He tucks his hands into the pockets of his jeans. "Not on purpose. I think I've been waiting for you all along."

My breath catches in my throat. When the leash tugs behind me, I find Slipper chasing a flower petal. "What…"

One must have blown away from the batch spread around the pitcher's mound. Now that I'm close, I can see the colorful petals surrounding Lee. When I look back at him with a question on the tip of my tongue, he bites his lip with a bashful look on his face.

"I know they're cheesy, but I wanted to make sure we had a part of everything that brought us together."

"I don't remember there being flowers." I finally reach him and quirk an eyebrow.

He reaches out to stroke a strand of hair away from my cheek, his gaze drilling into mine. "They're for your mom."

"I-I don't understand."

He hasn't said anything, and I'm already dangerously close to crying again.

Taking both my hands in his, he studies our connection. "Slipper pushed you into my lap. Lincoln brought you to baseball where I'd stand on this field and have to fight with myself to not find you in the sea of faces just so I could stare at how pretty you are. And if you weren't out there watering those flowers your mom planted, I never would have asked you to come over."

"Lee."

His shoulders rise and fall with a deep breath. "You once told me night makes you think of your mom and that they're a little lonely and sad. I'm here to reclaim your nights."

On the same mound my brother plays baseball, Lee drops to a knee in the clay dirt at dusk. Tears fall freely down my cheeks, partially hidden by the dark surrounding us. I squeak around a sob as he pulls a black box from his pocket.

"Juniper Kelly, you've been through so much already in your life. I wasn't a part of most of it, but I want to be there for the rest. For every minute you feel sad and lonely, I want to remind you you're never alone. For every illness, I want to nurse you back to health. For every moment of self-doubt, I want to be the one to remind you how incredible you are. I want your mornings with hazelnut coffee and to be lucky enough to fall asleep with you at night. But most of all, I want to take away the last piece holding you to a past you never deserved. I promise to protect you from all harm, and that includes the hurt you feel every time you sign your name."

The breath leaves my lungs in a whoosh. "Yes."

Lee's mouth tilts in a sinful smirk. "I haven't even asked the question yet."

"I don't care. My answer is yes."

His voice is a raspy growl when he asks, "Will you do me the damn honor of becoming a Powell and marry me?"

I charge into his chest, and he grunts. "Yes." I lean down and seal my answer with a kiss while he slides a square-cut diamond rock onto my left ring finger.

He grips my hips to steady me and gazes up at me with so much love my heart hurts. "We'll get rid of his last name as soon as we can."

"I don't care. As long as I have you, nothing else matters."

"I love you, Juniper. I don't know how you did it, but you snuck right in my fucking heart and made yourself at home."

"It's because you're a good, deserving man." I stroke my fingers through the hair at his neck. "I love you too."

Slipper gives a woof and tugs the leash in my fist taut, forcing us apart. She strains heavily in the direction of the dugout where Lincoln stands awkwardly, digging his toe in the dirt.

"Hey, bud. Get over here," Lee calls from his position still on the ground.

Lincoln keeps his head down. "Are you two done with the gross stuff? I didn't want to interrupt."

I can't help but notice his voice sounds a little sad.

"Come here," Lee says again.

With a huff and an eye roll, Lincoln saunters across the field. "Yeah?"

"What's on your mind?"

Lincoln continues kicking dirt, avoiding Lee's eyes.

"You shoot straight with me, kid, you remember that? And what did I tell you?"

"That you'd be straight with me too," Lincoln mumbles.

The relationship between the two has really been

something beautiful to witness. Ever since Lincoln shared our secret to Lee, they've formed their own bond. This year, Lee signed up to coach Lincoln's team without coercion, and they've spent time together at the sanctuary and fishing. He easily became the role model I wished last summer Lincoln would have.

Lincoln scrubs his hand over the back of his neck and adjusts his hat. "What happens to me when you guys get married?"

"We've been living in the same house for the last year, so I really hoped we'd become a family, if you'll have me."

My brother's head shoots up, and he stares at Lee with so much hope I nearly start crying again.

"Oh, goodness," I fan my cheeks with my free hand.

Lee cuts his gaze to me with a grin before turning back to Lincoln.

"It's just I have a dad. He's not a good one, but sometimes he was all right."

Lee settles his hand on Lincoln's shoulder. "I'm not going to be your dad, just like Juniper isn't your mom. If it's okay with you, when I marry your sister, that actually makes me your brother-in-law."

Lincoln beams back at Lee. "Ollie is going to be so pissed I get his favorite uncle as my brother."

A warm laugh bursts from Lee. "I'm not sure you were supposed to tell me I'm his favorite uncle."

"Forget I said that." Lincoln grimaces in the dark.

"How does that sound to you? You aren't going anywhere and we'll continue just how we are."

Lincoln quickly nods. "I like that."

WHAT TO READ NEXT

WHILE WE WAIT FOR CORJAN'S STORY, CHECK OUT MY OTHER CONTEMPORARY SMALL TOWN ROMANCES

Where We Meet Again

An unexpected pregnancy by a man wielding sweet words and empty promises forced Cami to flee from home.

At sixteen, she gathered her torn and tattered heart, determined to construct the best life for her daughter.

Years after settling down in Arrow Creek, West Virginia, her life flourishes in all areas but one—love. She's convinced the sacrifice is necessary to keep her daughter happy and a roof over their heads.

Until she stumbles into her childhood best friend Lawrence 'Law' Briggs at the local coffee shop, and a painful confrontation ensues.

Their long-buried feelings for one another quickly

resurface and challenge a carefully constructed reality. Her strength wavers as Law's reappearance exposes half-truths, and memories flood through the barrier.

Her daughter is a gift she'd never regret, even if it meant she lost him forever. Dark secrets hold them apart. The deepest betrayal imaginable.

Years of hurt and suffering can't disguise that Law's love remains, and Cami's is equal in measure. But is love enough to find a way forward through their murky past?

When Morning Comes

There are worse things than getting knocked up by your best friend. Right?

Kiersten won't make excuses for living her very best life. But being the life of the party has its downsides—like waking up naked next to her best friend.

Ever since Nathan's wife died a few years ago, he's avoided commitment. He went from living the family life to a one-and-done mentality. Until Kiersten breaks the news.

She's pregnant with his baby.

She shoves him back in the friend zone. But there's no

return to normal when he's already falling in love with her.

Convincing her that his affection runs deeper than their new reality isn't an easy feat. Not when her lips are his addiction, and her touch is a brand. He's determined to become more than friends.

Kiersten wants to play it safe, but Nathan is ready for risks. The problem is relationships can go south fast.

And they might learn the truth about what's worse than getting knocked up by your best friend.

Losing them forever.

What Tears Us Down

Rhett Senova could charm a woman out of her panties and in the next breath, thank her mother for dinner.

Smooth doesn't even begin to cover his moves. But the hottest playboy in Arrow Creek wasn't always this way.

He had dreams of a one-woman future, and the cry of his firstborn brought him to tears.

He never thought his wife would cheat on him with her boss.

Each day is a feud over the dream home he had built for his ex and learning to raise his young son without the jaded lens now coloring his world.

Starting over in his thirties isn't on his agenda. Not now that he's raised impenetrable walls. His ex left the sour taste of infidelity in his mouth, and he's not sure he can trust anyone new.

That is until he meets a vision passing through town and nearly gets mauled by her she-demon dog.

Her sassy wit makes other women seem inadequate, along with those luscious curves and burgundy curls.

The fact she hides beneath her tough exterior that she might be in trouble sends up red flags he'd be smart not to ignore.

Using his charm to win over the pit bull is the easy part. The question is whether he wants to win over the guarded redhead too.

Where Our Turn Begins

Caiti Harris thought her story ended the night her husband died.

She packed their history away like trinkets in an old box and held steadfast to the ache. Life granted her one love, and after he was cruelly ripped away, she knew there wouldn't be anyone else.

When a tempting bartender invites her to stay for a drink after closing, she agrees to one night, not a lifetime commitment. His sinful smile promises to chase away the pain of the past while his chiseled body guarantees to ward off the unrelenting chill.

Her love life ended, but that doesn't mean she's sentenced to an existence of total solitude.

Dane's world is exactly the way he wants. Tidy. He keeps a watchful eye over his bar, and remains a pillar for the people he cares for most. So when the woman he's dreamt about for three years shows up at his door with a toddler in tow, he's ready for the challenge. The two come as a package deal.

Caiti only wants to establish a connection with him in the event something happens to her. A backup plan to keep their daughter safe. She didn't expect to be whisked away in an ambulance before she could explain her sudden return to Arrow Creek.

Dane's vision soars beyond an eighteen year commitment. He sees a lifetime of settling down. And he's not ready to give up his turn without a fight for their daughter.

Or her.

ACKNOWLEDGMENTS

Book number twelve.

Wow.

What a journey this has been.

I can say with certainty that this year has been the best, most inspiring one of my entire career. I closed out a series I never intended to write and at a moment when I expected to be lost, I really wasn't. Because immediately after I finished the last book in the Arrow Creek series, the characters for the Powell family came fast and clear.

All six of them.

Plus Juniper, Ollie, Lincoln, and the large pack of dogs.

For that, I have to start off by thanking my newsletter subscribers. Without you, Lee and Juniper wouldn't have been the first book in the series. I never expected one little poll about which book to write next would have such an impact. (If you haven't figured it out yet, the other option was Corjan, and I'm really excited he gets to go next.) His storyline has me REALLY excited!

My husband - my dear old man, the one who always scolds me for the tight deadlines because he doesn't want to see me stressed but supports me through them anyway. Thank you for having my back and being my #1 fan.

To my children - who always seem to forget they have a second parent in the house when I'm on a deadline and call for me 3,440,498 times. I love you guys. Yes, you can have a snack. No, I won't get it for you. Please take the dog that you wanted so desperately out to go potty.

The team at Grey's Promotions - You are rockstars! Thank you for making my book releases 100 times smoother than they are when I do them myself. I don't know what I'd do without you.

Jenny - Thank you for always giving my stories a beautiful polish and making them shine. I also still can't remember the difference between passed and past so thanks for fixing them!

Tiffany - You worked magic with this cover! Thank you for taking my very vague vision and creating something beautiful.

Alex - Thank you for sprints and support and for always being a quick message away at all times. I hope we support one another through many more book releases.

Jill - Haha you will never see this but I'm writing it anyway. Thank you so much for the continued support. For the "max two compliments". For calling me badass when I don't feel like I am.

To my ARC readers, bloggers, and friends - Thank you for taking the time to read this book before release. When there may still be a pesky typo or two standing in your way. Thank you for your kindness. For the shares, likes, comments, and support during one of the most vulnerable times of book publishing! I appreciate each and every one of you.

ABOUT THE AUTHOR

A. M. Wilson is a *USA TODAY* Bestselling Author. She loves infusing her stories with real life--the good, the bad, and the steamy parts. There's something special about that pivotal moment when two characters realize their love for each other, but she likes wading through a little angst to get there. When she isn't furiously typing on her computer, she can be found searching for her next all-consuming read. A. M. lives in Minnesota with her husband, two children, and black lab.

Visit her website at http://amwilson.net
Subscribe to her newsletter

- facebook.com/A.M.WilsonAuthor
- twitter.com/AMWilsonAuthor
- instagram.com/amwilsonauthor
- goodreads.com/amwilsonauthor
- bookbub.com/authors/a-m-wilson

Printed in Great Britain
by Amazon